See What Flowers

By Shannon Mullen

But here there is no light,
Save what from heaven is with the breezes blown
Through verdurous glooms and winding mossy ways.

I cannot see what flowers are at my feet,
Nor what soft incense hangs upon the boughs,
But, in embalmed darkness, guess each sweet

-John Keats,
Ode to a Nightingale

Prologue

"Struggling and suffering are the essence of a life worth living. If you're not pushing yourself beyond the comfort zone, if you're not demanding more from yourself - expanding and learning as you go - you're choosing a numb existence. You're denying yourself an extraordinary trip."

-Dean Karnazes,
Ultramarathon Man: Confessions of an All-Night Runner

Emma: May 10, 2014, 9:30pm EDT

The party is over. I'm floating weightlessly through the sky like Mary Poppins, grasping my flamingo pink birthday balloons so tightly that my nails puncture the skin of my sweaty palm.

Supercalifragilisticexpialidocious!

Startled by the sound of myself giggling, I release the balloons. They float to the ceiling as my feet hit the floor but the giggling doesn't stop. Instead, it becomes louder, more honest: the yelp of a dog off-leash, the squeal of a toddler chasing butterflies, the height of sexual pleasure, the subconscious release of something raw and visceral, something undeniably, yet unexplainably true.

It's like I've pierced a small hole in the balloon, sucked in the helium and exhaled delirium. I'm under the effect of something, certainly too much Malbec, but perhaps also too much happiness.

After more than a decade of cramming for exams, late nights at the library, taking risks, and making tough decisions, I've become lighter, like in the way sticking to a running program burns excess fat. The lightness teaches me that struggle lifts us up rather than weighs us down.

I take a blue recycling bag from underneath the sink and start cleaning up empty tall cans--Steam Whistle, Mill St., Muskoka, Great Lakes, Kichesippi and other Ontario Craft beers that I've never seen before. Every time I go to the Beer Store, there's a new microbrew on the market. With so much competition, what makes one product last and another disappear? By the time I've tossed a dozen or so empties into the recycling bag, the giggling has stopped and I'm overcome with exhaustion. I check the time on my phone. 3:30 am. There's a missed call from Adam.

Where is he?

He'll be upset that I already washed all of the dishes—the plates and forks we used to serve my DQ cake, the wine glasses, and the Starbucks mug that that Katie used for her Cab Sav because we ran out of glasses. Adam wouldn't make me clean up a mess on my birthday. He'd remind me that a real partner shares the responsibility, and that since I'm the BDG, I deserve to let him pull the weight.

I tug on the ribbon dangling from one of the balloons floating against the ceiling. I want to set it free, let it fly into the wild like a caged parrot being released in the jungle, so I put the recycling bag on the floor and collect the ribbons from all three balloons. How high will they soar before bursting to the ground?

I shiver slightly as a draft of cold air floods the apartment the second the front door opens, like winter has suddenly arrived even though summer is just around the corner.

I spin around to see who it is. I already know.

Adam.

He's holding a couple of pink tulips in his hand, freshly picked from the neighbours' garden. His eyes are glowing with the droopy haze of booze and he looks like a maniac, a wild dog. We are both high on the energy of the party and the awareness that we are on the brink of something wonderful. As I float towards him, a nagging question tugs me back; I want to swat it away like an annoying mosquito. But it keeps buzzing inside me.

I shiver again.

Is there such a thing as being too happy?

He hands me the tulips, luscious lips in full bloom. As I accept the flowers, I release my grip on the balloons, and they bounce gently against the ceiling the way they did before—hovering, annoyed, frustrated, contained by the ceiling and disappointed by the limits of life.

He hugs me tightly and an electric current shoots through me as though he's resuscitating a heart that's already beating. We hold each other, our bodies linking in the courtship ritual of dragonflies; our brilliant green darners hover as one above our apartment. Our home.

"This is the happiest I've ever been," I whisper.

It is.

Part One: Ten Days Later

"Seeing is limited by two borders: Strong light, which blinds, and total darkness."

-Milan Kundera, *The Unbearable Lightness of Being*

Adam: May 19, 2014, 6:00am PDT

The darkness terrifies me.

It pins me to the cement floor. Suffocates me. I don't fight back. I can't. My body's numb. Paralyzed.

Move your fingers. Nothing. Wiggle your toes.

Nothing.

Blink goddammit.

Nothing.

My head pounds, screams, a steady *beep-beep-beep* of an alarm clock.
Even the pain won't wake me up.

I gasp—short, effortful breaths that taste like iron.
I try to move my right arm to feel the wetness—blood— around my face but can't move it.

Suddenly, I'm overcome by a putrid stench.
Rotting cheese left in a hockey bag. I gag, spewing vomit out of the left side of my mouth. My eye stings. It swims in my own puke.

I'll kill whoever did this to me.

Where am I? How did I get here? What day is this? Why is my head pounding? Where's everyone else? How long have I been here? Why can't I move?

Get up.

Get the fuck up!

I shout at myself over my screaming head. I'm a prisoner, desperately banging on the iron gates, but who could help me if they tried?

My muscles contract, wanting to move. My heart rate rises as blood pumps to my muscles. Nothing happens. All I can feel is the pounding in my head, like someone's cracking my skull with a sledgehammer.

Am I awake or asleep?
Alive or dead?

I try to think of yesterday or the day before.
Anything.
My mind moves slowly, a few memories mix together like dirt and rainwater.
Mountains. Ocean. Wilderness. So wild and beautiful and terrifying.
The pounding in my head becomes more intense the harder I concentrate.
What time is it?

I have to call Jeff. I won't be able to work like this, or maybe my headache will disappear in time. Did Regionals happen without me? Our competitors would have been screwed if I wasn't there to coach them.

This is the happiest I've ever been.
This is the happiest I've ever been.

Our friends. The party. The surprise. The dancing.
It's all a blur.
This is the happiest I've ever been.

Was it yesterday? Last night? Last year?

At once my body tenses to the sound of a key turning in a lock, followed by the creak of a metal door opening.

Get up!
Stand up and defend yourself. Fight like a MAN.
But I can't move.

The darkness surrounds me so tightly I can't breathe.

It is not the darkness of shadows: one that follows you, haunts you, terrifies you.
Instead, it consumes you, becomes you, weighs you down.
It IS you.
It is comforting. Familiar.
I have walked with it. Eaten with it. Loved with it. Smiled with it.
Yet I feel it destroying me.
Like cancer.
But I can't remove it. It stays inside of me, taunting me to kill it, myself, but it does not realize that this seduction keeps me alive.

Footsteps:
One. Two. Three. Four.
Then nothing.

Who's there? It's too dark to see.

Then slow deep breaths, the terrifying rasp of a mongrel, hungry for flesh. I wait, preparing for the unrestrained torture of animals.

I close my eyes.

Be strong. Embrace the pain.

Nothing happens. Seconds pass before I hear another breath. Then silence.
The breaths are slower now, muffled.

"Yo, buddy."

A man's voice bellows over me. Is it just one man? Or is it a man with a dog? Or a group of men?

"Get up. You're lying in your own shit. It's fucking disgusting and it smells like ass. I'll get sued if I let you choke on your puke and die, so I've gotta make sure you stay alive in here."

I breath deeply now.
Relief.
There's comfort in his voice.
Concern. I don't know who he is, but he will not kill me now.
Not yet.

His footsteps get quicker and softer.
He moves away from me.

"Hey, Steve!" The man shouts.
"Can you get something to clean this up? This guy puked all over himself."

I open my eyes.
It has gotten brighter now, as though someone turned on a light somewhere. I see the outline of another man walk down a long narrow corridor towards what looks like a door to a cage.

"He can clean it up himself when he wakes up. You'll have to ignore it until the morning."

Emma, May 19, 2014, 11:30am EDT

"Would you fuck him?" Melayna passes me her iPhone and takes a sip of her coffee. I scan a picture of a burly Roots-model type wearing a University of Toronto football uniform. He's flexing his biceps, two perfectly sculpted grapefruits.

Chris, 28. About Chris: Sports, beers, good times. Tough exterior, soft interior.

"Yuck, too much muscle," I admit.

"Really?" Melayna replies, "I thought you'd like a man with muscle, considering your psycho workout routine. Adam's pretty ripped, eh?"

"Mel!" Eliza scolds. She gives Melayna a "what-the-fuck-are-you-doing" look and then rubs my thigh with loving concern.

"Omigosh. I'm so sorry, Em. That was insensitive," Melayna nearly spills her coffee as she reaches across the table and snatches her phone from me. Then she shoves it into her pocket and smiles sheepishly. "Em, you just seem so put together that I guess I forgot what you're going through. Any news?"

"It's okay. I'm trying to keep my life as normal and structured as possible right now."

I can't stop. Can't think. Just gotta keep moving forward.

"A group of friends and concerned citizens are meeting at 7:00 tonight to search between Dufferin and High Park. But it seems like everyone's giving up hope."

They both look at each other awkwardly; neither of them really knows what to say. Sometimes you just gotta accept that hope is gone. I can't give up, though. Not yet. I refuse to believe that someone I've loved for over a decade could just disappear, without warning, without explanation.

"That's so tough, Em. I'm so sorry," Eliza says, "I saw that the "HELP FIND ADAM" post you shared has hundreds of likes...hopefully someone will be able to give the police a lead."

"Yeah," I agree, even though we both know that any news at this point, ten days after Adam disappeared, will likely be bad. Really bad.

"Let me see that picture again, Mel," I extend my hand towards her, gesturing for the phone.

Anything to distract myself. (As long as Adam doesn't pop up in one of the pictures. OMG. He wouldn't, would he?)

"Nah, not my type. WAY too much muscle." I force a laugh at the picture of the guy flexing his biceps on one arm while he takes a mirror selfie with the other.

"Clearly, this guy just wants to get laid," I tell them. My throat clams up, my shoulders tense, and my breath quickens like I'm having an anaphylactic reaction.

Is this going to be my future if Adam doesn't come home? Swiping through pictures of self-obsessed dudes on the Internet?

Melayna takes the phone back and swipes left a couple of times quickly. "Well, I'm not really looking for a relationship. Like we have time for anything serious with this job."

Deep breaths. Deep breaths. I tug uncomfortably at the collar of my lab coat, trying to calm myself down. My throat has constricted so much that I'm on the brink of a full panic attack. I can't stay and listen to my friends talk about how shitty the Toronto dating scene is. Then I notice the Emergency Exit sign across the hallway, beside the waiting room for X-rays. Against the antiseptic white corridor, it's like an alarm blinking: *"Leave! Leave! Leave! Escape while you still can!"*

But where would I even go if I left? Home? To my Dufferin apartment without Adam? To my parents' place in Parry Sound? Out West? Adam was my constant amidst all of the chaos. My rock. My best friend. My family. Wherever I run to, there's no escaping the fact that he's gone and might never come back.

"I think it's a shallow app," Eliza responds. "At least with online dating sites, you can find people with common interests and values. I wouldn't have messaged Meaghan if I didn't know that she also played the saxophone."

"Well, I think you can tell a lot about a guy from his pictures. I don't swipe right for anyone who takes a shirtless mirror selfie. Or anyone who poses with his mom. Or smokers. Or guys on motorcycles. Maybe Meaghan would've put a picture of herself playing the sax."

"Oh, I highly doubt Meaghan would go on Tinder. She's too serious to swipe…"

"Let's be honest, you only approach guys…" says Melayna before she glances at Eliza, "or girls… in bars if you find them attractive. What's the difference? At least this way, you can narrow it down to the ones who are looking. Besides, I tried the online thing and not too many guys messaged me. I think it's because I listed 'doctor' as my occupation. Guys are freaked out by that."

"It's true," I say, thinking about how lucky I felt about being with a man who respected and admired my career as a doctor. Guys often run away at the bar when my single friends tell them that they're doctors.

Despite all of the social advances in women's rights and the push for gender equality in the workplace, it seems like modern men still want a woman that they can take care of at home. Instead of being attracted to our confidence, intelligence, and work ethic, many men seem to be intimidated by women in high-powered careers, like that it makes them feel emasculated in some way. I never thought that my professional status could actually hinder my relationship status.

"That's not something I have to worry about," Eliza laughs, "Hey, maybe you two overachievers should start putting 'nurse' as your occupation instead of doctor."

"Yeah, right," Mel groans, "they're all married or total overconfident assholes. Like Neil. The way he talks to women is borderline sexual harassment."

"He's definitely the type of guy who'd be all over Tinder," Eliza says.

"No, he seems more like Bill Cosby," Melayna tells us. "Charming, but totally using his status as a superstar doctor to get away with inappropriate comments."

"Oohh, what about this hipster?"

Melayna flashes us a picture of a guy with wavy dark hair, a Mr. Monopoly moustache, a plaid red shirt, black skinny jeans and Ray-Bans. He's holding an espresso cup up to his lips and sitting on a bench underneath a sign. *Sam James Coffee Bar.*

Reid, 34. About Reid: "Nothing is so necessary for a young man as the company of intelligent women." --Leo Tolstoy, War and Peace

"Oh, no! This guy is way too Robert Pattinson."

She shows me the photo. "Now that's TOO skinny!"

Eliza takes the phone and stares at the picture for a while. "This guy DOES seem a little hipster for Mel but I just don't think you can tell much about a person from a picture. Maybe he's your future husband."

"No way!" Melayna waves her phone at us. "It might not look like it right now, but lately I've been thinking that maybe I should just accept that I don't *need*... or maybe *don't even want* to get married."

"Really?" Eliza raises her eyebrows.

"You're the one trolling the Internet on your coffee break," I remind her.

"Yeah, but I have no intention of marrying them!" Melayna cries defensively. "I just want someone to have fun with. Women used to *have* to get married. For economic reasons. But why get married now? I have friends. The idea that you're supposed to find ONE person to settle down with feels a bit… suffocating."

"Suffocating because you haven't found the right person yet, so keep swiping!" Eliza explains. "I know I don't *need* to get married, but for me, marriage is like a… a commitment to someone that you'll be in their corner no matter what happens."

"There's so many guys..." Melayna laughs, "I mean, people out there. How can you pick just one?"

"Until I met Meaghan I thought there were a lot of people I could be with. I think we'll probably get married eventually, but does that mean she's THE ONE? I could have a happy life with girls—don't tell Meaghan that, though!" Eliza laughs nervously.

"I think it's rare to find a real spark," I mumble. Then I pretend to check my phone so they don't see the tears start to form in my eyes. The emerald green emergency exit sign is blinding now, as though going through one door will magically erase the past and transform the future. Adam and I felt so real. So honest. So true. But the past feels like one big lie. Why would he come back into my life if he was going to leave me? I remember watching *Sex and the City* and thinking how cruel it was of Big to prance back into Carrie's life claiming his marriage was falling apart, and then not pulling through.

I genuinely believed that we were each other's family. Now it's like everything I knew crumbled in an instant, like a betrayed wife must feel after reading about her husband's infidelity on Ashley Madison. *He's not that kind of man. There must be some mistake. My partner's one of the good ones. Right?*

The taste of vomit in my mouth is putrid. I try to stifle it, stomach the past with a whiff of sterile, purified hospital smell. How can any of us even know what to believe anymore? Our culture's full of so much phoniness and deception. Companies advertise products to make us believe that we will be more beautiful, more healthy, or live longer by consuming their products. We are seduced by lovers who feed their porn addictions when we're asleep. We're taught to believe that if we work hard and take risks, that we can achieve our dreams, yet youth unemployment is the highest it's been in decades. Fairytales tell us that true love exists, but half of all marriages end in divorce.

At work, I can do everything I'm trained to do and the patient still dies. I want to stay optimistic, but it feels like every time I start to believe in something, all I'm left with is soul crushing emptiness. Maybe the truth doesn't exist if you look the other way.

Melayna swipes her thumb across her phone a couple of times, then holds up picture of a Zac Efron lookalike funneling a beer.

Cory, 26. About Cory: I make six figures and own a condo in Liberty Village. "Work hard. Play hard."

"This dude...would hide in bed with you, or ask you to fight off the burglar yourself."

I need to get out of here. STAT. I can only keep a smile on my face for so long before I start to feel like a pathetic clown at a kids' birthday party. The taste of vomit is strong and awful and I need to run because I don't know what else to do. I sprint to the washroom as quickly as I can and slam the door. *Adam, please come home.*

Crouching down, I place my hands on the toilet seat, supporting myself in case I throw up. Instead a few tears roll down my cheek, the first signs of grief settling into my body, the way a light frost overtakes the earth before a winter storm. As my head hangs over the toilet bowl, I close my eyes, and take a deep breath.

"Don't go," I whimpered as Adam stuffed a few more warm layers into a bag: long johns, a fleece pullover, the warm socks I'd brought for him from my parents' house. His eyes were glowing with the same energy I'd witnessed in him before big rugby games. A crazed blend of excitement and aggression. Utter fearlessness.

In a few hours, he'd be heading north for about a month, to the wild, on a fishing trip in the Yukon, right on the Alaskan border. I'd be going back to Calgary for my last year of med school, with no idea where I'd be working next year.

Marcus and I had our fingers crossed that I would get a job in Calgary. Or at least somewhere in the area. With Marcus, I felt safe. Secure...but also restless at times. Seeing Adam again made me feel like I was showing my petals after a dormant winter. It's like all of the old feelings I thought I'd moved on from came pouring back the moment I saw him. Was it nostalgia or something more? How could I even consider becoming something more when I had someone who loved me out West?

"I really need this trip, Em. I don't know what to do with myself now," he'd explained. "Rugby was everything to me."

I understood, but I longed to hold him, squeeze him, pull him tight to me and never let go. I wanted to scream at him: "Don't go! Come with me!" But I said nothing. How could I? I had responsibilities to the hospital in Calgary. I had another boyfriend.

As he continued to pack, I whispered, "Adam. It's been so nice to see you again."

Memories keep coming back. Flashbacks. They creep up unexpectedly. In the middle of the night. During work. On my morning runs. I'm trying to stay strong but it feels like my brain's searching for some proof, a moment, a missed conversation, something to help me understand what has happened to him. It's a dark shadow following me around, whispering that "red flags" had been there for months or years, and that I'd been too blind to notice.

"Hello?" A knock on the door snaps me back to reality. I close my eyes again. *Inhale, exhale.* The bathroom door handle rattles, an impatient intern testing the lock.

"I'll be a minute."

My distressed voice cracks slightly. Then I stand up and stare at myself in the mirror. The emptiness is blinding. Right away I splash water on my face, wiping away my tears. I don't know where Adam is but I feel him everywhere I go.

He's the aching in my heart. The watering in my eyes. The tension in my neck. He's a virus infecting me. There's no treatment, no cure. As the time passes, I become more and more vulnerable to his absence, more and more desperate.

Adam: May 19, 2014, 9:00 am PDT

"Davison, clean up your shit."

I'm awake but I close my eyes as his footsteps approach.
Something terrifying inside me tightens its grip.
I know this man is dangerous: a terrorist, or drug lord. I am his hostage. If I close my eyes maybe he will disappear.

Who am I fooling? Bad dreams never end. We just pretend they aren't there.

I've been here before.
Not this exact place. Not on the cold concrete floor. But I've felt the horrifying emptiness.
Numbness where I should feel pain.
Wanting to disappear.
So I went north. Whitehorse.
But now I'm trapped in the nightmare.

I hear the rattle of keys and the slow creak of a heavy metal door. He has access to me. Not I to him. I hear the clunk of something drop on the floor.

A voice directs itself towards me.

"Davison, I brought you a cloth and a bucket to clean up your shit. Fuck. This is nasty, man, and I've seen some nasty shit in here before, but nothing like this… This is what happens when people don't give a fuck about themselves."

He raises his voice.

"It better be cleaned up by the time I get back."

Then his footsteps get further from me. The door clangs shut. I'm locked in.

Trapped.

I am completely lost in here, in myself, in everything.

My head throbs and my heart beats loudly, a *thump-thump-thump* reminder that I'm still alive even if only half-alive.
I'm so thirsty.
My mouth is a crust of puke and blood.
My tongue feels like sandpaper.

I bite down and feel a bolt of electricity shoot through my gums and into my head.
The brain freeze you get from slurping a slushie too fast.

Finally, I open my eyes. I don't know where I am or what I've done or most of all how to get out of here. All I know is that I'm fucked.

The room is small and dark and rectangular. There's a metal bench and a toilet and no windows and nothing on the walls. I understand where I am now but there's nothing to tell me why I'm here.

I press myself deeper into the grave I've dug for myself.
What's the point of getting up?
I'm a fuck-up.
I deserve to rot away in my own shit. So I just continue to lie in my blood and puke and despair. They will punish me for this but I can't move.

I can't feel.
I can't hurt.

I can't cry.
I can't remember.
I don't care.

I close my eyes and try to disappear.

Eventually I fall asleep.
Sleeping is much safer than the nightmare I'm living.
When I sleep I feel nothing and I do nothing and I see nothing and nothing matters and no one cares. There's no one to hurt or disappoint or notice when I'm low and I don't need to face anyone not anyone in the world or not even myself.

"Davison."

I hear my name.
"Davison."
I hear my name but don't really know who I am anymore.
I have no job.
No money.
No girlfriend.
I'm a fucking IDIOT.

"Davison. Get the fuck up."

I can hear keys jangling in a lock.

"Fuck. I told you to clean up your shit."

I keep my eyes closed.
I do nothing and say nothing and feel nothing.

"You're really going to make me make you clean up your shit? As much as I'd be happy to let you continue to lie in your puke and let you die, there's laws in place that say I can't do that."

"Warren!" He calls out to someone. "Help me get this fucker up!"
"Ya, sure Steve. You got it."

More footsteps.

"You got left side. I got right."
"Yup."
"Fuck this is gross."
"Yup. He's been like this for almost twenty-four hours."
"Shit."
"Yeah."
"Ok. One. Two. Three. Lift."

I'm pulled onto my feet then dragged across the room and slammed up against a wall.

"Come on, Davison, stand up."

They are pressing my back against the wall and holding me up under the armpits.

"You're meeting with the judge later this afternoon and he'll determine if you're eligible for bail, so if you want to be released, you better start cooperating."

I open my eyes and see that I am face to face with a tall, middle-aged man who looks like he may have worked in the army when he was younger and fitter.
I know I should be intimidated but I'm not.
"This is serious." The other man says.

I look at him.
He's young and keen and twenty-five and he is still excited about life.
I don't take him seriously.

"If you want a chance to be with your friends and family while you wait for your trial, then you need to show that you want to get out of here."

The thought of Emma seeing me like this is worse than the thought of never getting out.
These guards can do what they want to me.
I don't care.

I hang my head, looking at my feet.
Whose shoes am I wearing?
Shiny.
Black.
Leather.
They look expensive and fashionable, like the ones worn by CEOs or big shot lawyers, not a gym rat. A jobless criminal.
Then I notice my pants.
Charcoal dress pants.
When's the last time I wore dress pants? My graduation? Jeff's wedding?

Confused, I check out the rest of my outfit. I'm wearing a charcoal suit jacket to match the pants and a white dress shirt underneath. Both are covered in puke and blood. The puke's mine but I don't have any cuts.

Whose blood is this?

Emma: May 19, 2014, 2:30pm EDT

I check on Hillary, a 21-year-old who was brought in after she was found passed out at a nightclub on King Street West. I can just picture her last night. Her short sequined dress. Black heels. A duck face selfie on Instagram. (#girlsnite #yolo #hotties #dressedtokill) I bet she'll make a mockery of this whole situation in her next post. (#blackedoutdrunk #shots #oops #ninelives #hotdoctors #sorrynotsorry)

She had a University of Toronto Student I.D. card in her wallet, so maybe she was out celebrating the end of her exams. Or maybe it was a regular night out for her. I shake my head. Too many smart and beautiful women have spent nights in the ER after self-induced benders, partying 'til they puke like Miley Cyrus or Lindsay Lohan.

"Do you remember the nurses stripping you down?"

"No," Hillary replies, embarrassed.

"Luckily, the bouncers at the club found you and called an ambulance. You could have passed out on the street and anyone could have taken your clothes off and brought you anywhere. You could have come here in a body bag."

My train of thought breaks as I hear my name in an overhead page. "Dr. Watters to resuscitation bay, please!" I hustle to respond to the next emergency, relieved with how busy the day has been. If I stop moving, I'll think of Adam. I'll freeze.

As I put on my mask and gloves, Neil comes over to me. I assume he wants to review our roles for the situation. He steps uncomfortably close to me, so that he's directly behind me. He whispers in my ear, his hot breath causes the hairs on my neck to rise. I quickly pull away. *Not so fast, Bill Cosby.*

With his dark curly hair, olive skin and blue eyes, Neil bears such a striking resemblance to Patrick Dempsey that many of the nurses call him McDreamy, like Dr. Shepherd on *Grey's Anatomy*. But I think he's almost too good-looking, like an indoor flower arrangement that you have to get really close to in order to determine if it's real or fake.

"How long is the mourning period?" he asks. I'm assuming that he's referring to a patient's death this morning.

"I'm not dwelling over it. We did everything we could have. There's nothing I would have changed. I've let it go already."

"That's not what I meant," he replies. "I mean, when is it no longer inappropriate for me to invite you to my place for a drink?" *Is this guy for real? Just because you were at my party does not mean that I want ANYTHING to do with you outside of work.*

"Don't ask me. Ever. I'm not interested," I say, irritated that he would think that right now is a good time to hit on me, as though we don't have a life or death situation on its way.

"I'm only trying to help you. Get you back in the game. Have you been on any dates yet? Are you online, at least? "

He grabs my right shoulder gently, turning me to face him. He looks at me directly. I immediately avoid his gaze. "You're one of the most beautiful women, if not, *the* most beautiful woman in this hospital. You shouldn't be holding out for some loser who took off. Make sure you remember that."

"It's none of your business," I say, turning away from him.

"Hey, you don't still think it's my fault, do you? I swear, I never saw drugs at the party, and if people did take something that night, it had nothing to do with me."

Whatever you say, Neil. Luckily, we're interrupted by the news that the ambulance has arrived. Our team gets into place as the paramedics wheel the man in on a stretcher while continuing to perform CPR. Mike, the chief paramedic and a George Costanza lookalike, updates us on the patient as the paramedics work with the team of nurses to transfer him and begin hooking him up to the monitors. No heartbeat.

"Man was asystolic on arrival. CPR's been ongoing for about 20 minutes. He's had 8 doses of epi. He's had an amp of bicarb and about 500 mL of fluid."

"Thanks," says Neil. "When was the last epi?"

"About 3 minutes ago," Mike responds.

Neil turns to one of the nurses. "Meg, give him another milligram of epinephrine, please."

I conduct the primary assessment, checking his vitals and looking for any information about the patient's condition and medical history.

Neil pauses for a moment then directs the team. "Ok, hold CPR for a sec." One of the nurses stops CPR. "Dr. Watters, do we have a pulse?"

I look up at the monitor as my fingers search his neck for any sign of a pulsation. His ECG is completely flat. There's no cardiac activity. "No, no pulse." I pause, then outline the next step: "Dr. Wilson's going to do a bedside ultrasound to get a confirmation."

The man is still pulseless after we run the tests to rule out any reversible conditions. One minute he was out enjoying the sunshine on Lake Ontario and the next he's being given CPR. I wish that there was something that we could have done to help, but he was already gone when he got to the hospital. We just have to step back and let him go.

For a perfectionist like me, letting go is not easy. I always try to find another way to fix things, change things, make things better, but I've learned that there's times when you have to accept that there's nothing else you can do to help someone, and move on.

Finally, Neil speaks up, "Dr. Watters can you call it?"

I nod, "Time of death: 11:49 am."

"I'll go talk to the family to let them know the CPR efforts were unsuccessful. Let's clean the patient up and remove all of the lines so the family can come in and see him if they want to," Neil suggests. "It can be very difficult for people to move forward if they don't have closure from the people they love."

I feel him staring at me as he says it.

Adam: May 19, 2014 1:10 pm PDT

I stare at Ken, the Duty Counsel, a legal aid lawyer who is going to help me with my bail hearing. I'm in disbelief. I take a deep breath, close my eyes, and try to recall something, anything, that I have been accused of.

It's all a blur. The party and the dancing and our friends and the surprise and Emma.

This is the happiest I've ever been.

I remember the mountains. The ocean. The wilderness.
The hotel. The protest. *Fuck*.
Nothing makes sense.

Why am I in Vancouver? How did I get here? Why was I wearing a suit?

Did I black out from partying?
I've barely drank since I stopped playing rugby.

He must have the wrong guy. He has to. I know I'm not a criminal.
I look directly at him.

"I live in Toronto so I don't even know why I'm in Vancouver. The person you're describing can't be me. I wouldn't do those things."

Ken opens a folder and passes me a picture.

"The taxi driver took this after you jumped out of his cab at a red light. Is this you in the picture?"

It definitely does look like me, wearing the same suit, someone else's suit, I was wearing when I woke up this morning. But it can't be me.
That man has a beard. Someone must have set me up.
I stroke my chin, expecting to feel a bit of stubble.
What the fuck? My beard's soft.
How long have I been in Vancouver?

I've never been in jail before so I don't know what I'm supposed to do or say, how honestly I should be speaking to this officer without a lawyer or something. But I remember from watching movies like *Shawshank* that you have the right to remain silent.
 Or maybe that's for when you're getting arrested.

So I say nothing.

Ken looks down, referring to some notes in the folder.

"I recommend you tell the truth here. Judges don't have sympathy for liars. They want to see that people can hold themselves accountable for their actions."

"I'm not lying." I feel a spark. Confidence. "I honestly can't remember anything you've described."

"When people are under the influence of drugs or alcohol they often do things that they would never do sober," Ken explains.

"You'd be surprised by some of the crimes people have committed when they were drunk or high. You probably blacked out. Maybe you were intoxicated the whole time you have been in Vancouver. You have been puking on and off for the last 24 hours so there was definitely something in your system. Do you remember taking any drugs?"

He must be wrong. He has the wrong person. I've done stupid things when I've been drunk before but nothing like what he is describing.

Again, I shake my head.

Ken thinks for a moment.

"Well, all of those details will be examined at your trial. We need to focus on getting you bail. Otherwise, you will have to wait in custody while you await your trial. Have you ever been arrested?"

I shake my head. I'm no criminal. Or, I thought I wasn't.

"Do you have a job?"

I tell him about my gym but hold out on the detail that I've probably screwed the business.

"Good. I imagine the judge will want you to get back to work right away. It's a little tricky since you're an Ontario resident. You'll have to ensure that you will return to B.C. for your court date. The judge will probably request that you have a surety, someone who agrees to be responsible for making sure you follow your bail conditions and get to trial.

Since you're from out-of-province, he or she will likely have to pay a sum of money to the court if you don't follow your bail terms. Is there someone in your family that would agree to this?"

My first instinct is to ask Emma, but I don't want to burden her with any more financial debt. So I suggest my mom.

"I'll get in touch with her right away to let her know what her responsibilities as surety would be. Usually, the judge would want to interrogate her as well. But I'll try to get a written statement from her now to help your case. What does your mom do for work?"

"She's a kindergarten teacher."

"Does she live close to you?"

"Not too far. Parry Sound. It's about two and a half hours from Toronto, where I live."

"The judge might prefer you have someone else who lives near you. Can you think of anyone else?"

I shake my head. I don't want Emma or any of my friends involved. I don't even want my mom involved.

"At the very least, your mom will need to be able to check in with you once a day. Can she do that?"

I nod.

"Good."

Ken checks his notes.

"Since you have had no prior arrests or criminal record, I anticipate that you may be let out on bail if you're lucky. Usually, accused held in police custody must see a judge within 24 hours for a bail hearing. However, we had to adjourn your hearing since you were in such rough shape when you came in here and we needed to wait for you to sober up before putting you in front of a judge.

Right now, you need to follow orders and remember that everyone's watching you. One wrong move and you could blow your chance at bail. Do you have any questions?"

I have so many questions, but again I shake my head 'no'. I don't know what to believe or what actually happened or how to find out. I'm so ashamed that I just want to curl up in my cell and die. I just want this nightmare to be over.

"Have you been in contact with your family or friends since you've been in Vancouver?" Ken asks. "Does anyone know where you are?"

I'm guessing the police took all of my personal stuff—my wallet and phone–when they brought me here.

"I don't know."

I remember how worried Emma was when I didn't call her after I stayed at Jeff's after his bachelor party. And now, from what Ken has told me, I've been in Vancouver for over a week.

This doesn't make sense. I have no money, no friends and no business in Vancouver. Why the fuck am I here?

Emma: May 19, 2014 5:45 pm EDT

I pour myself a glass of wine and return to my Netflix binge. Despite working more than twelve hours each day, I was able to finish Season 1 of *Orange is the New Black* in four days. I'm fascinated by the main character, Piper Chapman, a WASPy woman whose life gets turned upside down by a criminal conviction. When I watch her struggle to cope with the gritty prison life, I often wonder if I'd survive in a similar situation. Maybe. Probably.

I lived my own episode of *OITNB* once by having a near-fling with a convict. When I was in my third year at Queen's University, I met this Channing Tatum lookalike at Stages Nightclub, who turned out to be an ex-con on parole. Neither of us were drinking and were both about to leave. Instead of buying me a drink, he suggested we go to Pizza Pizza for a slice of Canadian.

He seemed so chivalrous. Rugged. A gentle giant. He even held the door open for me when we entered Pizza Pizza and bought me a carnation from a kid who was selling them on the street. Since it was so busy, we didn't realize that some drunk student had claimed the pizza we'd ordered, and were told we would have to wait about fifteen minutes for the cook to make another. However, my "date" told me he couldn't wait, revealing that he needed to get back to the halfway house before his 11pm curfew to check in with his parole officer. My friends and family all laughed when I told them about my 'near-date' with a prisoner. *At least it wasn't Pizza Pizza Man! Life could be worse—you could have dated a convict, like Emma almost did!* It's kind of like the running joke whenever anyone has a bad relationship.

He stroked my hair gently, then pulled me closer, our naked bodies fitting back together as though they were never apart, small of my back pressed against his chest, his cheek next to mine, his left arm wrapped around my waist, our fingers meshed together like perfectly fitting Jenga blocks. As he squeezed my hands tighter, an electric current ran through the palms of my hands, through my bloodstream, and into my heart.

"Do you miss Marcus?" Adam broke the silence.

I hesitated for a moment, unsure how to answer. The truth was both painful and liberating and I wanted to approach it carefully.

"Yes," I wrapped myself tighter in Adam's arms. "Yes, I miss him."

I take another sip of wine, urging my mind to detach from the memories that keep showing up, unannounced, haunting me. Again, I put the wine to my lips. This time I notice a more acidic flavour, a hint of vinegar. I swirl the liquid around in the glass. It looks a little cloudy, browner than before. Putting my glass down, to let the wine set for a moment, I return my attention back to the show. Just as Piper meets her new roommate, an activist who looks more like a pretty flower than a convict, my phone rings. *Unknown number.* I usually screen calls and make them go to voicemail if I don't know the number, but ever since Adam disappeared, I pick up after the first ring.

"Hello?"

"Emma? Are you ok? You sound out of breath?" I recognize the deep, husky voice. *Neil.* How did he get my number?

"Hey, ya. I just got out of the shower," I lie.

"Nice. I'm picturing it now. Anyways, I noticed that you left the hospital quickly after the ischemia situation and wanted to make sure you were okay. Two deaths in one day can be a lot to handle... especially if you have no one to come home to."

What a bullshitter.

"Well, thanks for the call. I'm fine. Just tired. I needed to get out of there. I've been working a lot of overtime lately and felt like I'd hit a wall. It was time to leave."

"Emma, I'm worried about you. How about you have dinner with me, so you don't have to be alone right now?"

He should have been an actor instead of a doctor. Dr. McDouchebag. We all feel the need to put on a show every now and then, and I almost want to let him continue, just for the entertainment. So I answer him bluntly and honestly, a pan from the critic, "No. I already told you, I'm not interested."

In general, ER doctors are not the type of people to back down from a challenge and Neil is no exception. "Ok, I understand that you might not want to leave the house right now if you are upset. What if I come over? I can bring some take-out and keep you company."

"I'll see you at work tomorrow, Dr. Wilson." I hang up before he has a chance to respond. A good doctor knows when to call it.

I get up and pour my glass of wine down the sink. Then I turn my attention back to Piper's irritation with her happy-go-lucky roommate. Within seconds, my phone rings again.

Unknown number.

Neil again. I worry that if I don't answer, he might be bold enough to come over, to 'check up on me.'

"I told you, I'm not interested," I assert, the way I would to a telemarketer, before Neil has a chance to speak. I'm about to hang up when I hear a woman's voice. *Press one to accept the charges.* Did I hear her correctly? Why is Neil calling me collect?

Confused, I press one.

"I said, I'll see you tomorrow. Now please stop calling me," I demand anxiously, feeling the temperature in my cheeks rise with the combined effects of red wine and emotional overload.

"Emma?" I hear a meek, scratchy voice. I recognize it immediately, although it sounds distant.

I think I started believing that I'd never hear his voice again. I spent nights with my phone resting on my pillow like a teddy bear kept close for comfort, so anxious for the call that I stopped believing it would actually come. *He's alive.*

"Adam? Adam is that you? Are you okay? Where are you? When are you coming home?"

"Um, Emma?" I can hear the quiver in his voice. Whimpers. Then there's a long pause. Is he hurt? Maybe he was kidnapped or tortured, and is only being kept alive for ransom. How do I make sure he doesn't hang up?

"Adam? Are you there? Please, please answer me! Please tell me where you are so that we can get you home safely!" Then, frantically, I add, "I love you," as though it might be the last time I'm able to say it. Does he hear me?

"Emma, I know you....urgh....oh God....oh Emma, I love you too. I'm so sorry. I'm so sorry. I didn't want you to get hurt....I...I...I don't even know what happened."

He's sobbing now. In the fifteen years that we have known each other, I have only heard him cry once and that was when his cat died. This is bad. This is really bad.

"Adam, please tell me where you are so that I can help you and bring you home. I love you."

There's another long pause. Are they hurting him? I know that at any point they can make him hang up. I need to keep talking, keep the conversation going.

"Adam, I love you. It's going to be okay. Please. Please. Tell me where you are. We have all been so worried about you. If it's money that they need, we can try to find it. I will do whatever it takes to make sure you get home safely. Please tell me where you are!"

"Em, baby...I'm....I'm in Vancouver."

Adam, May 19, 2014, 3:05 pm PDT

I fall under the silence, waiting for her to say something.
Anything.

Lubdublubdublubdublubdub.
My heart.
It's beating beating beating beating beating beating.
Like drums awaiting the sound of her voice.

I hear the beat of my heart and I want to feel.
To feel to feel to feel.
I want to feel the pain that comes once I tell her I'm a fuck-up and a criminal and I've ruined her life.

I'm a fuck-up and a criminal and I've ruined her life.
This is the happiest I've ever been.
I'm a fuck-up and a criminal and I've ruined her life.

I want to feel the suffering she'll feel.
The shame and the guilt and the despair and the rage.
The horror and the humiliation.
The bottomless pit of disappointment.
My loneliness.
Her loneliness.
Our loneliness.

I feel nothing.

Lubdublubdublubdublubdub.
I'm empty but I can hear my heart.

It beats it beats it beats and I feel nothing.
It's screaming at me--YOU'RE ALIVE!
But I'm dead.

"Adam."

I hear the voice of an angel.
My heart. Oh my heart.
I want to feel.
But the void is getting bigger.

Even she can't save me.
She'll want to try.
But she can't help.
It's pointless.
There's nothing to be done.

It's over.
For her.
For me.
For both of us.

"Adam..."

Her voice cracks slightly this time.
She fights tears and tries to be strong.
I heard the crack but I feel nothing.
She's suffering and I don't care.

"Adam? Are you there? Why are you in Vancouver? Are you okay?"

I hear her desperation. Her fear. Her broken heart.
I don't say anything.
There's nothing to say.
Nothing will make it better.

Nothing.

"Adam, please, say something, speak to me, please! Can you come home? I've been so worried about you. I love you."

I don't feel for her. She can't feel for me.
She can't worry. She can't 'fix.' She can't love.

Words explode out of my mouth.

"Emma. I'm not coming home! I'm a FUCKING CRIMINAL. It's OVER!"

My temperature rises.
I've lost control of myself of my life of everything.
This conversation needs to end.
Everything needs to end.

"Adam, why are you saying you're a criminal? Are you okay? What happened?"

Why does she have to care so much?
If she didn't care, she wouldn't be suffering.
Stop caring. Stop caring. Stop caring.
Stop loving. Stop loving. Stop loving.
Leave me alone. Let me rot.
She's young and beautiful and it's not too late to find a better man.
She should be with someone else.
Not me.

"I FUCKED EVERYTHING UP!!! YOU NEED TO STOP!"

I catch my breath before shouting at her with everything that's left of me.

"STOP WORRYING ABOUT ME. STOP THINKING ABOUT ME. STOP LOVING ME. MOVE ON WITH YOUR FUCKING LIFE!!! I DON'T LOVE YOU! I CAN'T!!! IT'S OVER!!!"

I'm breathless.
I want to hang up but I can't.
This needs to end.
Her pain her love her fear.
Everything.

Emma: May 19, 2014, 6:10 pm, EDT

I don't love you.

The words pierce my heart. I wait for him to speak, to say something, anything, to give me some clue as to why he's in Vancouver. The silence is torture. It's so loud that I can't hear myself scream.

I don't know how to respond, so I say nothing. So many emotions run through my body—anger, fear, terror, rejection, disappointment, despair, and sadness jumble together with the tiniest sliver of hope. I don't know what to feel. *Stay strong, Emma. There's always hope.*

Something's wrong. This is not Adam but a madman or a monster, or maybe he really is just some big asshole and I'm the fool.

The only time I can remember him exploding irrationally at me was when we were at a party at Jeff's cottage in Muskoka. It was the summer after our second year of undergrad and he freaked out when I wouldn't fight this girl for bumping into him and spilling red wine on his white Tommy Hilfiger golf shirt. I'd never met the girl before—she must have been Nancy's friend. He came inside the cottage in a fury. *Go out there and beat her up. She's a fucking drunk idiot! I'd do it myself, but I can't hit a girl.*

At first I laughed, thinking he was joking. Sweet, polite, friendly, me—Little Miss Sunshine!—was supposed to go to the beach, seek out some girl I didn't know and smash her face for accidentally stumbling into my boyfriend at a party. Sure, I can lift a lot of weight at the gym, but I'm not a 'bully.' I didn't think Adam was, either. But he shouted at me. I cried. Our friends didn't really know what to do. It was so out of character for Adam to yell at *me*. His best friend, Jeff, intervened and calmed Adam down. They went for a walk on the beach together and when they came back, Adam apologized.

I'm sorry. I don't know what happened. Maybe I'm drunker than I thought. No excuse though. It's like I just snapped."

He seemed confused, like he lost control of himself. I figured he must have been under a lot of pressure since he was waiting to hear if he had been selected as a starting player for Team Ontario, so I didn't make a big deal of it. But since then, he's really laid off the booze, especially when I'm around.

"Emma, are you still there?" A feeble voice whispers into the receiver, so softly I can barely hear it over my throbbing heart and spinning head, but I recognize Adam in it. He seems distant, like he's lost within himself.

"I'm here. I'm not going anywhere," I say calmly. "Please tell me what happened."

I opt against asking him about all of the charges to his credit card. After he went missing, I called his bank in hopes that they could give me some information about his spending history. Unfortunately, since we don't have joint bank accounts, it was nearly impossible for me to get any information. However, the employee I spoke with told me that they had been trying to get in touch with Adam about some unusual spending. Since they flag any suspicious activity as possible cases of identity theft or fraud, the bank froze his accounts.

I immediately called Jeff. He looked into unusual spending on the company credit card and called me back to report that Adam—or someone—had spent over $2000 on a suit at Harry Rosen on West Georgia Street in Vancouver on their company credit card. We figured it mustn't have been Adam since he wears sweats to work, the old-school kind with the elastic around the cuffs. (He refused to wear the Lululemon pants I bought for his birthday!) *"I'm a man. I don't do tight!"* he'd explained, and then scoffed when I told him how sexy I thought that the men in my yoga classes looked when they wore their Lululemon pants. *"I can't stop checking out their asses in the downward dog,"* I'd joked. *"Real men aren't afraid of tight pants."*

Jeff e-mailed a picture of Adam to the store to see if they could recognize him as the person who purchased the suit. Unfortunately, the salesperson who sold the suit said that it had been really busy that weekend and, while Adam's picture did look familiar, that several men with dark hair, dark eyes and scruffy beards had been in the store recently, and that he was unsure whether it was him. He said that the store doesn't have cameras, either, so he couldn't double check. The signature matched Adam's, though. But signatures can be forged. It couldn't have been Adam. It didn't make sense. Someone must have stolen his wallet.

"Emma. Can you call my mom and Jeff and tell them that I'm okay and that I'm sorry?" Then he adds, "I'm so sorry, Em. I've ruined your life. I've ruined everything."

Just tell me where you are and what happened! Just tell me! Please!

"You haven't ruined anything. It will be okay. I told you that. We'll get through this. I will tell them, though. They are both very worried about you. We all are."

"I can't call them now. I don't have much time. I just wanted to tell you that I'm okay. I'm, I'm…"

He hesitates, as though carefully choosing his words, like a witness reluctantly testifying against his best friend to save his own skin.

"I'm in….I'm in…. JAIL. It's all my fault." Then there's a long pause. I'm not sure if he's hung up. I don't know what to say.

Did I hear him correctly? Adam's in *jail*? This can't be happening. There must be some mistake. I'd been preparing to hear him say, "I was abducted," or "I'm having an affair," or "I was diagnosed with cancer and needed some space," or even "I panicked because everything was going so well between us and I didn't want to screw it up."

"Adam? Adam? Are you still there?"

"I'm not the person you think I am." His voice is quieter, more broken.

I can't believe that a few weeks ago, I was hoping that he would propose to me. Maybe I've been dating Pizza Pizza Man all along. Or Walter White. My life's become an episode of *Breaking Bad*.

The feeling of rage is so visceral that I feel heat rising up from my abdomen into my chest and up into my head. Why did he have to do something so stupid?! He's SUCH AN IDIOT!

I erupt so hysterically, that I know if we were both in the kitchen, I would start breaking whatever I could find in his cupboards, like that scene in *Sex and the City* where Samantha's girlfriend, Maria, becomes outraged over Samantha's passionate sexual history and smashes all the plates in Samantha's kitchen to prove what a 'firework' she can be. If Adam wants drama and fireworks, I can show him fireworks!

"What the heck, Adam?!" *Smash!*
"What were you thinking?" *Blip!*
"After everything we have been through, how could you do this to me?" *Tinkle.* A little plate for dramatic effect, just like Maria. *"You don't even cook," she said.*
 "I'm so thankful that we didn't get married. Now I'm not stuck with you and your mess!" *Smash! Smash! Smash!*

There's a long pause. I catch my breath and wipe tears that have scattered out from the corners of my eyes like the shards of Samantha's plates. A calmness has come over me, like Maria accepting her relationship is over after the fireworks show. I exhale deeply then continue to question him gently.

"What did you do to get yourself in there, anyways?"

"Emma, it's all a blur. I'm so confused. It doesn't make sense. I'm sorry." I can hear his muffled cries. "I'm so, so sorry, Emma."

What's happened to the Adam I know? The man who planted tulips in our front garden a few weeks ago to brighten up our home? The one who organized a surprise party for my thirtieth birthday? My roommie. My best friend. My family.

"Adam, please don't lie to me. What happened, really?"

"I honestly can't remember...I remember coming to Vancouver but I don't know why I came in the first place. I only remember bits and pieces of the last week. I can't remember doing the things that the officer said I did."

"Which is what? What did you do?"

"Listen to this. Listen to the lies they're telling me. They say I: 'Jumped out of a cab. Assaulted a man on street corner. Ran from cops.' I would never do that. What in the hell is this? I have to go in front of a judge later today for a bail hearing. What am I supposed to say? I know I'm not crazy, but I can't remember any of this stuff they are accusing me of! Emma, I don't know what happened. I don't know why I'm here. I'm so sorry."

"How can you not remember? Own up to it, Adam." *Be a man.*

He must have been drinking or on some sort of drugs. But that still doesn't explain why he went to Vancouver in the first place. *We watched* Breaking Bad *together, Adam. If you're cooking meth, it's better if you just tell me.*

Adam, May 19, 2014 3:05 pm PDT

I hang up the phone and collapse to the floor like I'm having a heart attack.
She doesn't understand me.
I would cry if I could but I can't. I have no more tears no more soul no more hope.
Nothing.
I'm a mass of scar tissue, destroyed beyond repair.

There's no hope.
No silver lining.
No reason to keep going.

I want to fucking die.
It wouldn't matter.
I'm already dead.

It would make it easier for everyone else if I was gone.
Emma will stop worrying.
She'll move on.

I close my eyes.
The darkness surrounds me like a blanket.
I clutch it desperately. My knuckles turn white.

I'm drowning myself in a sea of something big and black and horrifying.
Falling deeper into a place worse than death.
I want to wrap myself in it and never wake up.

I awaken to footsteps.
Must be Ken coming back for me, or another guard.
How long have I been asleep?

At once I'm slammed face down into the floor.
I whimper as a boot kicks my gut.

"Shut the fuck up, you fuckin' pussy," a gruff voice snarls.

I close my eyes and escape into the darkness.
As the real nightmare begins.

Emma: May 19, 2014, 7:00 pm, EDT

Finally, I slump onto the couch with my wine and continue the unfinished episode of *Orange is the New Black*. It's a bit terrifying to think that at this minute, Adam might be wearing coveralls and will have to find a way survive amidst psychopaths like Suzanne or thugs like Vee. I hope the show isn't a realistic portrayal of prison life, with all of the sexual abuse and violence and gangs, but I'm reassured by the fact that the show is set in New York. Canadian prisons must be safer, right?

Ok, Little Miss Sunshine, pull it together. The waterworks need to stop. Nothing makes sense. This person who's in Vancouver is not Adam. What's going to happen to us now? To him?

I guess all of the late night Netflix binges made me believe that real love is something that can endure any plot twist. (I mean, it took six seasons for Carrie and Big to figure out their relationship, and **ten** seasons for Ross and Rachel to end up together!) Adam and I have something that's hard to find offline and in real life, or so I thought. But do 'soulmates' even exist anymore?

The world's changed so much since *Sex and the City* and *Friends* ended. Maybe relationships have changed, too. I mean, Carrie and Big's, and Ross and Rachel's relationships all developed before the age of the Tinder swipe! Perhaps love in the digital age is more like Netflix binge-watching: we enjoy bursts of fantasy, and then move on to something else when it's done. Like browsing for a new series on Netflix, if the relationship doesn't fit perfectly, you can trade it in for something new with the click of a button or a swipe on your phone.

But it can be really hard to let go. And I can't let go yet. There must be some mistake. Some explanation for what's happened. Adam must be in some kind of trouble.

Jeff picks up after the first ring.

"Hey Jeff, it's Emma calling to let you know that I've heard from Adam."

He pauses. "What, he's okay? How do I get a hold of him?"

"Um….you can't call him. Adam's in…uh…he's in jail. He might be getting bail today but I'm not sure. When I spoke to him, he didn't have a lot of information."

"WHAT?!? REALLY? For what? How would Adam find the time to get himself in prison? We've been way too busy with work for him to get into any kind of trouble! This just doesn't make any sense to me. How could Adam possibly be in JAIL? He's too honest!"

I can hear the shock in his voice. He is clearly as dumbfounded as I am, which rules out the possibility that Adam went there for business. Did Adam really do all of those things he's been accused of?

"Are you going to go see him today? Do you want me to come with you?" Jeff's concerned. "Obviously, they've got the wrong guy. The General's the man we all look to for guidance. How could he possibly be in jail? It just doesn't make ANY SENSE."

"Yeah, I'm as confused as you are. But, actually, I can't go see him today. He's in Vancouver."

"WHAT? Why is he in Vancouver? Does he even KNOW anyone out there?"

There's silence on the other end, like he's trying to searching through the memory bank for a name, a comment, a sign, ANYTHING to suggest why Adam may have gone to Vancouver. I'd done the same. I'd stalked his Facebook, checked his search history on his computer, and looked through his text and call history on his cell. But I couldn't find any clues to his disappearance. It's like he hadn't even planned on going there in the first place. *He must have been kidnapped! There must be some explanation for this.*

"So those charges on the company credit card were his after all?" Jeff asks hesitantly. He doesn't want to believe that Adam would put their company in debt. Neither do I. It's just so unlike him. Someone else, the real criminal, the kidnapper, forced him, or stole his credit card.

I pour myself another glass of wine. The image of Adam, held at gunpoint by a drug dealer/sex trafficker, is really stressing me out. I don't know how Skylar held it together for so long after she found out that Walt was cooking meth. Does Adam expect me to go into business with him like Skylar did with Walt?

"Emma, are you there?! Did you hear me? What was that sound? Are you drinking?"

Shit. I figured he wouldn't be able to hear me pour that glass of wine.

"Sorry, Jeff. Yes, I'm here. I'm not 'drinking,' just having a post-work glass of wine to unwind. It's been a long day."

"You know that exercise is much better medicine! Let's go for a run and talk things out, figure out what the next steps are here." Jeff is the best. He is such a good friend for Adam, always convincing him to get outside, and go for runs or sailing on Lake Ontario whenever Adam gets bummed out about work.

"No, thanks though. I was going to go for a jog but I think I'll just stay in and watch Netflix or something."

I hang up the phone and take a small sip of wine. Then I pick up the glass and chug it in one gulp and pour myself another. The thought of having to call Nicky, Adam's mom, makes me feel sick. So I cop out and send her a text: *Heard from Adam. He's ok. Talk soon.* Then I turn off my phone, toss it to the other side of the couch, and resume the episode as I lock my fingers tightly around the stem of my glass of Malbec. I know I should be calling Nicky, my parents, my friends, the local police, and put an update post on Facebook for everyone who's been trying to help figure out where the fuck Adam's been over the last ten days. I just can't handle having the same conversation over and over right now. *It doesn't make sense to me either. I don't know why he's in Vancouver. I never pictured him as the criminal type. There must be some mistak*e. I'll make the calls later. Tomorrow.

I resume watching *OITNB* so I can disappear from this nightmare. But the episode only makes my reality more terrifying. The image in front of me makes me feel sick: Piper on the prison phone, dressed in orange coveralls, speaking desperately to her partner on the outside. She looks tired, hardened, and helpless. Her relationship is falling apart. Of course it is, she's a fucking criminal! *Like Adam. No, he can't be. There has to be some kind of mistake.* If not, Adam and I will be over, like Piper and Larry.

I inhale my wine. *This is a mistake. It has to be.*

Adam, May 19, 2014, 7:00 pm, PDT

I look at the floor.
"The next station is YVR Airport. YVR Airport Station."

Everyone is staring at me.
Dirtbag creep. Homeless criminal.
People only notice you at your shittiest.
No one cares about you when you want to be noticed.
Emma didn't even put her birthday flowers in water.
It was like she didn't even care.

I just need to get home.
(Where is home now?)
Emma and I are done.

I've already risked breaking my probation.
I had to sneak on the SkyTrain.
Goddamn bankcard wouldn't work.
How do I get home if I have no money?

Fuckin' bail conditions.
Get back to work.
Stay in Toronto.
Don't contact victim. (I don't even know the guy!)
No drugs or booze.

I have no idea how I'm gonna pay for this stupid plane ticket.

I step off the train onto the platform.
Then stare out at the parking lot full of cars.
So many people coming and going.
Visiting people who care about them.
So many people.
The ones who care about me will stop wasting their time.

I close my eyes.
I still feel his warm, rancid breath on my ear.
Fuckin worthless piece of shit.
His rough hands on my skin.
Get up. Davison, get the fuck up.
I couldn't. I couldn't get up.
Escape.

I stare at the parking lot then stare at the mountains.
Rugged snow-covered peaks.
How easy it would be to get lost in them.
So wild and beautiful and terrifying.

What if I don't go home?
Head north. Up the coast of B.C.
To the Yukon. Like I did after undergrad.
How freeing it would be to escape.
Become a lone wolf in the wilderness.

Emma.
My throat tightens.
Thinking of her suffocates me.
I'll think about her when I want to forget her.

No, I could never escape.

I loved her.
I ruined her life.

I won't forget her.
I can't forget her.

She's gone but not gone. I'm the one who should be gone.

I watch a train pass by.
How easy it would be to lie on the tracks.
Disappear forever.
Erase my memories my life myself.

I think of the pain.
The pain in my head my heart my life.
Unrelenting pain.

I feel my heart race in anticipation.
Oh my heart.

I look at the ocean.
I hear the wind echoing from the mountains.
Laughing.

I don't belong anywhere.
Not in the vast and empty wilderness.
Nowhere.

I'll lie with my head turned towards the mountains.

Beauty will be the last thing I'll see.

Another train approaches.
Faster than I thought. The impact will be great.
Now I see the light.
I imagine myself lying on the tracks.
Awaiting the end of this nightmare.
Awaiting freedom.

People get off the train after it comes to a stop.
A man in a suit.
A young family.
A couple of girls with backpacks.

Too many people.
I'll have to wait until it gets dark.

I stare at the tracks as the train leaves.
I see my crushed body spread across the tracks.
What will happen to it?
Who will scrape it off the tracks?
Will they send it to Ontario?

I know Mom will want a funeral.
She'll want the body.
Canada Post? Fed Ex? UPS?
Or will she have to come here to get it? Maybe they'll burn it before they send it.
Cheaper shipping.

There doesn't need to be a funeral.
What would anyone say?
"Here lies a man who fucked up his life."
No funeral, Mom.

I step closer to the edge.
Looking at the mountains.
So much beauty.
So wild and beautiful and terrifying.

I can feel myself rocking back and forth slightly.
On a precipice.
Drifting with the breeze coming off the ocean.

Another train stops.
I watch the passengers step off.
A couple with bicycles.
A mom with a baby on her back and a large suitcase.

A couple with a cat in a carrier.
Too many people.
Maybe I'll wait another hour.

"Sir." I hear a woman's voice. "Excuse me, sir?"
I keep staring at the mountains.
I'm already gone.

I feel a tap on my shoulder.
"Sir, are you lost?"
"Sir, can you hear me?"
"Sir, do you need help?"
The light fades as the sun disappears behind the mountains.

I turn towards her.
A blonde middle-aged woman in a blue jacket.
A bright yellow safety vest. *SkyTrain Customer Service*.
"Sir, I notice you've been staring at the trains, but going nowhere. Do you need help?"

Fuck.
FUCK!
I thought I was a ghost.
Faded into the wind.
Disappeared into the wild.
But I'm a flashing warning sign.
DANGER! DANGER!

I tell her I'm going home.
Back to Toronto.

She walks with me off the platform.
Down a long hallway.
Towards an elevator.

"This will take you up to the departures. Have a great flight. There's nothing better than going home," she says cheerfully.

I take the elevator up and look back.
She's still watching me, making sure I'm okay.

I guess there's always the TTC.
But the views from the Toronto subway are nothing like the SkyTrain.
Or maybe the Yukon.
Escape.

I find the flight schedule.
Departures.
Vancouver to Toronto.
West Jet. 9:35pm.
Air Canada. 11:50pm.

I walk to the West Jet ticket counter.
The blond woman's got too much lipstick.
Like Emma's friend Katie.
I fuckin hate red lipstick.

"How can I help you, sir?"

Too smiley. Too cheerful.
A nauseating happiness.

"Can I have a one-way ticket for the next flight to Toronto, please?" I ask, her phoniness rubbing off.

"I can certainly look into that for you," she replies. A robotic voice.
She does a quick computer search.
But it feels like hours pass.

"There're a few seats available for the 9:35 pm flight in economy class. Would you like me to book one for you?"

I nod, giving her my information.

"That will be $550.30."

I hand her my credit card.
She passes me the machine.
I type in my PIN.
And wait.
I stare at the screen.
Come on come on come on.

Card declined.
Fuck.

"Uh oh. It looks like that didn't go through. Would you like me to try again?" 'Happy-go-lucky' asks.

I look through my wallet.
I hand her the company credit card.

"Try this one instead."

Once again, I type in the PIN.
And wait.

Jeff will understand.
I'll pay it back eventually.

Card declined.
What the fuck?

"I'm sorry. I'm so sorry," I say. "I don't know what is going on."

I don't know what is going on.

"Can I use your phone? I'll have to ask my company to book this for me."

"I'm sorry, sir, the phones are for staff only. However, you are welcome to use the pay phone over there," she says, struggling to hold her smile as she points towards the payphones.

Fuck.
When you're down on the ground, people just keep kicking.

I walk towards the pay phone.
I pick up the receiver and make a collect call to my mom.

"Hello?" A muffled voice.
She's been crying.
It's all my fault.

"Hi Mom, I'm so sorry. I'm so sorry."

"I know, sweetie," she says, "just come home and we'll figure it all out then."

"The thing is…oh God…I'm so sorry, Mom…"

What thirty-year-old man still needs his mommy to bail him out?
She had no help from anyone when she was my age.
And she supported both of us.
I can't even support myself.

"I can't buy my ticket. My credit cards aren't working."

"Of course they wouldn't. Emma called the credit card company when you went missing. She...urgh, *we*, thought that you may have been the victim of identity theft or something crazy. They had already frozen your accounts by the time she called. I guess they had been trying to contact you about some unusual spending. We can work that out when you're home, though."

"So, uh, Mom, I'm not sure if you're near a computer, but I need you to book a flight for me Toronto. There's seats available on West Jet. The 9:35 flight."

"Shoot. I didn't even think that you wouldn't be able to pay for your ticket home. I'm surprised the judge didn't consider that, either. I'll get the ticket right away, but call me if there are any problems."

I'll never be able to pay her back.
Not for raising me.
Not for loving me.
And definitely not for this.

"Thanks, Mom."
"Have you told Emma you're on your way home?"
"No."

I'm a fuck-up.
A criminal.
I've ruined her life.
What's there to say?

"Just focus on getting home safely. I'll get you the ticket. I promised the judge I made sure you got home. I can't come to

Toronto to pick you up at the airport since I'm taking my class on a field trip to the farm, so you'll have to take TTC. Please call me when you get home. I'll come to see you as soon as I can."

Emma: May 20, 2014, 5:45am, EDT

My alarm goes off and I wake up to the worst hangover I've had since Frosh Week. I spent most of my first semester at Queen's getting wasted like everyone else. I crammed into residence rooms in Vic Hall and did shots of vodka, rum, or whatever I could get. I even did a few keg stands at house parties in the Student Ghetto. *Chug! Chug! Chug! Chug! Chug!* It makes me sick just thinking about the gallons of nasty PBR that were consumed that week. During Frosh Week, I started playing a part, like a character on a TV show. Emma Watters: Meredith Grey by day, Kim Kardashian by night.

The Kardashian in me took over. I'm embarrassed by that now, but every gal's got a little Kardashian in her, right? I failed my Chemistry 112 midterm. I failed my Biology 102 midterm. I failed my Math 121 midterm. I failed my Physics 117 midterm. The only midterm that I passed was HLTH 101 but that was because I'd gotten my hands on a copy of last year's exam from a second year student who I almost made out with when I was drunk.

One morning, I slept through my 8:30 am Chemistry lecture for the third week in a row because I'd closed the bar dancing at Ale House. When I woke up, I was covered in puke. It was terrifying that I could have easily choked on my vomit and died. After I got out of the shower, I looked at my flabby body in the mirror for a long time. The "Frosh Fifteen" I'd gained from all of the booze had transformed my previously toned abs, hips, and thighs into jiggly blubber. I didn't know who that walrus in the reflection was. Not Meredith. Not Kim. Not me.

I knew I had to stop drinking. How was I going to get into med school with failing grades? By November, I quit drinking. Instead of boozing it up, I'd curl up in bed with my laptop, like a kid with a book, and escape into another place. New York. California. An island in the South Pacific. The first Thursday, Friday, and Saturday nights were lonely when my friends went to the bar without me. I joined some intramural sports teams, like basketball and inner tube water polo to take a break from studying and make some new friends. (On the plus side, my walrus weight helped me float!) But the games never seemed to be scheduled on bar nights, so I started watching TV shows that I'd downloaded onto my laptop the old fashioned-way. (This was about 10 years before Netflix came into existence.) *The OC*, *Sex and the City*, *Lost*, *Grey's Anatomy*, and *House*. Each show taught me so much about life, love, and relationships, while *Grey's* and *House* taught me a bit about the medical profession. I often felt that I learned more about life from watching an episode or two on my laptop than I did during a lecture for one of my courses.

Ding-dong. Despite my pounding head, I'm spurred into action, quickly putting on my spandex shorts and t-shirt. *Rain or shine. Get up and run.* Katie and I are committed to running 10km three times a week in the mornings. Without running, I'm not sure how I would manage the stress of working in the ER. *Ding-dong.* She's getting impatient! I rush into the kitchen to get a glass of water and notice the empty bottle of Malbec. *I drank the entire bottle?* No wonder it's painful to think. Shit, what did I do to myself? I thought I was stronger than this mess.

Finally, I open my door and greet a smiling Margot Robbie look-a-like. Regardless of the circumstances or the time of day, Katie always looks stunning. I'm never quite sure if she takes the time to put on make-up before running because she looks so put together in a way that's almost too perfect.

"Hey, sorry I'm late. I had a bit of a rough night. It might be a bit of a slow run for me."

Katie looks me over and scrunches her face in concern. "Are you okay? Your eyes are really puffy."

"Yeah...well...I'm not sure." I lock the door and then discreetly put the key in the mailbox. "Adam called me last night."

"What? *Phfewf!* He's alive!" She hugs me tightly. Then she pulls away and looks me directly at me. "Was it a ransom call? Is he safe?"

"It wasn't a ransom call," I reply. "Let's just start and I'll tell you on the run… I had a couple glasses of wine last night and need to sweat it out."

"Oh, don't beat yourself up over it. We've all done that. I never told you this, but when Mike broke up with me, I had to call in sick one day because I was so hungover… but to be honest, I felt more heart-broken when I lost the account in Beijing. It's hard to admit, but we can't be superwomen all of the time."

"Yeah, well, I never thought I could just lose it like that. Ok, let's do this." I start my watch.

We jog slowly down Dufferin Street towards Bloor. My legs are iron dumbbells, my gut is wrenching and my head feels like it's going to explode, but I force myself to keep moving. Once I commit to something, there's no turning back, no matter how much energy it takes to keep going.

"So what happened with Adam?" Katie asks.

"I don't have much information right now. But he's in jail and he's in Vancouver. It doesn't make any sense."

"What? Yeah right! Adam's in jail? What did he do?"

"I don't know. He claims he doesn't know either. But he must be lying. The cops don't just arrest people for no reason."

"Uhhh...unless you're a black man in a hoodie!" Katie adds. "Sorry, I had to say it. I've gotten a bit more sensitive about the whole racial profiling thing since I started dating James. Totally inappropriate right now. Are you going to go to Vancouver? To talk to him?"

Huh? I didn't even consider flying to Vancouver. I mean, I shouldn't have to take time out of work or pay money out of my pocket when he's the one who screwed up. Besides, I've only been working at Toronto Western for a couple of months. I don't want to ask for favours or time off this early, especially if it's to pick up my boyfriend from jail. Imagine that request!

"No," I reply. "Anyways, he mentioned something about possibly being released on bail while he awaits his trial. But I haven't heard anything."

"Wow, this is so crazy. How could Adam have possibly gotten into this much trouble?"

"I don't know. I've come up with a ridiculous list of possibilities, though. What if I've been living with Walter White all along?"

Katie laughs. "Imagine. Yikes! I'll admit I did start questioning your taste in guys after you dated Pizza Pizza Man."

"What? We never dated. We danced at Stages. Then we shared a slice of pizza. Period."

"Sure, sure," Katie teases. "I'd be surprised if Adam was up to something this whole time. You guys have been friends since forever. You would have noticed if something was up. Also, his MaxFit is doing so well. He's a popular coach there. Everyone loves him.

I just can't believe he would break the law. He seems too… too honest. Remember how he called you from Cancun after he kissed that American girl on Spring Break? He felt so guilty, and you guys weren't even together at the time!"

Katie's right. "I know. Adam takes commitment very seriously. That's why all of this is so confusing."

We jog on the spot as we wait for the light to change at Bloor Street. Katie stays quiet. I can tell she doesn't know what to say. I don't blame her. I wouldn't know what to say to me either. What prepares someone to give advice to a friend who is dating a criminal?

"So, what are you going to do?" Katie asks me.

"What do you mean?"

"Well… I don't know how to say this… everyone is different and I'll totally support you through whatever you decide…but are you, uh, are you thinking you guys will get through this? What if Adam has to go back to jail?"

I think back: Skylar tried to stick with Walt at first but she dumped his ass once he turned out to be a real hardened criminal. Larry asked Piper to marry him and she ended up sleeping with her ex-girlfriend. It seems that crime changes the person you love no matter how much faith you have in them to redeem themselves.

"It's silly to believe that there's any chance now. He did a really shitty thing. I do really love him, though. I thought that we were going to make it. This is all so confusing."

"Do you want to slow down?" asks Katie. "You sound exhausted. We could always turn around here and walk home."

I need to keep up the routine. I can't slow down. If I stop moving, I will crumble.

"No, I need to get through this. No matter how hard it is," I admit, "and besides, I want to see the cherry blossoms in High Park. I don't know if they'll still be in full bloom next time."

"Oh, yeah. They only last about a week or two," Katie agrees. "James and I went to see them on the weekend."

Katie continues, "You know, Mike and I tried really hard, too. Even though it sucked, him dumping me was one of the best things that happened to me. I invested five years into the relationship, I wouldn't have given up on us. It would have been like quitting a challenging job. It's not me just to give up. When things get hard, I just try harder. I make things work. But sometimes people just aren't compatible. Or it's bad timing."

Or a criminal conviction.

I remember being shocked when Mike ended things with Katie. He'd told her that he wanted to be with someone who needed him more, someone he could take care of. Somehow, Katie, with her movie star looks, great career, adventurous spirit, and bubbly personality, made him feel like "less of a man." I guess he prefers the kind of girl who will get dolled up and hold his hand at the bar when the Jays were playing. Idiot.

Is that what Adam wanted? Something simple? Was being with me too difficult? Too much of a climb? I thought that we had something special by pushing each other to greater heights than we could reach ourselves. Although I worry that the guys who settle for less will only end up like Big when he realized that all Natasha wanted was BEIGE! BEIGE! BEIGE. (Boring.), I'm not going to be there to clean up their messes like Carrie was.

Katie continues as we turn west onto Bloor Street, "Then I went online and learned that there are so many other guys out there, better matches for me. Like James. Mike and I just weren't right for each other. All of those fights Mike and I had seem ridiculous. I realized that the problem with our relationship is that I tolerated too much. I kept forgiving and trying to find solutions to our problems when the right thing to do was give up."

"Well, it's hard to know when to stop fighting for someone you love."

While it's great to see Katie so happy, I wonder how long 'perfect' can last. Carrie and Aidan were perfect at first, too, and look how that turned out. But Katie would definitely choose Aidan over Big. In her opinion, Carrie's a horrible role model for women: she's too self-absorbed, she's too materialistic, she's too dependent on men for emotional validation, and she's addicted to toxic relationships. I, on the other hand, wonder if Carrie simply embraces the fact that love is messy and tries to follow her gut, even if that means breaking the rules.

"All I can say is that with James, it's so simple. So perfect." I hear the voice of Carrie telling her friends about Aidan. *"It's smooth sailing. Nothing but calm seas and blue horizon as far as the eye can see...We adore each other. We have fun together. We mesh!"*

A wave of nausea comes over me as we begin our loop through High Park. I slow to a walk, lean down for a few seconds, and put my hands on my knees. *Pull it together, you've gotta keep going.* I spit a mouthful of phlegm to clear my throat.

Katie pats me on the back. "Emma, I think you should call in sick today. You're in rough shape both physically and emotionally. "

I think I've only ever called in sick once before, when I worked as a lifeguard at summer camp and had caught the 24 hour flu. I remember feeling so guilty about having to call in sick, but there was no way that I could sit for eight hours in the heat. I know that some of the doctors in the ER will call me weak if I take the day off, but Katie might have a point. I'm not in the best state to deal with trauma. A day of binge-watching a new show might be just what I need to recover from the nightmare of the last two weeks, although I worry *OITNB* might trigger more panic about Adam.

"Let's at least make it to the cherry trees," I say, noticing the beautiful white blossoms as we jog down the hillside along Grenadier Pond. "With everything that's happened lately, I forgot that they were in bloom. I'm glad we did this route today."

"James told me that the trees were a gift from Tokyo in appreciation of Toronto accepting relocated Japanese Canadians after World War II. Did you know that?" Katie pulls out her phone to double check her facts. "Yeah, Wikipedia says that the Sakura, the cherry blossom, is the national flower of Japan."

"Haha. I had no idea," I admit. "Sometimes I feel like I don't know anything about anything that doesn't involve hospitals or illnesses or diseases… or Netflix!"

We slow to a stop and I read a plaque in front of the tree: "This Japanese Cherry Tree was planted by His Excellency Toru Hagiwara, Japanese Ambassador to Canada and His Worship Nathan Phillips, Q.C., Mayor of the City of Toronto. One of 2000 presented to the citizens of Toronto by the citizens of Metropolitan Tokyo on Wednesday, April 1, 1959."

I'm amazed. I always thought these were the most beautiful trees in the city, but now that they have a history, they have even more significance. There is a story behind them, one that the Japanese ambassador decided should not be forgotten.

"Aren't they wonderful?" I turn and see a senior with dog stop and admire the blossoms. He reminds me of Chief Webber on *Grey's Anatomy*: wise, caring, yet stern--someone you could joke with, but not mess with.

"Yes," I agree, "my friend just told me about their history. I didn't realize they meant so much to the city."

"They mean more than you'd think. Due to their short bloom time, Sakura blossoms are a metaphor for life itself: beautiful yet fleeting. You'll realize when you're as old as me to hang on to the good times because they won't last forever."

Despite my sweaty hangover, I force a smile, "I guess things can't be beautiful all of the time."

"Yeah, these trees are absolutely stunning right now, but the rest of the year, you don't even notice them," says Katie, Instagramming nature's wonder. (#spring)

The man continues, "In Japan, there's a legend that each spring a fairy maiden hovers low in the warm sky, awakening the sleeping cherry trees to life with her delicate breath."

He takes what looks like a small piece of bacon covered in plastic wrap from his pocket and unwraps it. Then he bends down and scratches his dog around the jowls before feeding him the treat.

"While they aren't always at their peak, they're always the same trees," he reminds us, "Even when they're not flowering, they're still full of life."

Adam, May 20, 2014, 9:30 am EDT

I stand outside our wooden porch, staring up at the three story red brick house.
Home. It *was* home.

Lots of men have lived here.
Better men.
Corso Italia.
I was never meant to live here.

I don't belong. Not here. Not anywhere.
I'll go in, get my stuff, and leave.
Leave her. Leave myself. Leave everything.

I unlock the front door and walk up the stairs slowly.
One flight. Then two.
I'm breathless. Out of shape. Useless.

I reach our apartment.
Do I knock? Ring the doorbell?
No. She's at work.

I unlock the door and go inside.
I see the pictures and memories and love.
She is everywhere. We are everywhere.
I'm here but not here.

I walk into the kitchen and turn on the tap.
I take a glass out of the cupboard, fill it with water.
And see the wilted tulips on the table.
A bouquet of dead birthday roses on the counter.
The empty bottles of wine.
Only the horse piss remains.
I put my glass on the counter and go to the living room.

Collapse on the couch where we made love when we moved in.
We couldn't wait until we got upstairs to our bedroom.
We were so happy.
I don't even know what happiness is anymore.

The assault. The suit. The booze.
Why did I do those things they said I did?
I don't fucking love you!
Why did I say that?
Who was that man out west?

I hug my arms around my knees.
Curl into a ball.
I pull the blanket of darkness over myself.

Emma: May 20, 2014. 1:00 pm EDT

The last thing I remember before I fell asleep was watching Frank Underwood put a dog out of its misery. *"There are two kinds of pain," he said. "The sort of pain that makes you strong. Or useless pain. The sort of pain that's only suffering. I have no patience for useless things. Moments like this require someone who will act. To do the unpleasant thing. The necessary thing..." He breaks the dog's neck. "There, no more pain."*

Both terrifying and frightening, Frank reminds me of Adam's high school rugby coach, Michael, an old-school drill-sergeant type who used to keep track of how many times the guys dropped the ball during games and made the whole team run suicides for each error. "Move it or lose it!" he'd yell. "If you're not working, someone else is!" When Michael named Adam captain in grade 12, he started referring to him as "The General" and the nickname stuck with him ever since.

I press pause as Frank manipulates another politician into taking the fall for a failed education bill. *"What a martyr craves more than anything is a sword to fall on, so you sharpen the blade, hold it at just the right angle, and then 3, 2, 1—"*

If I can fall asleep watching political scandal and Shakespearean tragedy in the White House, then I probably wasn't in the best shape to be working in the ER today. I needed to take a break from *Orange is the New Black* and watch something to distract me from my life of hospitals, jails, and failed relationships. So I started *House of Cards*. All of my friends are hooked so why not use the day off to see what all the hype's about?

Feeling a bit like a zombie, I walk downstairs into the kitchen. Weird. Did I leave the tap on after my run? I must have been more exhausted than I thought. I open the fridge. Other than a few half-eaten take-out containers and yogurt, it's basically empty. I gotta get a hold of myself. Knowing that I should at least eat something, I pour myself a bowl of Cheerios (Adam's) and mix in some yogurt. Pretty pathetic meal, I think, but at least I have an afternoon of binging ahead of me.

As I walk through the living room, I see a body lying on my couch.

"What the fuck?" I shout, dropping my Cheerios onto the floor. "Adam, what are you doing here? Your mom told me that you were going to be released, but I didn't think you'd come here. Not today, anyways. Why didn't you call?"

He must have been released on bail after all. Frank reminds me to be ruthless, to keep the upper hand: *"Power is the old stone building that stands for centuries."*

He rolls over so that he is facing me and opens his eyes but he doesn't look at me. He says nothing. He looks awful: a skeleton of his previous self, he has dark black circles under his eyes and some bruising on his face. He smells like a homeless person.

I wasn't prepared for this sight. Not on my day to take care of myself. I can't give in so quickly after what he did to us. I need to stay strong. Claire would tell Frank to leave, right? I just stand there dumbfounded and stare at him.

Finally, he looks at me. I'm haunted by his eyes. It's like he's looking through me. Is he high?

"I'm so sorry. I'm so sorry," he whispers with words barely audible.

He looks so… broken. My eyes start to tear up as I begin to feel his pain, my heart heavy with compassion. The sight of him looking so defeated reminds me of the time one Christmas during our undergrad when Adam and I came across a deer lying in a helpless heap at the bottom of a steep limestone cliff face while were cross-country skiing in the Bruce Peninsula. I remember how sick I felt at the sight of the blood-stained white snow surrounding the deer. By the way it was positioned, it was obvious that one of its front legs was broken. It was still alive, but didn't make any noise or try to move, just lay in the snow as though it had become part of the frozen river. I'll never forget how its eyes whimpered at us the way a stray dog begs for food.

"We should help it," I told Adam, *"maybe we can tie a scarf around its leg to stop the bleeding."*

Adam looked at the deer for a long time while I desperately searched around for a stick that was strong enough to splint its leg, beating myself up for leaving my cellphone in the car. (Adam didn't even have a cellphone back then!)

"It's a wild animal, Em." Adam said at last, *"the only way we can help it now is by killing it. There are some things that you just can't fix or help, no matter how much you want to. It's going to die and there's nothing you can do about it."*

"We're not killing it," I told him firmly. *"But we have to do SOMETHING. We can tell one of the Ontario Parks guys when we get back to the parking lot or call someone from the car."*

"Ok," Adam agreed. We skied away in silence, both knowing that we had left the animal to die alone, still hoping that it would find a way to get back up on its own.

"Adam, what happened?" I ask softly, focusing my attention back to the frozen body in front of me. "You can tell me. Whatever it is, we can fix this. Everything is going to be okay."

He says nothing and I stand in front of him for several minutes, not sure what to do. The man lying on the couch looks more like Tom Hanks in *Castaway* than the General. It hurts me to look at him, so I crawl onto the couch, turning away from him and drape his lifeless arm around my body. I cuddle myself into him, pulling him around me like a blanket, the way we often sleep at night. His body warms me as it always does, but the heaviness is almost unbearable. I feel the pain in his heart pushing me deeper, like he's burying me beneath him.

"Just hug me," he says, in a distant whisper, chilled by the cool breeze sweeping across the Bruce Peninsula.

I turn towards him and hug him tighter, trying my best to squeeze him back together, adding another layer to protect him against the dead of winter. Physically, we couldn't be any closer, but it's the loneliest I've ever felt.

Adam, May 20, 2014 4:00 pm EDT

Slowly decaying.
Rotting.
A rift between body and soul.

I know the sun's setting.
The moon's rising.
But there's no light.
No stars.
Nothing.

I'm possessed by something alien.
A parasite. A tapeworm.
Eating me from within.
Swallowing me whole
Engulfed by darkness.

It's pressing me into myself.

Crushing my ankles, my wrists
Pinning my shoulders and waist.
Grinding my bones, my mind, my courage.
It's sucked my tears dry.

Pulverizing my strength.
Do it now. Just kill me.

Can't move.
Can't think.
Can't feel.
Can't cry.

So low.
Can't face her.

Can't face myself.

Leave her.
Can't lift her arms off me.
Can't move.
Can't feel her or me or anything.

Emma, May 20, 2014, 5:30pm EDT

    I feel my phone vibrate against my thigh. I loosen my grip on Adam and reach for my phone in my pocket and read the text.

Katie:	*How was day off?*
Me:	*Ok.*
Katie:	*Have u eaten?*
Me:	*No.*
Katie:	*I'm coming over. Let's order pizza!*
Me:	*Adam's back.*
Katie:	*WTF?*
Me:	*Ya.*
Katie:	*Wanna go out?*
Me:	*Nah. Called in sick.*
Katie:	*Can I come over then?*
Me:	*Uh...I guess...*
Katie:	*Great! C u in 20 min.*

    I'm not really in the mood for a visit right now but Katie's not one to take no for an answer. I'd rather her not see Adam like this, though. He's still lying in the fetal position on the couch with his head facing me. Strangely, his sleep doesn't look peaceful; rather, he looks like a zombie who's returned to the grave. I pull away from him gently.

"Adam. Wake up," I whisper. He's worse than Peter Russo: he can't see how good he's got it. *"Everyone in that room wanted to cross you off the list."* He doesn't even flinch. *"I said no. I stuck up for you."*

Then I shake his shoulders slightly. "Adam, come on. You need to get up and go upstairs to our, er, the room."

He still doesn't move. I put my hand on his shoulder and shake him again. He smells sour, like the milk he left in the fridge. *I said, "Peter Russo, he's got potential. He's young. He's capable. He's going places."*

"Adam, come on, get up, Katie's coming over. You need to get up and go upstairs. You can sleep all you want there," I pause, "and maybe take a shower."

Again, he ignores me. I know he can hear me. He's the world's lightest sleeper, constantly complaining how the "goddamn Dufferin bus" keeps him up all night.

"Adam, what's going on?" My voice cracks, tears are forming. "Can you please, just...just snap out of it? Where's my best friend?" *"I'm the only person who believes in you, Peter, but maybe that's one too many."*

I shake him harder. Tears pour down my cheeks. I must stay strong. "Adam, get up! Get up!" I start whacking him violently on the hips with one of the pillows from the couch. "Get up! You are such an asshole! What's wrong with you?"

Finally, after several minutes of whacking him and shaking him and yelling at him, he opens his eyes and stares off into the distance. I am sobbing now. Angry. Frustrated. Breathless. He avoids any eye contact with me and continues lying on the couch, staring off into space, for several minutes.

Eventually, my crying slows to a drizzle. *"It's up to you, Peter. Oh, and if you decide to take the coward's way out, cut along the tracks, not across them. That's a rookie mistake."* "Come on, let's go upstairs," I say as I sit down on the edge of the couch and drape Adam's arm over my shoulder in an effort to force him up. *One, two, three.*

"OFF!"

Out of nowhere, he swats me away in irritation, still avoiding eye contact. Then he gets up and walks upstairs, hanging his head in defeat, like an injured soldier.

"You can't treat me like this. Do you know what I've been through over the last couple of weeks?" I call after him.

He doesn't turn back.

WTF? I feel like such a fool. *"Why did I believe in you, Russo? I risked everything for you."*

I get some Febreeze from the bathroom and spray it over the couch, wondering if Katie will notice Adam's residue. I feel my phone vibrate in my pocket.

Katie: Here.

I open the door and greet Katie, who brought Erin along with her.

"Thanks for coming, guys. Ignore the pyjamas and hair!" I say, gesturing at my flannel pyjama set: pink with cows, and my frizzy ponytail.

Erin looks around then whispers, "Katie said Adam came back. Is he here? Are you okay?"

"He's upstairs sleeping," I whisper back, "It's all so confusing. I don't really know what to do or what's going on. Adam doesn't seem to either."

Katie pulls me in and gives me a big hug. "Like I told you this morning, you can't be superwoman all of the time. You've been through a lot." She gestures to a tub of Ben & Jerry's. *Peanut Butter Half-Baked.* My fave. "And there's nothing ice cream can't fix!"

We laugh, remembering how we used to shamelessly binge on the Ben & Jerry's that we'd buy from the 24-hour Metro on Princess Street as stress relief during midterms at Queen's. Then the next day, I'd always go to the gym and do intervals on the treadmill. For me, eating junk food is kind of like drinking: it feels good at the time, but you feel like shit the next day. I always do whatever it takes to purge toxins from my system.

Erin hugs me and then hands me a bouquet of flowers. "The man at the flower shop told us that daffodils mean new beginnings and happiness...I know it's been tough, but you'll get through this."

I'm touched by the gesture. Adam always keeps fresh flowers in the house, but since he left I hadn't been replacing the wilted ones. "Thanks. I can keep it together at the hospital, but when trauma happens in my own life..." I trail off.

Erin pulls a Blu-ray out of her purse. *Frozen*. "Oh, and have you seen this movie? We thought it'd be good for you to watch something silly to forget about everything. Even if it's just temporary."

Katie immediately bursts into song, flares her chest, and spreads her arms out wide likes she's performing on a Broadway stage. *"Conceal, don't feel. Don't let them see. Be the good girl you always have to be. Conceal don't feel, don't let them know. Well now they know..."*

She winks at Erin and the two of them belt out the chorus. *"Let it go! Let it go! Can't hold it back anymore. Let it go! Let it go. Turn away and slam the door."*

I clap my hands at their performance, trying to stay positive and hold it all together when all I want to do is plunk down on the couch and sob. "Nice singing ladies. I've heard the song but haven't seen the movie. I've been watching *House of Cards* all day and could use a break from American politics."

"Oh, Kevin and I watch *House of Cards*," Erin says. "We just kept watching episode after episode...it's so addictive. Don't you think Frank is such a manipulative scumbag?"

"He's ridiculously power hungry," I say. "I'm so inspired by his relationship with Claire, though. They're a real team, like power-couple of the year."

"Oh no, no, no. You gotta keep watching, Em. Frank and Claire have serious issues. They're just really good at maintaining their public image."

"Well, there goes all my hope for happy marriage. Relationships are getting more and more fucked up nowadays. Nothing is ever what it seems."

"Seriously," says Katie, gesturing upstairs. I know what she means. My life has become so unbelievable these days that it's like I'm watching myself on TV. (Horror!)

Erin nods her head in agreement. "I hope Obama isn't as evil as Frank."

"I doubt it. The writers probably exaggerate Frank's character to keep us interested. A real leader would never get away with the stuff he does."

"Oh, I don't have time to read the paper or follow the news much," Erin replies honestly, "between work, yoga, and my social life I don't have much time to follow politics. Haha, I do scan the odd article that one of my friends posts on Facebook."

"Sometimes I listen to CBC Radio on my runs. But it's hard to find time to keep up with all the news," I turn to Katie. "Have you seen *House of Cards*?"

"No, I don't have Netflix."

I'm shocked. "Oh you've gotta start. Even Obama watches it. Apparently he even compared his wife to Frank Underwood. So maybe politicians are like the Underwoods after all."

She smiles. "I know what it's about because everyone at work is always talking about it. My sister lent me the DVDs for *Homeland*, though, and it's pretty addictive. Have either of you seen it?"

We shake our heads.

"It's about this bipolar CIA agent who works for the counterterrorist unit and tracks al-Qaeda terrorists. Pretty intense. Sometimes I come into work with raccoon circles under my eyes and my co-workers think I've stayed up late working, but I really had to watch one more episode."

"I've heard it's good," Erin says, "but it doesn't sound very realistic that the CIA would let a crazy person work for them. I mean, it's probably even stricter in the States, but I remember when my friend from high school applied to work for CSIS, someone from the agency interviewed me for, like, two hours in attempt to uncover all of the 'skeletons in the closet'."

"Yeah, I was confused about that too at first," responds Katie, "but she keeps it well hidden. She's completely brilliant but also really messed up. She even fucks an American marine who she suspects to be an al-Qaeda operative."

"Talk about forbidden love," Erin laughs.

I go and get three spoons for the ice cream from the kitchen then motion at them to sit in the living room. I lower my voice to a whisper. "Adam's totally out of it. I could barely get him off the couch."

"Maybe he's in shock," Erin suggests, "but I guess you'd probably be able to tell better than me. You're the doctor."

"He seems a bit drugged out. His eyes are totally glazed over and he's just been lying around on the couch all day in a catatonic state."

"So what did you say to him?" Katie asks.

"I couldn't really say anything. I asked him what happened and he wouldn't speak to me. He basically came home and passed out on the couch."

"What a jerk! You don't deserve to be treated like that," Katie responds in anger, and scoops up a big spoonful of ice cream.

"I know but it's so confusing," I tell them, "He's been really ignoring me and then he asked me to hold him and we cuddled for a long time. I think something's wrong but I don't know what. He refuses to tell me what happened."

Katie squeezes my hand. "What did the police say?"

Shoot. The police. I hadn't even considered calling them when Adam came back. "I haven't spoken to them since this morning. I told them he was in jail in Vancouver. They said they'd contact the Vancouver Police Department and look into but I haven't followed up. I guess I should call and tell them Adam's home, and his mom."

"You should post something on Facebook, too," Katie reminds me. "Lots of people have been rallying together to support Adam's safe return, and don't forget about all of those people from his gym who went out looking for him."

"Do you think they'll make him have a psych eval?" Erin asks.

"I don't know. I imagine that he must have had some sort of screening in Vancouver if they granted him bail. I was thinking I should take him into the hospital. But you know Adam, he's not one to accept help very easily."

"Maybe one of the doctors would come here," Katie suggests. "There must be perks of working at the hospital!"

"I don't know if he'd go for that either," I respond. "Besides, Adam's been my best friend for so long. Don't you think I would know if he had some sort of illness?"

"Definitely," Katie agrees.

"It's more likely that he got himself mixed up in something illegal. It's really sad."

"It's okay if you're feeling overwhelmed, Em. This isn't something that any of us are prepared for. I'm sure Adam would understand if you needed to take a break for a while. Relationships shouldn't take this much work," Katie tells me.

It's pretty clear that she thinks that I should end the relationship. I can't make any decisions about that right now. All I want is to understand what happened!

Erin looks at her. "Maybe you guys *should* break up. But I don't think that anyone should expect relationships to be easy. Kevin and I've been married for almost ten years now and while it's been great, there's always ups and downs. He's my best friend but sometimes I want to kill him."

"Really?" I look at her in confusion. To me, her and Kevin are the perfect couple, like Carrie (Bradshaw) and Aidan when they first start dating. I lick the ice cream off my spoon. I can't even picture them (Erin and Kevin) fighting. I'd cast Rose Byrne to play Erin in a movie: a sweet and edgy Grade Five teacher with a sense of humour and a contagious positive energy. For the role of Kevin, I'd cast Ryan Gosling: a hot engineer with quiet strength and underlying roughness.

Erin/Rose: *Honey, you are so hot/nice/awesome it makes me sick. I hate how you make me breakfast in bed, do the laundry and cook dinner for us when I have parent-teacher interviews.*

Kevin/Ryan: *It's a problem. You are so sexy and make me laugh all of the time. I've developed a compulsion for doing nice things for you so that our sex life stays as steamy as it is now.*

Erin/Rose: *I think we need couple's counselling.*

Kevin/Ryan: *You're right, sweetheart, you're always right. Let's go to therapy. But first, [he grabs her] let's make passionate love.*

Erin rubs her thumbs and fingers together, fidgeting uncomfortably. "I'm not sure if I told you girls, but Kevin and I go to counselling regularly. Ever since we've been trying to get pregnant, there's been tension between us. I wasn't prepared for marriage to be so hard."

She continues to look at her hands, carefully choosing her words. "This is going to make me sound wimpy, but I guess...when you come from a loving family, and are told you can reach your dreams if you work hard enough, you think you can imagine a certain life, and achieve it like that!" Erin snaps her fingers. "You blame yourself when things go wrong. You're not prepared to handle disappointment. But sometimes life just sucks. I mean, what if I can't get pregnant?"

Her eyes fill with tears and I reach out to rub her thigh in support. "Sorry I'm making this about me when you're the one who's been through a couple of traumatic weeks. What if you and Adam go to a couple of therapy sessions? I'm not saying it will 'fix' things. But it might help you understand why he left in the first place."

Is she suggesting that I might somehow be to blame for Adam's disappearance? I never did anything or said anything to make him leave—that was his choice. For the first time, things between us felt, well... perfect before he left. At once, I imagine Erin/Rose Byrne leaping off the couch and strangling me. (Who would play me? I guess the logical choice would be Ellen Pompeo, as most would pin me as the Meredith Grey type considering my profession, but my top choice would definitely be SJP: what Gen Y gal didn't dream of being Carrie Bradshaw?)

"Adam would never go for that. He's too macho to admit that he needs help. Like, remember when he played rugby for U of T? He had the physiotherapist tape his elbow up so he could play with a hairline fracture!"

"Yeah and like you said, he was probably on drugs at the time and needs to be punished for his actions, not babied. You're the one who gets the sympathy card here, not him. Let's not try to make excuses for him," Katie argues.

I tell them about the conversation I had with Nicky this morning. "She has to act as a...um.... 'surety'... someone who makes sure you follow your bail conditions and makes sure you show up at your trial. I think she had to pay a bunch of money for Adam to get released. Anyways, she said he's facing up to two years for what he did."

"Shit!" Katie exclaims. Erin stays quiet.

"Yeah, I thought he would go to her place, but he just showed up here. What am I supposed to do? Wait around for him? At this age? What if we had kids and he just disappeared like that?"

I start crying, thinking of the future I thought we'd have together. Two weeks ago, I was thinking he was going to propose and now he might be spending the bulk of my child-bearing years behind bars.

"Yeah, that's a tough one," Erin admits.

"You've gotta put yourself first here, Em. I know that you're a really caring person, but you have to look after yourself. If he's mixed up in something, you could be at risk now too. Maybe you should ask him to stay at his Mom's until this whole thing's cleared up" Katie suggests.

"Well, what if Adam needs help?" asks Erin. "What if something is seriously wrong with him?"

"He's a thirty-year-old man. 'The General,'" Katie replies. "He can take care of himself."

Adam, May 21, 2014, 1:00pm, EDT

Crawling.

Away from the voices.
The General's strong.
A man.

Away from the pulsing.
The flicker in my skull.
Tingling.

Away from emptiness.
Towards emptiness.
Through the endless black pit.

Away from the burning.
The invisible flames.
The pain of feeling nothing.

Tears do nothing.
Stop crying, pussy.
The General's dead but not dead.

The fire burns brighter.
The darkness pulls stronger.
I close my eyes.

Emma: May 21, 2014, 2:00 pm EDT

This day couldn't be passing any slower. I thought that work would distract me, but so far all I've done today is put splints on fingers, read x-rays, prescribe medication, and reassure parents that their children are healthy.

No matter how much I try to get the image out of my head, I keep picturing Adam lying on the couch like a rag doll. At one point during the night, I even tried to rub his back and cuddle with him, but he pulled away aggressively, as if he had a contagious disease and didn't want me to catch this version of him.

I examine an x-ray of a fractured clavicle. *Sorry Jonathan, season's over.* I better make sure his mom understands the dangers he assumes if he decides to keep playing. He's going to be devastated. Most of the rugby players I know—girls and guys—suffer from a major invincibility complex on the field, flaunting their bruises like warrior wounds. They convince themselves that their injuries aren't serious in order to prove their dedication to the team. I look at Jonathan's x-ray in my hands. *Bones do break, boys! You're not as tough as you think.*

When we were in Grade 12, Adam sprained his ankle in the qualifying game for the Provincial championship tournament. The doctor told him that he would be out for the rest of the season. He refused to listen. *"A little ankle injury can't stop me from playing. The only way to prevent me from playing in the championships would be if I was dead!"* he told me. But what else was the guy to do when he walked around school wearing a shirt that said *Give Blood: Play Rugby*?

When he returned from the tournament, unable to walk, I was so frustrated with him for risking life and limb for a sport, even if he was scouted for the Ontario U19 team. He couldn't even slow dance with me at prom like I imagined, but he was proud that his crutches made the photos. *"So everyone can remember how tough I am,"* he'd boasted.

Fortunately, he managed to hobble-dance with his crutches, and we ended up having such a fun night, topping it off with a chilly 4:00 am swim in Lake Huron, which was Adam's suggestion. *"Swimming's so freeing—I almost forgot I was injured! Which one of you clowns wants to race a gimp to the cliffs?"* Even I, the Energizer Bunny, struggled to keep up with him.

His wild, carefree attitude about his injury didn't last, though. In the first game he played for Ontario that summer, he bulldozed the opposing flanker from Alberta and tore even more ligaments in his already injured ankle, putting him out for the rest of the season. He was so bummed out that he acted like a mopey couch potato and lazed around all day playing *Call of Duty*. Eventually, I had to encourage some of the rugby guys to go to his mom's house and "kidnap" him so that he'd come out to a beach party. It was heartbreaking to see him throw his summer away because of some silly ankle sprain!

"Injuries are part of sports. They happen to all athletes. You can't allow a little setback like this to drag you down so much," I told him. But he became even more determined to make the varsity team at U of T and began training like a madman the minute he was able to hobble around without crutches. That's Adam, though. He keeps pushing himself past the point when everyone else would have quit.

"So you've miraculously gotten better?" A deep voice makes my spine tense and snaps me back to reality. *Neil.* I turn around, not sure of what to say.

"I'm not 100%, but I'm glad that I took the day off," I tell him, studying the x-ray more carefully as though to appear busy.

"Diagnosis: broken heart?" he says in an overdramatic voice, performing a poorly written script. I ignore him. If Piper can stand her ground when Crazy Eyes stalks her, gives her flowers, and affectionately calls her "Dandelion," then I can fend off McDouchebag.

"You know," he says, "as someone who has such high expectations for herself, I'm surprised that you'd let yourself get so sentimental over someone who's not in your bracket. A beautiful woman like you deserves everything she wants."

I get what Neil's saying. *You deserve better. Move on. You can't fix everyone* (even if you are a doctor!). He's talking like my high school guidance counsellor, Mr. Wilson, when I told him I was thinking about taking a year off after high school to travel. *"Don't settle! You have the ability to be a heart surgeon. What are you going to do? Work at a surf shop in Australia or at café in Paris? Sure, they seem glamourous now, but what are you going to do when you come back? Everyone else will be ahead of you! You owe it to yourself to reach your potential!"*

Once I started my degree, I'd met several other people who'd taken a year after high school to travel, mostly Brits or Aussies who'd taken a "gap" year. They'd worked at restaurants, hotels, bars, or cafés: whatever they could do to pay the bills and fund their adventures. Instead of being "behind" as Mr. Wilson suggested I would be, they seemed "ahead" of me. They were more mature, more worldly, more independent, better prepared to handle the stresses of university life. Now I wonder if I owe myself anything other than following my heart, and my heart is telling me not to give up on Adam. Not yet! Am I just supposed to ditch the man I love when things get hard?

Of course, I don't want to be with someone who lies to me and mopes around all day, but this person in my house is not Adam. At the same time, I can't help Adam when he won't even tell me what's wrong or what happened. Even House has trouble diagnosing illness when he can't see the symptoms clearly, and he assembled a whole team to work for him.

"Excuse me, I have to get back to my patient," I assert, walking past Neil with the x-ray in my hand. He turns and catches up to me, pulling on the elbow of my white lab coat.

"Whoa, relax there, Katniss! I'm just trying to be a supportive friend. I have two tickets to the Jays game on Friday night. I'm not taking no for an answer. Come with me... as two co-workers releasing some steam."

"Thanks," I respond, "but I'm working."

He replies quickly. "No, you're not. I already checked the board. Don't think you're going to get out of this that easily. What else would you do? Stay at home, watching *Grey's Anatomy* by yourself while waiting for your estranged boyfriend to call you? That's pretty desperate."

"There's nothing wrong with being alone," I remind him, "Not all women are characters in *Desperate Housewives*."

Then without thinking I add, "But actually, Adam's back now. He's safe." Neil's face immediately softens. It's the way a child looks when he visits his Grandpa who's had a serious stroke. At first, he's filled with questions: *When are you coming home? How come you're talking funny? Can you come to my hockey game on Saturday? Do you like the hospital food?* Then he's overcome with anger at the realization that Grandpa's life is different now and there isn't anything he can do about it. *I want Grandpa back! It's not fair! I hate doctors!*

"Wow. Okay. Emma I'm so relieved. I was getting a little worried for you. Do you know what happened?"

"No. I'm just letting him rest now. He's really tired." *Hopefully, the police will have some answers for me soon!* I reach into my pocket and glance at my phone briefly, surprised that the cops haven't contacted me already. Am I supposed to nag them?

"Ok…" Neil responds hesitantly. "I've been thinking about Adam a lot. He seemed like an honest guy. I don't think that he would just leave you for now reason. Have you considered that maybe there's something wrong with his brain? Like maybe he suffers from addiction. Like performance enhancers or something. My friend, Tanya, who trains with him, says he has this superhuman amount of energy sometimes."

When I confronted him about the drugs at the party, he insisted that Adam was clean. Now he's suggesting Adam's an addict? Is this so I don't blame him if the police detect drugs in Adam's system? *Sorry, Neil. The results from his tests in Vancouver were all negative!*

"Thanks for your concern. But I'm sure I would have noticed if Adam showed signs of addiction. Besides, he treats his body like a temple! He doesn't even eat red meat or white bread anymore."

"People hide addictions from those they love all the time." He's right, but I've been friends with Adam for over a decade. Wouldn't I know if he was hiding something from me?

Neil touches my forearm gently; the way some of the nurses squeeze their patients' hands during surgery to let them know that they are not alone. He lowers his voice as though he's about to share some confidential information.

"Or have you considered that he might have had a psychotic episode? I know Adam's in great physical shape, but maybe his brain chemistry is imbalanced."

Good try, Neil, but other than some mild depression, anxiety, and shock from the arrest, the psychiatric assessment he had in Vancouver didn't reveal anything either...yet who's the zombie on my couch? Something's off with him, for sure.

"Honestly, I think addiction would be more likely. Adam's so mentally tough it's ridiculous...Besides, Adam's 30. The majority of mental illnesses develop before the age of 24, and they don't just happen out of the blue. We both know that."

"Relax. I'm only trying to help you as a medical professional..." he looks at me directly. For the first time, he doesn't seem to have an ulterior motive, "...and as a friend. I know there's lots of stigma attached to mental illness, but if you need advice, or anything at all, I'm here for you."

"Thanks...I've known Adam for a long time. I'm sure I would have picked up on the symptoms if he had been suffering something major."

Other than some possible slight depressive symptoms, which he's always pulled himself out of (we all get sad every now and then!) Adam's only ever been ridiculously healthy. "Anyways, I have to go tell my patient that his rugby season's over," I scurry away, clawing the x-ray results so tightly that I can feel my nails piercing through the file folder.

"Dr. Watters!" Neil calls out. Urgh. What does he want now? I should ignore him but for some reason I stop and turn around. I don't say anything, just look at him like a patient with a chronic illness. *You can try to help, but really there's nothing you can do. Sometimes life is just shitty.*

"Symptoms can be masked…just, uh…just remember that."

Adam, May 22, 2014, 9:20 am EDT

I hear the buzz vibrate on my phone.
Everyone keeps calling me. My mom. Jeff. Emma. Mark. Tyler.

I'd turn it off but Mom said it's part of my probation to keep my cell on.
She needs to be able to check in on me to make sure I'm following the rules.
I know she's lying. She's the one making all of these rules.
She keeps checking in. *Are you okay? How's your day? Is Emma taking care of you?*
Like a 30-year old man can't take care of himself.
It's fucking annoying.

My phone vibrates again.
I pull the covers over my head and ignore it.
I'm an angry bear in midst of hibernation.

Then it starts buzzing constantly.
And buzzing.
And buzzing.
I bury myself deeper into my cave.
Fuck off! Leave me alone.

It's probably Emma.
I don't want to talk to you or see you. Stop.
Grr. If I don't respond to her texts, she keeps calling and calling and calling.
Aren't doctors too busy for personal lives?
Why does she care anyways?
Two more weeks then I'll be out of her life.

I'll go back to Parry Sound.
Paddle out to the jagged cliffs off the coast of Georgian Bay.

Dangerous. Exciting. Terrifying.
I'll take a bunch of pills and end it with one leap.
I need to time it so that I minimize the pain.
Jump. Hit the water. Don't come back up.

The phone keeps vibrating.
Fuck. *Just give up already!*
Finally, I reach for it. *Jeff.*
The business is over. I fucked it up. He's gotta accept it.

I hear knocking on the door downstairs.
The phone vibrates in my hand. Jeff.
Fuck man. Give it up.

"Hey Adam. Get up, buddy. It's time for work."
He shouts through the door, waking up the neighbours.
Fuck. I pull the covers tighter, cocooning myself.
Go away. Stop. It's over. It's all over.

I tried to go to work the other day.
I showered. Got dressed. But I'd lost all my energy by the time I got downstairs.
I collapsed on the couch. Exhausted. From nothing.
Swaddled myself in a blanket and just lay there.

He tries calling me again. I stare blankly his name—Jeff—flashing on my screen.
Mr. Happy-Go-Lucky is finally pissed about something.
Having to get up early and coach my 6:00 am CrossFit workouts.
Even though he's up all night with his crying baby.
I hope Emma meets someone like him when I'm gone.

Bang. Bang. Bang. The knocking is getting louder.
He's frustrated. I'd be frustrated with me too.

I'd want to beat the shit out of me. I deserve it.
If that's what he wants, he can have it.

Slowly, I pull myself out of bed.
I throw on a hoodie and some track pants and look in the mirror.
I look like shit. My cheeks are hollow. There are dark circles under my eyes.
I'm a shell of myself.

My phone rings again. Fuck he's persistent.
I walk down the stairs, slowly and carefully like an injured soldier.
Step. Step. Step. Step. Right foot. Left foot.
When I get to bottom of the stairs, I look at the couch.
Then I look at the front door.

Bang. Bang. Bang. He won't give up.
"Adam. Hey, it's Jeff. Want to see how you're doing."
Don't sit down. Keep walking forward. Open the door.
My phone vibrates in my pocket. Can he hear it?

When I get beside the couch, I freeze.
A wave of panic takes hold of my body and I can't continue.
What will he say? Or will he just start beating the shit out of me as soon as i open the door?
The man has a fuckin' kid and I've destroyed his life.
He doesn't need me.

Be a fuckin' man, Adam.
Open the door. Face him.
You fucked up, now you've gotta own up to it.

I take a few steps forward, reach my right arm towards the doorknob. Then I hesitate. I can't do it. I can't. *Shit.*

My phone vibrates again. He must be able to hear it now.
I turn the doorknob and face him.

He puts some groceries bags on the floor.
Then he lifts his arms.
I close my eyes, bracing for the assault.
This is it. I'm sorry. I'm so sorry.
Jeff. Emma. Mom. Everyone.
Then I feel him pull me towards him.
His giant 6'4" frame will crush me with one squeeze.

Very softly, very gently, he hugs me.

"Nice to see ya, buddy. It's gonna get better for you. You're not alone. The gym will be fine. Don't worry."

For weeks, I've been too dead to cry.
But suddenly, I begin to sob uncontrollably.
He doesn't let go. He just keeps rocking me and holding me.
"I'm here for you, man."

Several minutes later, I stop crying.
He picks up the groceries and comes into the apartment.
"Are you hungry? I'm gonna fry up some bacon and eggs."
I nod.

I go into the living room while he starts cooking in the kitchen.
This time, I don't flop onto the couch into the fetal position.
Instead, I walk to the window and stare at the flowering lilac trees.

Emma, May 22, 2014, 7:30pm EDT

Dinner. Yoga. Groceries. Laundry. I go through my 'to-dos' and focus intensely on the sidewalk as I cross Bloor St, making every effort to avoid looking at the pixelated rainbow of coloured tiles in the bright, spacious entrance of the newly renovated Dufferin Station. I can't bear any attempts to sugarcoat life. Not today. No matter how much colour, culture, and vibrancy we add to the city's darkest spaces through public art displays and revitalization projects, sometimes life just sucks.

Dinner. Yoga. Groceries. Laundry. Dinner. Yoga. Groceries. Laundry. Dinner. Yoga. Groceries. Laundry. I repeat the list over and over in my head, like I'm calming myself to try to fall asleep. I concentrate on my breath, as I say the words, the way I do at yoga: *Allow your experience to be felt. Then return to your breath.*

But I can't get that horrifying image out of my mind. A smashed watermelon covered in brake grease and dust. Blood everywhere—soaking what was left of his hair and clothing. His right arm severed at the shoulder. Massive head and chest trauma. Exposed ribs. Bones shattered in both legs. Extensive hemorrhaging. Crushed, but not quite dead.

Dinner. Yoga. Groceries. Laundry.

I went on autopilot when the paramedics brought him in, working quickly to control the bleeding, assess the damage, and stabilize his vitals. It wasn't until after he was taken to the OR that the shock of what I'd seen started to sink in.

Matt, a veteran paramedic, rubbed me on the back when he saw how upset I was. He looked pale, likely in a bit of shock himself after having to remove the man's mangled body from underneath the train.

"This won't be the last subway suicide attempt you see in your career. It happens more than you'd think. Apparently there were close to thirty jumps last year."

"I can't believe he survived the impact," I said honestly. "I wonder why he did it. What drives someone to do something, so... so violent?"

He shrugged grimly, "He probably thought that the impact of the train would result in sudden death. But only a third of suicide attempts in the TTC last year were successful. So those ones who aren't put in body bags are brought in here."

I said nothing, thinking of how I felt when Adam went missing, how I'd worried he might end up in the ER. I never expected to see something like this, though. The man looked to be about Adam's age as well, at least from what I gathered while assessing his disfigured body. So many lacerations and bruises. So much blood. I wonder who spoke to the man's wife? Probably one of the surgeons.

What did they say? *Your husband's lucky to be alive. But he's suffered extensive brain damage and severe deformation. He'll experience a lifetime of chronic pain and require extensive care.* I can't even begin to imagine how she must feel right now. Why did her husband try to take his own life? What caused him to feel so desperate?

"I can't say what goes on in someone's head," Matt says, "but bodies are not meant to withstand the impact of more than 200 metric tonnes. I wish we could do more to prevent these tragedies from happening. The man has no history of mental illness or anything, so maybe he was faced with some setback. I guess there's only so much you can do to help someone, though."

"Yeah, I guess. It's hard to help someone if you don't know that what's going on in their head. It's so tragic," I said, not knowing what to do, what to say, how to help, how to grieve, how to forget, or how to move on.

"It's tragic for everyone. The victim. The families. The friends. Even for the first responders like us. One of my buddies drives a train on the Bloor Line and he's hit two jumpers. One was a fatality. He had to take a leave of absence and underwent six months of counselling. I didn't think he'd go back to work. He completely shut down."

I feel sick, shaken, saddened, and I'm only a doctor who responded to a tragedy. I'm not personally involved or invested in his life or death. I hope I never have another case like this one, but I guess I can't control what comes into the ER.

I approach our front steps. Home, finally, home. But what comfort is there in coming home anymore? Nicky's car's not here so she must have gone back to Parry Sound. Did she take Adam with her? My heart breaks a bit more every time I open the door.

"Hey, Adam!" I shout, as I walk into the house, pretending this is a few weeks ago, before he disappeared. A glimmer of optimism hits me and I wonder what Adam might have cooked up for dinner tonight? Fettuccine Alfredo? Shrimp Pad Thai? Roast Chicken? I remember when there was always something delicious waiting for me when I got home.

Right now, I need him to hold me, hug me, and tell me he loves me and that everything's going to be okay. We'll have a hot bath together or cuddle in bed. Feel safe with each other as we used to.

But instead, he doesn't even acknowledge me. His eyes are glued to the TV, remote control in hand. I stare at the screen for a moment. *Dinner. Yoga. Groceries. Laundry. Breathe.*

"Aw, fuck off, man. Really?" He groans at the TV, still ignoring me. I step closer towards him and put my hand on his shoulder. He swats it away in irritation. *"Time to step it up, Russo. Be a man."*

"Come on, fuck off." Is he speaking to the TV or me?

A white sports car races through a suburban housing community as Adam steers from the couch. It's raining, there are mountains in the background and the car drives up a hill. From what I know of *Grand Theft Auto*, Adam's bout of road rage is likely happening in LA. Maybe his video game addiction inspired his crime spree out west. Violent video games influence guys, right? Didn't a gamer shoot a couple of cops somewhere in the States?

At once, the car pulls to a stop and the driver gets out with a sniper rifle. From the top of the hill, he zooms in on a target in the community and opens fire.

'Fuck yeah! Take that, motherfuckers!"

"Oh, no. What the fuck? Where are you hiding, asshole?" he shouts at the TV as he dodges bullets coming from the side of the house.

I pretend this isn't happening. Does he even see me? My eyes start to tear up but I don't cry because I'm too pissed off. I can't take this. Not now. I need a hug! But what is he doing? Participating in some virtual shoot-em-up bullshit. Right now, I'd be better off if I had a cat than a man. At least a cat would let me hug it and cuddle it. Can I Tinder swipe for cat cuddles?

"Adam, your mom popped by today when I was working. It was a bit hectic today so I didn't get to talk to her for that long. I was hoping to be here when the cops came to chat with you. She said everything was okay? We all just want to help you, Adam."

"There you are. *Bam*!" He opens fire and a body is sent flying to the side of the house. I look at the TV then look at him in complete disbelief. *"You really fucked it up this time, Russo."*

Breathe. Breathe. Breathe. I'm going to explode. Why can't he just answer me? I walk into the kitchen and see a mess of plates, pans, and a grill covered with grease. No dinner cooked for me, just a big mess for me to clean up. Seriously? After the day I had, I can't handle extra stress. Not right now.

I open the fridge to find something to throw together for dinner. I don't know why I even opened it, since I already knew there was no food. I open the freezer, pull out some bread, and pop two slices in the toaster. You'd think I'd be done with PB&Js after med school.

"You could've gone to get groceries, you know."

I'm friggin' pissed off at him. I can't even look at him, sitting there, shooting pedestrians, and robbing banks. He doesn't look at me, either, or acknowledge my criticisms. Instead, he just keeps thumbing away on the controller with this eyes glued to the screen.

"You've just been lying around like a zombie and now that you finally seem to have gotten your energy back, you sit on the couch and play video games? I guess I've been expecting too much from you all along."

He keeps playing his game as tears begin to run down my cheeks. "I had the worst fucking day and you're just going to sit there? Really?"

I look at the clock. 8:05 pm. *Shit*. I'm going to miss yoga.

I run upstairs to change quickly into my gym clothes. Of course, the bed's not made. Adam's pyjamas, t-shirts, and track pants are on the floor along with some dirty socks and underwear. Who does he think I am? I didn't work my butt off at university for ten years to be a maid and clean up his shit.

I grab my yoga mat and race downstairs. So he'd prefer to touch a virtual hooker than pay attention to me. He's like Stu in *The Hangover*: he'd rather marry some stripper he met in Vegas than me. His partner in crime. His love. His best friend. Awesome. I stayed away from the frat boys at university for a reason.

"Adam," I call towards him like a mother speaking to a rebellious teenager, "I'm off to yoga. By the time I come home, I expect the dishes to be done and our room to be clean."

He keeps playing, ignoring me like a rebellious teenager would to his parents.

Adam, May 23, 2014, 5:30 am EDT

My alarm goes off. *Get up, get dressed, go to work.*

I look at the empty spot in the bed beside me. Emma's gone running.
Again.

Last night it was yoga. When she's not working, she's working out. Yoga. Pilates. Running. Spinning. Bootcamp.

Or, she's watching *Desperate Housewives* or some other shitty soap-opera.

Always busy. Sooo busy.
Everything with her needs to be perfect.
Perfect body. Perfect job. Perfect boyfriend.

Fuck perfect.

I can't make her happy. I've ruined her life.
When I leave, everything will be better for her.

She'll find herself the perfect man she always wanted. A real man.
Someone who won't take off. Who will provide for her.
I just bring her down.

Fuck. Why did I have to fuck everything up?

I'm a big fuck-up like my shitty dad, wherever the fuck he is, whoever the fuck he is.

I should find him and make up for Mom's suffering, my suffering.

Mom said she met him one summer at some music festival out west.

He played guitar in a folk band, the hippie, knew it was love the moment he saw her, promised to write to her and call her when he was in Toronto for a show, blah-blah-blah. *Fuckin' lying asshole.*

He never did. All he did was ruin lives. Hers. Mine. Everyone's.

I'm so fucking mad at him. I'm mad at my mom for getting duped by him. I'm even madder at myself and at the world. FUCK!

I pick up a pen from the bedside table and chuck it across the room.

"It was a whirlwind love," she'd said. *"I couldn't stop myself."*

I told her it wasn't real. She fell for some fairy tale.
Love's not a whirlwind, just a slow fucking grind.

I look around at the pictures on the walls of Emma and I.
Smiling. Happy. Holding hands. Together. In love.
Paris. Victoria. Banff. Dublin. New Zealand. Fuckin' fairy tales.
No happy endings.
Just a slow fuckin' grind.

I pull the covers around me, and close my eyes to sleep a bit longer.
Fuck, I thought I could do this.

C'mon, Adam.
Get the fuck up.

The business will be fine. That's what Jeff said, right? He wouldn't lie to me. He doesn't need me. He could buy out my share or declare bankruptcy and move on. He'll do better without me. Everyone will.

Paddle to the cliffs. Take some pills. Then jump.
A better resting place than in the TTC.

Somehow I manage to pull off the duvet and sit up on the bed.
I stare at the my feet. *Walk.*
Then I stare again at the pictures. *Fuck.*
Shit. Am I my mom *and* my dad? A deluded groupie *and* a fucking loser?

I stare at my feet. Then I stare at the pictures.
We look perfect. Frozen in a happy place. Happy time.
Was it real then?
 I just stare. Paralyzed.
 Wanting to move forward, end it all, and wanting to go back. Start over.

Today is the day you will get to work.
Get the fuck out of bed.
Stand. Do it. Now!
Fuck you! Just do it. Do it now.
There's a plan now.
After what feels like an eternity, I get up.
Finally.

I look at myself in the mirror. I look like shit.
Like a ghost. A skeleton.
White skin. Sunken eyes.
A lumberjack beard.
Bruise on the right side of my face.
Cut above my eye.

When I played rugby, scars were the signs of a warrior.
But these ones look like I took a beating.
And it's even more pathetic because I beat the shit out of myself.

I'll tell the members I got in a fight. They should see the other guy. Phaneuf fan.
I don't know what he even fucking looks like.
I'll say he was drunk and weak and annoying. Now he's weak and annoying and ugly. And probably still drunk. They'll laugh. Pat me on the back. Then they'll get back to their workouts.

Shower. I'll shower first then go to work.
Be positive. Motivating.
I'll work them hard.

I hear the front door slam closed.
And then footsteps quickly bounding up the stairs.
The sound of rushing, desperation.
Panic that she might fall a minute behind the schedule.

"Whoa, Adam," Emma gasps, as she enters the room. "Didn't expect to see you up yet."

I watch her take off her sweaty running gear. Her Nike dry fit shirt. Her black tights. Her socks. Her sports bra.

Nothing happens. I used to get hard when I saw her naked body but now I feel repulsed.
She stares at me. I can see the hurt. The disappointment in her eyes.
She takes a minute, a whole fucking minute, to remind me what a fuckin' disappointment I am to her.

Of course, she doesn't consider I might be going to work. I might need the shower.
Why would she? All I've been able to do the last few weeks is laze around.
Can't get up. Can barely eat. Can't work. Can't answer the phone.
Fucking loser.

And then she goes to the bathroom and closes the door.

Another whole minute goes by. The she comes back out. Looks at me. The same look of disappointment. *You're right, Em. That's what I am to you. A fuckin' disappointment.*

"I'm thinking that maybe we could go see a doctor together after I get back from work. You know, get some help for whatever's going on with you. I don't know what's wrong but we can fix this."

HELP? You can't help. You can't fix. You can't love. No one can. Not you. Not me. Not my mom. And definitely not some doctor.

She goes back in the bathroom. I hear the shower go on this time. I hear her crying.
STOP. STOP. STOP.
Stop crying. Stop caring. Stop loving.

I trudge downstairs.
Get help. Make coffee. Do dishes.
She's worse than my mom.
Just leave me alone.

Shit. All of a sudden my energy is gone.
I feel drained. She sucked me dry.

I look at the kitchen. Coffee. Dishes.
Then I look at the couch.
Walk to the kitchen. Keep going.
Today is the day you are going to work.
Start the plan.
But I can't. There's no point.

I crumble onto the couch and lie there.
Then pull the blanket over my head.

Part 2: Two Weeks Earlier

"This is where it all begins. Everything starts here, today."

-David Nicholls,
One Day

Adam, May 9, 2014, 5:45am EDT

Two more reps. C'mon, pull. This workout is fucking killing me, but I won't quit until I'm dead.

Tyler stops the timer.

"Two minutes and thirty-eight seconds. New record, coach."

I shake my head, and then lift my arms above my head, pushing down on my left elbow to stretch my triceps. My heart's beating through my chest, and my torn muscles are burning. Sometimes the pain lasts for days. But it's a good kind of pain. Muscles must first break down in order to become stronger.

"Thanks. But I can shave a few more seconds off the time. I could have pushed harder on the sprints."

I hurry out to get set up for the 6:00 am class, organizing circuits of kettlebells and tires in the open concept gym that looks like a grungy industrial warehouse. The usual crowd of early morning exercisers, about ten members in total, are preparing to get their butts kicked.

"Alright team, this morning, for our Workout of the Day, we're gonna attack 'Jan.' She's a real bitch." I point towards the whiteboard where I have written out the exercises.

"We're gonna alternate between barbell thrusters and pull-ups. Three sets of each. Twenty-one, then fifteen, then nine reps."

"How much weight?" Tracy, a middle-aged Phys. Ed. teacher and mother of three, asks. She's dropped from 26% to 19% body fat since she started training with me six months ago and is a prime example of how anyone can change their life if they make it a priority.

"Great question. The advanced option is 95 lbs for men and 65 lbs for women. That's the weight you need to push if you're gonna be competing next week. Beginners and intermediate, make sure to go at your own pace. Sound good?"

There's a few sarcastic cheers from the pack as they try to pump themselves up for the WOD.

"Alright, time to get moving, team!" I command. "Matt, can you lead the team through a warm-up?"

"Sure thing, General." Matt, a MaxFit coach in training, says as he organizes the group into a circle and guides them through a Samson stretch, lunging forward with his right leg and resting his left knee on the ground. The rest of the members obediently settle into the lunge, and lift their arms above their head as Matt does for a deeper stretch.

"While you're getting warmed up, I'll write your PBs from the last time we did Jan on the board if I have them. Matt, Jeanne, Tyler, and Rosa, you want to push for less than three minutes. At this point in the game, you want to make sure you're practicing in competition mode so that you're prepared both mentally and physically for regionals."

"I'm so nervous," says Rosa as she lunges while reaching her palms towards the ceiling. Only 21 years old, Rosa is our youngest member. She'd never exercised before joining the team and has really leaned out since she started training with us over a year ago. Last year, she was worried that lifting little 5lbs would make her bulk up, but now she's doing power cleans with a 65lb barbell. MaxFit's transformed her body, her attitude, and her personality: the whole package.

"I wouldn't have committed to coaching you if I didn't believe in you," I say. "Sure, you might get nervous, stressed out, get injured, or even have a mental breakdown at some point in the next week. When that happens, look in the mirror ask yourself: am I going to go deeper into myself where I don't want to go? If you're a champion, you'll say, 'there's no way that this is going to be the thing that stops me,' then you'll come out swinging and stay in the fight."

I continue my pep talk as they march through the warm-up routine like gladiators preparing for battle. "I can spit platitudes at you and work you hard. But one day you're all going to hit a wall… either in the competition, at the gym, or in life. You've gotta make a choice: Will I rise above this or will I accept defeat?"

No one says anything as they swing their legs side-to-side, supporting each other, or holding the wall for balance. Since the energy level's a little low this morning, I turn the speaker on and crank the volume. The beats blast in a steady rhythm as the gym transforms into a 6:00 am rave party.

"Let's count 'em out together, folks. Time for sit-ups. Hit the deck," Matt demands. "Focus. It starts here, team. The warm-up sets the tone for your workout."

One. Two. Three. The team chants in unison as they execute the sit-ups, lifting their shoulders and upper backs off the floor to warm-up their abdominal muscles. I feel like a proud parent, watching them give it their all before the crack of dawn.

"Come on! Work hard. You got yourself here. You owe it to yourself to work as hard as you can."

Discipline's the number one value I instill in my athletes. So much of success is about showing up day after day, being unwilling to back down when everyone else wants to throw in the towel. This isn't like one of those gyms where you pick a setting on a treadmill and try to keep up to it. Here, *you're* the machine. You push yourself to be the best that you can be.

"Oh, and another thing to get ya motivated to burn some calories," I say as they finish the set. "I'm having a surprise party tomorrow night at my place for Emma's 30th. You're all welcome to join. Be there before 9:00 pm. We'll be coming back for dinner sometime around 9:30."

I glare at the team sternly. "There will be serious consequences if any of you suckers ruins the surprise!"

"Do you think Emma suspects anything?" Rosa asks.

"I don't think so. She's been working long hours lately so unless one of her friends spilled the beans, I think she'll be surprised." I reply.

"I know that Emma isn't one to be the center of attention," says Tanya, "but she loves surprises."

"She's lucky to have you, coach!" Rosa tells me, probably sucking up a bit so I'll go easier on her in the workout. "I wish a guy would do something like that for me. No one's romantic anymore. These days, guys just want to sleep with as many people as possible without having to do any work for it."

"Yeah, maybe you should offer a class that teaches some of those assholes a lesson in growing some balls!" Tanya adds.

"Seriously. I was supposed to have a date last Sunday afternoon with this guy I'd met online and he didn't show up and didn't even bother to text me to let me know. When I texted him to call him out on it, he just ghosted me. He never responded and we'd been texting for over a week. It happens all the time now." Rosa takes a sip of water from her Nalgene bottle dejectedly. She's become like a daughter to me since I started coaching her, so it hurts to see that guys have been treating her badly. Any guy who'd pass up on an opportunity to be with Rosa's a total idiot.

"Shitty. Don't take it personally. You're amazing. Those guys are losers. Ok. Just give us a list and Matt and I will hunt them down and deal with them for you," I promise, winking at Matt.

Matt shakes his head, determined to get back to the workout. "Let's go, let's go, let's go. Move it or lose it kids!" He shouts, stealing a line from my playbook.

I watch as Matt hustles everyone over to the chin-up bars to start their pull-ups and helps them get set-up with bands as needed. He'll be happy to cover if Emma and I take time off to go away next year. Somewhere hot. Jamaica. Or Cuba. Or maybe Costa Rica. It's been too long since either of us has been able to get away.

Emma, May 9, 2014, 10:30am EDT

"You married?"

Tanya, the curious translator, looking cool in her ripped jeggings and boyfriend-style plaid shirt, is already back to texting her friends by the time I finish splinting her grandfather's wrist.

"No," I admit. "But I have a partner. We live together."

"Oh," she scrolls through her phone. Her long dark bangs fall across her face, obscuring her vision. She huffs casually to blow them away. They immediately fall again. "Partner...like girlfriend?"

"No. A man. We're basically married."

Adam and I had talked about getting a couple of years ago, but he's a lot more into it than I am. *"I want to make my Mom proud,"* he'd argued. I think that subconsciously he longs to prove to his mom that he won't take off on me the way his dad did to her. Now, I think maybe it would be nice if Adam and I get married. We should celebrate the work we've put into building our life together with all of our friends and family. Something small, though. No princess weddings for me!

"I thought maybe you're like Mindy from *The Mindy Project*. Lots of bad dates," Tanya explains. "But actually, I think…." her thumbs tab quickly on her touchscreen, "Yep! Here. Look."

She flashes me a Google Image search of a blonde in a lab coat. "You're more like the girl from Spider-Man 2 than Mindy."

I take her phone from her and study the pictures. "Haha. Emma Stone. My boyfriend thinks I look like her as well," I tell her.

Ever since we went to see *Crazy, Stupid, Love.*, Adam's been calling me Miss Stone. I think she's gorgeous, so I've taken it as a compliment. Yet sometimes I wonder if he does it because he can't call me Miss Watters anymore now that I'm Dr. Watters. I guess I'll have to be prepared to have that fight about name changing if we DO end up getting married. When we were in high school, we had this ridiculous deal that I'd change my name if my husband made $10 000/year more than me.

"I'm richer than you, anyhow, Em. I have my own business and all," he'll say when I tell him that I'll marry him, but that I'm not becoming Emma Davison. We haven't actually compared salaries. It's a touchy subject. I highly doubt he's banking more than I am right now, but there's definitely potential for his business to expand across the city. I want us to become a family, but I'm keeping my own last name. At the very least, he'll want me to be Dr. Emma Watters-Davison, and he'll remain Mr. Adam Davison.

If I have to change my name, he should too! Maybe we should become the Davison-Watters. Or Watters-Davisons. Or Davitters. Or Wattison. Those all sound awful. I'd like to pick a new last name for both of us. The Parrys, like Parry Sound, where we met. Too cheesy. The Parks, for all the camping we used to do in Massasauga and Killbear Provincial Park when we were younger. The Bruces, for hiking on the Bruce Trail. Adam would never change his name. He supports women's rights and all, but his traditional side comes out sometimes and he wants to partake in patriarchal responsibilities like passing his family name onto the next generation. What about *my* family name?

My med school friend, Geneviève, told me that she and her partner planned on having two children and giving the first baby her last name (Lévesque) and the second baby his last name (Maisonneuve). So combined, their family would be the Lévesque-Maisonneuves, or Maisonneuve-Lévesques, yet each member of the family would only have one last name (either Lévesque or Maisonneuve). This way, both the mother's name and the father's name would be passed on to the next generation. When I told Adam about Geneviève's plan, he made some joke about Quebecers being too liberal. But it makes sense to me!

Tanya takes a break from her phone to look at her grandfather. *"Ela não é casada."*

Her grandfather studies my left hand and shakes his head in disbelief. He whispers something to his granddaughter and they both giggle like gossipy teenaged girls.

"He said he shoulda brought Diego for translation instead," Tanya explains, "then you can have a husband and not be lonely anymore."

"Uh, thanks," I reply, smiling awkwardly, then quickly change the subject.

"Now, Mr. Costa, there's still too much swelling in your wrist to put a cast on it today. So you'll have to go to see the orthopedic surgeons in the fracture clinic within a week. I'll send the referral and make sure they have a copy of your x-rays.

Judging from your ability to get yourself here, it seems like I should call your wife as well… to make sure you follow through with my advice."

I look up and see that neither patient nor translator is listening to me. Tanya scrolls through her phone the way my co-worker/friend Melayna does when she plays with her Tinder app. Her grandfather watches her intently, and shakes his head in disapproval after she flashes the screen towards him every couple of seconds.

"*Sim!*" Mr. Costa enthusiastically gives the phone the "thumbs up sign" with his unsplinted hand.

"*Este?*" Tanya stares at the phone, then holds it up to me. "See, my uncle. Look. Handsome."

"Cheeek. Mag-a-net," Mr. Costa beams.

I glance at a picture of a young James Franco circa *Freaks and Geeks*. Is this Diego's high school yearbook photo?

"You're right. He's very good-looking," I tell them with a smile. "But I have a boyfriend. So please tell your grandfather, 'thank you,' but I'm not interested."

"Yes, boyfriend. Your part-en-ner," she reminds herself. Then she whispers to her grandpa who smiles and asks me something in Portuguese that I don't understand.

"He says, uh… you love him, you should marry him. You love him?" Tanya asks. "You love him?"

I think of all of the little things that Adam does to make me feel special. The coffee he brings me in bed at 5:00 am before he leaves for work. The fresh flowers he puts in vases throughout the apartment, never letting them die. *"You need to be surrounded by life when you're dealing with death all of the time!"* He told me. The notes he leaves in the lunches that he packs for me at night while I'm tuned into *Grey's Anatomy*. There're no grand gestures like you see on TV. Adam didn't rush to the airport to stop me from moving to Paris like Ross did to Rachel. It's the little day to day actions that keep us strong. For us, love is a blanket we pull over each other at night, a hug after a long day, a shoulder to lean on when watching the sunset. It is something so comfortable and routine that we barely notice it in the moment, but it is the extra weight, the layer that gives these everyday moments meaning.

"Yes," I say speaking to Tanya, her grandfather, but most of all, myself. "Of course, I love him. He's my best friend."

"Don't worry. If you don't marry him, you can marry Diego," she says, with her eyes glued to her phone, "Or you can go on the Bachelorette!" *No thank you!*

I've been hit on by patients before, like the grandpa last week who offered to fly me to his condo in Florida after he regained consciousness following a life-threatening stroke. *You can quit your job! Live in paradise on the beach! You can even look at the young surfers. I don't mind!* However, this is the first time I've had a patient try to set me up with a family member. I wonder what Adam would say if he found out I'd become such a hot commodity?

Adam, May 10, 2014, 6:00 pm EDT

My fingers tremble around a bouquet of red roses. The bouquet's so goddamn big that I'm gripping it in both hands like a 30-lb dumbbell. I look around. No sign of Jess, the basement tenant, who often sits on our porch reading for her thesis. Surprisingly, Dufferin's pretty quiet for a Saturday evening as I return home from Jeff's after getting ready for the big night. Matteo, our twenty-year-old neighbour, usually sits on the deck with his friends drinking Moretti and cat-calling women as they walk down the street or get off the bus. *Sei! Quattro! Dieci! Dieci! Dieci!*

I don't get butterflies but I definitely feel a little tingle in my stomach as I ring the doorbell of the old Victorian-style two-story house that we rent on Dufferin Street. If all goes well, we'll be homeowners in a few years. Jeff and I will open a few more MaxFit locations across the city, or maybe expand across Ontario. Then I'll be able to afford the kind of house Emma deserves. One with a big piece of land where the kids will be able to run free, build tree forts, and play hockey in the backyard rink that I'll build for them in the winter.

I think of the ring hidden in my gym-bag. *What if she says no?* The uncertainty has been driving me nuts.

Pull yourself together, man. Just because you are ringing the doorbell like it's your first date doesn't change the fact that she's chosen to share a bed, a bathroom, a home with you. She picked YOU. Emma could be with any man she wanted. If she's still with you, it's because she wants to be with you. She wants to create a family with you and grow old with you and put up with your shit because she loves you, just like you love her.

I hear her bounce down the stairs. At once, I've stopped sweating and my heart has stopped racing and my hands have stopped trembling. When she opens the door in the red dress I bought for her, it's the best moment of my life. She doesn't need the red dress or the makeup or the wavy hair to make everything brighter and warmer and calmer. I want to take a picture and preserve this moment forever.

The roses. Give her the roses. I wasn't sure whether or not to give her flowers. Any man can give his woman flowers and Hallmark cards, so I outcompete the other dudes by giving her roses and more: a home, a family, a best friend. At the same time, Emma's Netflix addiction has gotten out of control lately. I don't want the night to seem fake by pretending that all we are is characters in one of those silly soap operas she watches like *Grey's Anatomy.* *("It's not a Soap Opera!" she argues defensively. "It's a Medical Drama!")* I can put on the shining armour and be that prince for her for a night. Let her have whatever fantasy she's been craving.

"Awww!!" Jess squeals from the sidewalk, breaking the spell. She lifts her bike up the steps and locks it on the porch. "You guys are precious, getting all dressed up and all. That's the biggest bouquet I've ever seen, Adam."

I take the opportunity to give Emma the roses. "Here. There's thirty. One for each year of your life."

Emma blushes. "Seriously Adam. Isn't this a bit much? You know stuff like this doesn't matter to me," she struggles uncomfortably to hold the massive bouquet of roses in both hands. *Come on, Em. Let me do something special for you for once in your life. You deserve it all and more.* How do I communicate to this woman that she means everything to me without pissing her off?

As if she could hear my thoughts, she looks up at me and smiles sheepishly. "I mean, thanks, Adam. The flowers are beautiful. And the dress, it's stunning. Did you pick it out yourself?"

She knows me too well. "Of course not. Katie found it online and e-mailed me the info. All I did was use my credit card."

There are a few things I'll admit to sucking at. Dress shopping is one of them. "Oh, and you have to give the shoes back. They're Katie's."

Emma would die if she saw how much the dress cost. She'd never spend that much on herself. Not that she's cheap. She just has a "more with less" mentality. *Well, Em, today's your 30th and I'm gonna splurge a little.*

"I'll have to remember to thank her," Emma responds. "It's gorgeous. You didn't have to do all of this, though. You know I'd have been just as happy to stay in and order pizza in our PJs," she winks at me.

Damnit. I casually wipe the sweat off my forehead as I feel myself get hard. The woman didn't even need to do anything and I'm already lost. *Get a hold of yourself.* "Well, my girl only turns 30 once…I mean, my WOMAN." I can barely look at her now she is so sexy. Just being around her turns me on.

Emma laughs nervously, "Adam! Don't make me feel old!"

"You two inspire me," Jess says. "I just had the worst date ever. I'd been chatting with this guy online for a couple of weeks and finally agreed to meet him at Bloomer's, you know, that great vegan café at Bloor and Ossington?"

"Yeah, the guy who owns it works out at my gym," I tell her.

"Well, the guy… JP… he's a writer and seemed super nice from his texts, showed up over half an hour late, saying it was because of some delay on the subway. So I had to sit there awkwardly, wondering if I should stay or leave. When he finally showed up, we had this awesome debate over whether or not Megan will be murdered on *Mad Men*."

"Ok, so this doesn't sound too terrible," says Emma. "I thought you were going to tell us that he told you he was a convict on parole, like Pizza Pizza Man."

"Ya, you told me about him," Jess replies. "It gets worse. After about an hour, he starts nervously checking his phone. Finally, this redhead walks in and he looks at her then looks at me, kind of sizing us up. I guess he thought she was the better option, because he turns all of a sudden and says it was nice to meet me but that his next date is here so that it would probably be best if I go."

"What a loser," I tell her, disgusted. "Show me a picture of him and I'll get some guys from the gym to beat him up for you. Teach him a lesson."

"Thanks, Adam," Jess says, "but we all know you'd never hurt anyone."

"So what did you do?" Emma asks.

"I didn't go right away. I couldn't. I went up to the redhead and told her what happened. I thought she'd think he was a total asshole. Guess what she said? 'So? It's all part of the game. I've already got a date lined up for tomorrow night.' Can you believe it?"

Emma looks at the roses. "Jess, you've gotta keep believing that you'll meet someone who deserves you."

"I know," Jess responds. "Guys like Adam remind me that the good ones are out there. But I've been on so many crappy dates lately. Last week, I went for drinks with a guy who admitted he was married and looking for something on the side."

When I hear guys at the gym bragging about how many girls they're playing at once, I secretly work their asses as hard as I can and make them suffer. Punish them in my own private way. It's like they think strength is only how much they can lift or how many push-ups they can do. Tanya's right. I should offer a class at the gym. Man Camp.

"At least he was upfront about it," I say. "There's this woman at my gym who was dating a guy for two years before she found out through Facebook that he was married."

Emma looks at me in disbelief, "How could she not know? How can you live with someone and not know that they're living a double life?"

"I believe her," I admit. "The man lived with his wife in Calgary, but came to Toronto for business a lot. She was a complete wreck when she joined the gym. She started working out to feel strong again."

"Geeez, Adam. How am I supposed to believe in love when you tell me horror stories like that?"

"Sorry," I say, "but I'm not going to sugar-coat things for you, Jess."

"Thanks for the pep talk, guys. I'm banking that I'll meet a hot doctor tonight at your birth---" I shoot her a threatening look. *Jess, you know it's a SURPRISE party. Don't spill the beans now!*

Luckily, she catches herself before blowing the surprise. "I mean, I'm pretty busy anyways with school and all, so it's probably better that I can have time to focus on my thesis."

Flustered, she opens the front door and hurries inside, then she pauses and turns back. "Whenever I have a bad date, I'll think of how perfect you two look right now, all dressed up for each other and I'll remind myself that the kind of love we see on TV and in the movies exists in real life."

I want to tell Jess that she's missed the point. Being with Emma's like a 6:00 am ass-kicking: 'Myrna,' 'Jan,' or even 'Lia.' It makes me stronger and when I'm stronger, everything else is stronger, too.

"So are you going to come in first, handsome?" Emma teases, gesturing for me to follow her inside. Her gaze warms every cell of my body. Of course I'll come inside. This woman is more than love to me. She's my fuel, my best friend, my soulmate, my purpose, my struggle, my life. I can do all the squats and cleans and push-ups that my body can handle but the only thing that will really make me stronger is her.

Emma: May 10, 2014, 6:45pm EDT

"Adam? Adam, are we late?"

I double check myself quickly in the mirror, grab my purse and phone, and rush downstairs. I squeeze into Katie's nude pumps. *How does she wear these things to work everyday?* (Thank goodness for Crocs!) I swing open the door to greet my man. Adam. The General. But all I see is a cab waiting in front of the house. I look closely at the cab. He's definitely not in it.

"Adam? The cab's here!"

Where is he? He was just here a minute ago!

I take off the pumps and run upstairs to check our bedroom and the bathroom. One minute, we're moving as one person, experiencing one of the most intimate moments of our relationship, then the next, he's Polkaroo, nowhere to be found. *How did this happen?*

"Adam? Did you hear me? The cab's here!" I try calling his cell. Nothing. Then again. Nothing. *Maybe he was hiding in the cab after all.*

I go back downstairs, squeeze back into the pumps, and rush out to the cab. When I open the passenger door, the driver, a cheerful older Pakistani man gestures for me to come in.

"You must be Miss Emma," he says, with a thick accent. "Mister Adam told me that I would be driving the most beautiful woman tonight, who looks like the famous celebrity Emma, Emma Rock."

Stone. Emma Stone. Hopefully, since the sun's set, it's too dark for the driver to see my face turn the colour of my dress. Crimson Red. That's what Adam said it was. Like any of us knows the difference between Red-Red and Crimson Red. But the dress is absolutely gorgeous. Katie's amazing. Adam's amazing—I mean, WAS amazing. I wish I knew what the heck's going on!

"Thank you. Do you know where Adam is? Are we waiting for him, or picking him up somewhere? He was just in our house a minute ago."

"All I know is my direct instructions from Mister Adam to bring you places. So I bring you places. Mister Adam meet you later."

Huh? When we were younger, Adam used to play tricks on me. He joked that by driving me crazy, that he would be able to stand out against all the "other guys" (?) who had crushes on me. I gotta hand it to the General for being overconfident—it worked! But he hasn't pulled any real pranks since my first year at Queen's.

We'd gone on the "Haunted Walk of Kingston" and were spooked by some real-life ghost stories that had occurred at various historic buildings around the city. Actually, I was freaking out, while Adam made fun of me for being so gullible. *"It's only storytelling. Just made up for entertainment,"* he said, unconvinced. I don't believe in ghosts. (Maybe?) But the stories the guide told sparked my imagination, and I've always been interested in what happens when we die, especially now that I witness death so often.

There was one story about Waldron Tower, my residence building, a former nurse's residence, that creeped me out. Apparently, years ago, a nurse named Betty committed suicide from the top of the spiral staircase on the 11th floor and continues to haunt the building. There had been reports of students who'd had their printers turn on in the middle of the night, had things like pop cans or books moved around in the night, had a TV switch on and off on its own: little things that might mean nothing at the time, yet when added together, made for a terrifying explanation. The guide said that a residence don even had a motion-activated candy dispenser that she had turned off before going to bed. Then in the middle of the night, it turned itself on and started dispensing candy. *"The guide's a DRAMA student. It's her job to make the stories sound believable!"* Adam reminded me after I'd squeezed his hand so much that I'm surprised his knuckles didn't break.

When we got back to my room in Wally, I was feeling a little chilly from the cold, so I had a quick shower in the shared washroom on my floor. When I came back to my room, Adam was gone. But he'd left a note: *Gone to get snacks. Be back soon.*

Weird that he didn't wait for me, I thought. But when Adam had a craving in the middle of rugby season, he acts on it. While I was waiting for Adam to return, I put on an episode of *Sex and the City*. Just after Miranda proposes to Steve, the light on my bedside table went off. (So did this mean, I won't propose to Adam in the future?!) I turned the switch on and off to test the light.

Nothing happened.

Then a hand grabbed my ankle. I screamed so loud that my neighbours, Andrew and Paul, came over to see if I was okay, just as Adam emerged from under the bed laughing. *"I couldn't help it, Em. Now you know the stories aren't real."* I didn't know whether to laugh or cry. So, I told Adam that he had to go outside and sleep in the car for a while. He came back an hour later with flowers and sour Jujubes, apologizing profusely. I knew he would never play a prank like that on me again.

So what's happening now? Where is he?

"Mister Adam, he your husband? My wife, she would kill me if she knew I was accepting women as beautiful as you into my taxicab." The driver examines me through his rear-view mirror then starts driving south towards Bloor.

"No, we're not married. We've been friends for a long time, though. Since high school."

"Yes, in the West you do things differently. The dating. The 'figuring of it out'." He makes quotation marks in the air. "What is there to figure out? It's simple. You get married. You have children. You take care of your family. Love happens on the way."

"I guess here we meet new people all of the time so we want to make sure we find someone who's right for us." Of all of my high school friends, only Adam and I, and one other couple, are still together, and Adam and I didn't think we'd get to this point!

"In Canada, you think you meet more people. In Punjab, where I come from, bigger population. Smaller land. More people to meet. There's no 'right person' for us. We pick. We commit. That's it. If there's a problem, our families and community try to fix. Me, if my parents requested it, I could have married another woman instead. I'm lucky, my wife. Very beautiful. I love her very much. Very, very much. With all of my heart. Good cook too!" He laughs.

I never really thought about whether there's one "right person" for me before Adam and I got back together. I guess I always assumed that I could be with different people, that it was a choice to be with someone or not. I was so invested in becoming a doctor that I didn't really have time to worry about "choosing my match" until more recently. *You aren't getting any younger!* My mom reminds me. *You're almost 30. When are you two going to get married?* Then I think of how much deeper and stronger Adam and I become when we got back together. All those on-again-off-again TV romances like Ross and Rachel, Carrie and Big, or Meredith and Derek, suddenly made sense. It seems like love can't grow these days without being lost then found again.

"I have two daughters. They do dating. Joe, Marc, Amir. I can't keep track. Do these boys come from good families, I ask? I don't even know their parents. Each weekend a different boy picks them up to go to the movies. I said no to the dating, but my wife, she put her foot down. She say arranged marriage is less religion, more culture, and we need to let them grow up the North American way even though we practice the Sikh tradition at home. So I said only the early show. No late show. Not until married. Well, my younger daughter, no dates yet. She does the texting, the Facebook."

He turns left, driving East on Bloor. *Ooooh*, okay, maybe we're going to go up the CN Tower and have dinner at 360, the restaurant with the panoramic views. I've been trying to guilt trip Adam into taking me there ever since we got back together.

"Why you and Mister Adam not married?"

There must be something about turning 30--everyone seems to be asking me the same question these days!

"Uh, we met each other really young so I guess it's taken time to make sure we were right for each other. We both dated other people before we got back together two years ago."

He studies me through his rear-view mirror. "Miss Emma. Miss Emma Rock. How old you were when you meet Mister Adam?"

"Fifteen."

"Ah, same age as me and my wife. The day I met her was the day we married. We had never even seen each other but love grew over time. Our parents, they arranged it when we very young. In Punjab, marriage is the coming together of two families. You and Mister Adam: your families, they friendly?"

I think of the few awkward encounters my ultra-religious parents have had with Adam's hippie mom. "They get along when they have to," I admit, "but they're not in any rush to merge as families."

"That is most unfortunate. Family is the most important thing in this life."

He stops the cab, pulling over on Bloor, just west of Bathurst, then he looks at a piece of paper. Craning my neck to try to see it, I make out Adam's handwriting.

"Mister Adam. He say you go in that café over there and pick a game you like. Tell them your name. They expect you. Pick one that," he holds the paper up to his face, "one that doesn't have too many pieces that will blow away in the wind."

"Sorry, I'm confused. Is Adam inside?"

"No, Miss Emma. This pit stop. You get game, then we continue. I wait here for you."

As instructed, I head inside Snakes and Lattés to pick out a game. The café is packed with couples and groups of friends drinking beer or coffee and playing games like *Settlers of Catan*, *Ticket to Ride*, and *Dungeons and Dragons*, as well as the classics like *Monopoly*. When I was in high school, I loved board games. During spare or recess my friends and I became obsessed with *Cranium* and often hung out in the room left over by Ms. Roberts, the drama teacher, and played while our classmates would go outside and smoke or walk to McDonald's.

"Can I help you?" I'm face-to-face with Mike, aka Dwight from *The Office* with his geeky vibe and square appearance. "You're looking quite lovely, Miss. Did you just come from graduation or something?"

"Thank you. I'm on my way out to my birthday dinner. My boyfriend, Adam, he sent me here with instructions to pick out a game."

"Oh, yes. You must be Emma. Happy birthday! Adam was here a couple times last week, trying to plan something special for you. He had so many wild and crazy ideas, like a massive *Cranium* tournament, a *Clue* re-enactment, and a costume party where everyone would dress up as their favourite board game. But eventually he settled on something more intimate and low-key."

He winks at me. "We usually don't rent our games out to customers. However, Adam convinced me to make an exception. What kind of game would you like to play? Fantasy? Classic? Trivia?"

He walks me towards the back of the store where they shelve the games. I was expecting to be able to choose from maybe twenty or so games. This place is overwhelming. There are hundreds. It's like what Blockbuster used to be for movies. I scan the shelves. What, there's a *Game of Thrones Monopoly*? *Harry Potter Trivial Pursuit*? *Subways and Serpents*: what the heck? I pick up the box and turn it over.

'Subways & Serpents is a chaotic, fast paced, 'hunt or be hunted' board game that takes place on an expanded version of Toronto's existing subway lines. The good people of Toronto finally got the expanded subway system they'd been waiting for. Getting across town is quick and easy! Or, it would be, if the tunnel excavation didn't unleash hordes of bloodthirsty Serpents..."

"This is hilarious. Whoever invented this game is super creative. It's like they imagined a whole new city."

"Well, that's what board games are all about. Giving people a chance to do things they can't do in the real world. Ride an efficient subway system. Build settlements or hotels. Slay the dragon. Win the lottery. Basically, be someone they're not."

"I didn't realize there were so many games. What's your favourite game?" I ask.

"That's easy! *LIFE*. Just kidding. No, my favourite game is definitely *Dead of Winter*." Then he lowers his voice to a conspiratorial whisper, "I'm really into zombies. Are you?"

"Uh, no."

"Hmm, well I thought you were someone I met at last year's Zombie Walk. But I guess it's hard to know who you meet at zombie gatherings because everyone's wearing make-up. You should check it out. Surprisingly, lots of hot chicks dig zombies."

There must be an episode of *The Office* where Dwight dresses up for Hallowe'en because the mental image I'm forming of this guy in a zombie costume seems like a déjà-vu. Suddenly I remember that the meter's still running on the cab.

"Do you have a section for two-player games?" I ask him. He walks me over to a section on the far left.

"Are you looking for a new game? Or something nostalgic?"

"I'd prefer something we both know how to play. It's always frustrating to have to take the time to learn how to play something new. I always want to just jump in there and start playing!"

"Okay, the classics are over here," he gestures to a shelf at the far end of the section. I skim through the options. *Backgammon. Battleship. Chess. Guess Who? Monopoly*...then I see it: *Operation*.

"I'll take this one."

Dwight takes the game from me. "So you want to play doctor?"

"Ha, ha. Actually I AM a doctor," I explain. "I used to play this game as a kid when I dreamed that I might become a doctor *someday*. Maybe I'm being nostalgic, but weirdly, it seems like an appropriate game to play on my thirtieth birthday... like I've finally gained the wisdom in my old age to get through life without setting off the buzzer!"

Adam, May 10, 2014, 7:25pm EDT

Putting up this tent's more effort than I thought, especially since 'Jan' tore apart my lats yesterday and I'm struggling to lift my arms.

Using a stone I found by the playground, I hammer a peg into the ground to secure the tarp. This is one luxury shelter. *"It doubles as a family camping tent or portable disco for rainy Cabana parties."* The guy at Mountain Equipment Co-op told me that when I rented it. *"This shelter's luxurious. The best we've got."* He's right. It *is* luxurious. But there's no way that sleeping in this five star palace is camping.

Two months in the Yukon. Fly-fishing for trout and salmon in St. Elias Lake. Carrying 80 lbs of gear on your back. Getting lost and then bushwhacking through boreal forest to forge your own trail. Taking precautions to protect yourself against grizzly attacks and goddamn mosquitos. Roughing it. Pushing yourself out of your comfort zone. Testing your limits. That's camping. Being inspired by the wonder and the beauty of the mountains, icefields, and valley glaciers. Long summer days. Such incredible light. *That's fucking living.*

None of this cushy, 'sip my Pinot Grigio in stainless steel wine glasses and call it camping because I'm outside' camping. It's like those people who go up the CN Tower once or go to Canada's Wonderland and say they've been to Toronto. Life's just cold beers and hot showers for them.

When you're in the wild, there's nothing to hide behind. No bars or credit cards or movie theatres or cell phones or credentials or security. You're just alone with yourself. You look around and lose yourself in the mountains, rivers, forests or tundra, but you can see nothing except for the chaos in your own mind. It is fucking terrifying and peaceful at the same time. I'd love to take Emma on a big canoe trip through Algonquin Park or even up the coast of Georgian Bay towards Manitoulin Island. It would be so great to spend time together before we have kids. Just the two of us, with nothing but the sun and the stars and our camping gear.

After I hammer in the final peg, I haul the cooler to the picnic table and get the food out for grilling. Steak. Asparagus. Mushrooms. Potatoes. Then I take out some Brie and crackers, place them carefully on the tablecloth I've spread over the picnic table, and take out the wine I've poured into a Nalgene so the cops won't think we're drinking. My girl and I are sneaking booze in Christie Pits like a couple of delinquent teens! We'll tell the grandkids about this night at their weddings: you know it's love when you're able to act like goofy kids at the park without feeling judged or ridiculous or pressured to put on any kind of show. You can just be yourself.

As I walk over to the public BBQ that I reserved online and check out the heat, I notice an orange and green cab pull around to the northwest end of the park. *I told him northeast, damnit.* The cab slows in front of a house and an older couple dressed in cocktail wear walks out from their house to meet it. Looks like they're going out for a night on the town. I wonder what Emma and I will look like when we're that age: 60? 70? The baby-boomers are looking so young these days I can't even tell. Like Wendy at the gym. What a woman, she's been retired for eight years and still exercising harder than most of the guys in their 20s. The way I see it, age, like health, is just a state of mind. We often stop ourselves from doing the things we want to do, finishing the set, just because we don't think we can.

It's hard to imagine where we will be in 30 years when I have trouble predicting where we will be in five years. I'd love to try to save up enough to move to Parry Sound by the time the kids are in elementary school, so they'll have the small-town upbringing that Emma and I did. I know Emma will grow tired of the pace of the ER and want to open a family practice, and I'd love to open a MaxFit club there. We'll have a family and grow old there together, spending our days going on hikes, paddling on the lake, and doing crossword puzzles.

Finally, the grill feels hot enough to start cooking. Perfect timing. A cab's pulling up to the northeast corner. Must be Emma. Anxiety begins to build inside me. Why am I so jittery? *It's the same girl you have dinner with every night. Relax, man.* I watch her get out of the cab, heels in one hand, board game in the other. She's even hotter in Crocs than those heels. Not many women could pull that off. Finally, I put a couple of tulips that I picked from our garden into a plastic cup.

"Adam! Are you kidding me? This is too much! You are crazy!" Emma shouts, skipping towards me. She'll never admit it. She's too modest. I know she's loving every fucking second of this.

After I propose tomorrow, she'll see how much being part of a family means to me. I'll promise to always be there for her and our future kids. I'd put my money on sons. How many will we have? I'll get them into sports right away. Hockey. Basketball. Rugby.

Daughters would be nice, too, but I have no idea how to raise a girl these days. Emma would obviously have more expertise in that area. I'd probably raise our daughter like her brothers: start her in sports young and teach her to stand up for herself. Women can do whatever they want these days, so it'll be my responsibility to help her see that she can do all of the things that men can and more. No boyfriends unless they have my permission. There's no way I'm going to let some shitty guy break my little girl's heart.

I bring the steaks over to the BBQ, place them on the grill, and flip the potatoes and vegetables. Emma is not supposed to feel guilty or stressed on her birthday, especially not about us. If anything ever goes wrong between us, I'll be the one to blame, not her. Nothing's going to happen, though. It can't. We've come too far. I'll be the best friend, lover, husband, father that she could ask for because that's what she deserves.

After closing the lid to the grill, I walk over to where Emma's standing in disbelief at this ridiculous setup. I wrap my arms around her. "Happy birthday, Miss Stone. I love you, Em," I whisper.

We both know that none of this matters. It's all just an act. But acting is part of every relationship. We're all just trying to convince each other that we know what the fuck is going on, and that our relationship will work out like we want it do. There will be lots of tests: financial struggles, problems with the kids, etc. We'll only prove our strength as a team if we're able to get through them. It will take lots of work, but I'm going to do everything I can to make sure I pull my weight and more.

I take a sip of my wine as I watch Emma cut a thick slab of brie cheese and wedge it on a Triscuit, then open her mouth extra wide so she can fit the whole appetizer into her mouth at once. As she bites down, part of the cracker breaks off and falls inside the top of her dress. Barely embarrassed, she quickly reaches down her top and fishes out the cracker. Instead of throwing it out, she pops it right into her mouth and eats it. *Classy, Em.* She's comfortable enough to be herself around me and that makes her even more beautiful.

"Adam?" I have trouble looking her in the eyes she's so beautiful.

"Yes, Em?"

"Do you still want to get married?"

Does she know about the ring? Or did Katie spill the beans when Emma called to thank her about the dress?

"Emma, are you proposing?" I ask, half-jokingly.

She's taken aback. "Ha, no. Don't you think I'd be doing something more romantic if I were proposing, like lighting a room full of candles like Monica did when she proposed to Chandler?"

"All I know is that when you put your mind to something, you do it. If you want to propose, then go ahead and propose, in whatever way you feel like."

All of a sudden she's shy and awkward and uncertain, traits I NEVER see in Doctor Emma.

"Ok, well. I just wanted you to know that I might want to get married now if you still want that."

Of course I want that. I reach for her hand and gesture for her to come towards me. Then I pull her in tight. I never ever want to let her go. The pretty girl with the long strawberry blond hair hugs me back and we sway back and forth in the park like we're in the middle of the gym at our high school dance. We're lost in each other, in the heart of Toronto, slow dancing to nothing but the beat of my heart and the sound of her breath on my neck. I know the subway trains are trembling beneath my feet and that we're amidst the constant buzz of city life, yet I hear nothing but my heart beating and feel nothing but her breath on my neck.

Emma: May 10, 2014, 9:30pm EDT

"So Jeff, you were in on this plan the whole time?" I ask as I help lift the cooler into the back of his truck.

"Yeppers, Em. When he told me that he wanted to do something special for you, I said, 'that Emma Watters, she deserves everything and more.' So I tried to help him with the 'and more' part. That *Snakes and Lattés* pit stop was my idea. We needed to distract you so we could get the tent set up. Did you lovebirds have fun?"

"It was one of the best nights ever," I admit. Everything about tonight was perfect: the effort, the food, the wine, the tent, the game, and the surprise. No crowd. No menus. No pressure. The simplicity made it romantic: the way he looked at me honestly and listened to me when I spoke, pulled me close to him, and hugged me like he never wanted to let me go. It felt like we were back in high school, a couple of silly kids who believed our love would last because there was nothing to tell us otherwise. I hope we're able to hang on to that feeling for the rest of our lives. Maybe love's more than the daily comforts: more than morning coffees and flowers and notes in my lunch bag and holding hands while watching the stars. It's about never giving up, believing in each other, and supporting each other through the good and the bad.

"The night is young, my lady," Jeff winks. "I know you both get up super early on weekdays, so you're probably getting pretty sleepy. Just remember that you only have one 30th birthday, so you may as well make the most of it. You are looking outrageously beautiful tonight, by the way. If I wasn't married to such an amazing woman myself, I'd definitely consider fighting for you, Em. Adam's a lucky man!"

He helps me into the passenger seat, while Adam squeezes into the back seat. I notice that he has his phone out. Who is he texting?

"What did you and Nance do for her 30th?" I ask Jeff.

"Same thing," Adam cuts in, "I totally stole the idea from him."

"Adam! You're the worst!" I exclaim. I know he's teasing. The General would never use an idea from one of his 'brothers'.

"Actually, Nancy's 30th was shortly after Emily was born, so we invited her sister and our parents over and ordered take-out from Thai Green Chili."

"That's pretty low-key," I said.

"Yeah, it wasn't very fancy, but it was special, especially since it was Emily's first birthday party! And the Leafs won, so that was a bonus."

"You made Nancy watch the game?" Adam asks in surprise. "It was her birthday!"

"She's a Leafs fan, too! We were both too tired to entertain anyone, anyways. So we put the game on, put Emily to bed, and zoned out a bit. Nancy's dad can get a bit too opinionated about us choosing to keep renting in the city now that we have a kid. He wants us to move to a nice house in the suburbs, like Mississauga or Oakville or something. But neither of us wants to deal with the commute. Whatever we can do to avoid that conversation, the better!"

"I get it," I sympathize, "my parents are always bugging Adam and I about moving back to Parry Sound. I'm sure they'll be pushy once we have kids."

"I always tell them that we're open to moving one day, but for now, we're happy in the city," Adam adds.

Great. We're totally on the same page. At least about the 'big picture'. The plan for tonight is another story.

What happens next? Adam, you're messing with me!

He kind of just shrugged off my marriage question, but the way he held me makes me think he wants it to. Or maybe he shrugged it off because he doesn't want to ruin the surprise. What if this whole night's leading up to the big proposal?

We pull up in front of the house. I catch Jeff wink at Adam in the rear-view mirror. *He IS going to propose to me after all.* Jeff got married a couple of years ago, so he'd definitely be the guy Adam would go to for advice. I stop myself from asking Jeff how he proposed to Nancy. That would ruin the surprise, right? Steal Adam's thunder.

"You go ahead, Emma," Adam encourages, "I'll grab a few things from the back of Jeff's truck."

He's getting some last minute pointers. *It's a no brainer, Adam.* Get down on one knee and present the ring. Ask the question. It's cute to see him so nervous. Usually he's very calm under pressure. Before a big rugby game, he'd always be the one reassuring people, pumping them up, making them believe in themselves. Now Jeff's the one encouraging him: *"I'm sure she'll say yes. She has to. She wouldn't have stuck with you all of these years if she didn't want to be a family with you."*

I put the key in the lock and open the door. Should I pour the champagne? Have it ready for an immediate celebration? Or will he want to pop the cork?

I hear some muffled noise coming from the living room. Maybe I left a window open.
"Shhshhhshh. She's here! Shshshsh. Cameras ready!"

The neighbours must be catcalling me again. I turn the light on--

"SURPRISE!!"

"Happy birthday to you! Happy birthday to you! Happy birthday, dear Emma. Happy birthday to you!"

Mom and Dad. Granny and Grandpa. Nicky. Katie and James. Erin. Jess. Mel and a few of the staff from the hospital. *(Who invited Neil?)* A bunch of friends from Queen's. A few friends from med school. Some guys from Adam's rugby teams. A handful of members from MaxFit. Basically all of my friends and family piled into our little apartment.

Tears form in my eyes as Adam comes from behind me carrying a Dairy Queen cake. *Happy 30th Emma!*

Even though there's no proposal (YET!), the best night of my life just got better.

Part 3: The Day After the Party

"Two years he walks the earth. No phone, no pool, no pets, no cigarettes. Ultimate freedom. An extremist. An aesthetic voyager whose home is the road. Escaped from Atlanta. Thou shalt not return, 'cause 'the West is the best.' And now after two rambling years comes the final and greatest adventure. The climactic battle to kill the false being within and victoriously conclude the spiritual pilgrimage. Ten days and nights of freight trains and hitchhiking bring him to the Great White North. No longer to be poisoned by civilization he flees, and walks alone upon the land to become lost in the wild."

-Christopher McCandless,
(From Jon Krakauer's *Into the Wild*)

Adam: May 11, 2014, 10:05 am EDT

Everything looks different from up above. I'm floating through one of those fun-houses at a summer fair, the ones with the mirrors that distort your body into weird shapes and have crooked kitchens.

I wave to Mrs. Rizzuto as I drift past. My hand's light, a balloon lifting me further and further into space. I can smell the tulips in her garden. Fruit juice mixed with black tea. *English Breakfast*. The kind my mom drinks.

I'm soaring now. Living the dream as I was always meant to. I'll never understand why was I rejected from Team Canada. The guy they picked over me is at least 20 lbs lighter, and definitely slower. He's skilled, but he lacks balls. On the pitch, I'm an assassin out for blood. I show no weakness, no pain. I conquer what cannot be conquered. I fight. That's what life's about, risking everything—your pride, your body, your heart—for the extra inch that drives the ball over the try line. All of those moments of struggle, despair, and suffering add up. They create warriors. They create champions. They made me unstoppable.

Within minutes, I'm at the grocery store. *Pancakes*. Toilet paper, $5.99. The good stuff. Silky double-ply. I toss a pack in my basket. Goldfish crackers. Like my mom and I used to eat before swimming lessons. *Goldfish can swim. So can you!*

I start grabbing items off the shelf and putting them in the basket, which is getting heavier and heavier by the second, weighing my arm down like a dumbbell. It's a few days since I've done a real workout. Tomorrow, I'll start training for the marathon or the Iron Man. Or cycling. These massive quads could fuel a thousand horsepower engine.

I toss groceries from my mental list into the basket: Syrup. Milk. Eggs. Five boxes of pancake batter. *Cake.* Vanilla? Chocolate? I pick up both. Orange juice. Pulp-free. Ice cream. I toss the cake mix high up into the air like I'm playing JACKPOT! at recess. But of course no one else is playing and the boxes explode in the aisle.

I was pretty fucked up last night, but my girl only turns thirty once. One minute we were in the backyard smoking cigars then the next I'm popping pills with some of Tyler's buddies. Apparently, the pills help them pass the wall in their workouts. I won't let myself get hooked. Can't have any shit in your system when you compete and real power isn't something that can be faked. But the pills definitely made the party more interesting. Did the Jays win last night? I bet Buehrle pitched another shutout.

Pancakes? Check. DQ Cake? Mental check to stop there next. Lots of other stuff. Check. I race to the checkout. An old man ahead of me removes items from his shopping cart by one, so slowly it's like time is reversing. I can see every wrinkle on his face, the crows feet around his eyes, the creases in his forehead, the smile lines.

People. Canadian Living. TV Guide. I scan the magazines on the rack beside me as I wait for the old man who brought thirteen items to the eight-item express line. (I counted.) You think he'd put the time he has left to better use.

ESCAPED KILLER'S CRAZED LUST FOR OPRAH: Winfrey tops celebrity targets of psycho who fled prison. That *National Enquirer* always distracts me in the checkout. If I was a psycho prisoner, I definitely wouldn't be lusting for Oprah. More like Scarlett Johansson or Beyoncé or Taylor Swift or Rachel McAdams or Jennifer Lawrence or even Kim Kardashian.

Canadian Geographic. Travel. I'm mesmerized by an image of crystal blue water surrounding a white sand beach. The photo is so perfect it seems to be fake, but I can already feel the sand beneath my feet. I twist, digging myself deeper into the sand. It's so hot that blisters start to form on my soles and under my toes.

Explore Phuket.

I drop the basket on the floor like a piece of hot coal. The cracking of eggshells is like the haunting shatter of breaking bones. I run towards the exit, hearing the *hey-hey-heys!* of the cashier calling out after me. Suddenly, I'm lighter, only half of who I was. I sprint down the street, even faster than before. Finally, a cab approaches and I wave frantically at it. I hop in, drenched in sweat, uncomfortable, but it's the most alive I've ever felt.

"Pearson," I tell the driver.

"Airport? You have no luggage?"

"I'm going to be late. Please get me there as quickly as you can."

Emma: May 11, 2014, 10:55 am EDT

I call Adam for the third time. I can hear a faint ringing coming from our bedroom. *Shoot, his phone's here.* His note says he went to get groceries for breakfast (how sweet!), but that was hours ago. I've already watched two episodes of *OITNB*. I bet he went to the gym first. To sweat out the booze from last night.

Take your time, Adam. I'm almost done Season 1 and want to find out if Piper and Larry stay together. (Spoiler alert!) I can't believe that Piper's rekindling the flame with Alex, her former lesbian lover who's the reason that Piper's locked up in the first place. Piper, you can't lower your standards just because you're in jail. The woman ruined your life. Bad relationships are a prison. They can lock you into a lifetime of misery. We shouldn't forgive so easily.

I've panicked a bit while watching Piper and Larry's relationship fall apart so quickly. Despite how much effort it takes to build a solid foundation, love can dissolve without warning. Are Adam and I that fragile as well? We broke up before, but things between us feel different this time around, much stronger. We both know what it feels like to lose our other half and we don't want that to happen again. Besides, circumstances drove us apart the first time, not lack of love. Well, that and Adam took it really hard when he got cut from Team Canada. Adam decided to stay in Toronto so that he could train with the Ontario rugby team in hopes of making the Team Canada training squad leading up to the 2011 World Cup. The only med school that accepted me was the University of Calgary. Maybe things would have been different if I'd stayed in Toronto. Been there to support him. Maybe not.

A couple of months after I moved to Calgary, Rugby Canada announced the longlist. Adam wasn't selected. Ever since he was in high school and started playing rugby, he'd dreamed of playing for Team Canada. It's like his whole life fell apart when he got cut. He gave up on rugby, himself, our relationship, and everything that went along with the future he'd envisioned.

From working in hospitals, I've seen people overcome a lot more in life than not making a sports team. Like Delilah, a patient I met during a med school placement who was diagnosed with breast cancer when she was only twenty. Sadly, after a double mastectomy and radiation, the cancer spread from her breast to her lymph nodes, and up to her brain. After she had been treated twice for breast cancer, surgeons found two brain tumors, including one the size of the golf ball. Usually, when you have a brain mass, survival is about a year.

Delilah underwent radiation. Despite the aggressive treatment, the tumor in her frontal lobe came back. Instead of becoming depressed and hopeless, though, Delilah went on a three-week trip to Spain with her mom and decided to continue living life to its fullest.

Dr. Orr was not surprised when Delilah asked him to try radiation again after returning from her trip with the familiar lust for life he saw in her. "Let's just get rid of it," she said confidently. This time, the radiation appears to have worked. Delilah has been cancer free for almost two years. I really believe that Delilah's positive energy helped her beat cancer. Her recovery sticks with me as a lesson that either we can choose to be victims of despair or we can keep fighting, so I didn't have sympathy for Adam lying on the couch sulking that he got cut from Team Canada when people like Delilah persevere in the face of death!

"Just snap out of it," I said. *"Don't let one rejection get you down. Didn't Michael Jordan get cut from his high school basketball team? If you work hard and have a good season this year, you might be able to make the list for next year. Don't give up. You're stronger than this."*

He said he was feeling low. *"I'm sorry. I can't talk to you because it just makes me feel worse. Everything is so hopeless."* After a month or so of him ignoring me, we broke up. It was really sad to see him so crushed, but it wasn't fair for him to take it out on me.

I'm not sure how long it took Adam to get back on his feet, but opening MaxFit has definitely given him new purpose. When we ran into each other (while running!) in Parry Sound two years later, I felt like I was reintroduced to the man I fell in love with. Positive, inspiring, go-getter Adam. The man who motivates everyone around him to become better. The General.

Last night was easily the best night of my life. We dressed up all fancy, shared a romantic dinner, slow danced in the park, and celebrated with our closest friends and family. Everyone there looked like they were having the time of their lives. Even Granny got up and danced with her cane once the living room transformed into a spontaneous dance party. It was like one of those really fun weddings that you never want to end. The night made me realize how much I really do want to get married to Adam, after all. I was sure he was going to propose, but maybe he's waiting to do it tonight when we go to Granny and Grandpa's for dinner.

I must've told myself that I didn't want to get married because I thought that medicine was *the love* of my life. My purpose. My soul. But there's room in my heart for more than one love. I want to continue my work as a doctor *and* build a family with Adam. Now it seems that having more love in my life makes me stronger.

Last night, after the party, I told Adam this is happiest I've ever been.

This *is* the happiest I've ever been.

Adam: May 11, 2014, 11:15 am EDT

I look at the airline departure schedules for the day: Bangkok, American Airlines, 3:30 pm. My flight. Or maybe Vegas. I'll go and play the slots and win my millions and never have to work again. *Beijing.* The world needs me. China's rising. How long it would take me to learn Mandarin?

The woman at the counter looks like she's in a car commercial. Her red lipstick is so bright I can see it sitting thickly on her lips. She doesn't know that she is speaking to the next Steve Jobs. Someday, she'll thank me. Is that a bug in her hair? I look away then look back and it's gone.

"Sir? Are you all right? Can you hear me?" The woman at the counter speaks loudly like a gym teacher using her outdoor voice.

"Yes, ma'am," I pull out my credit card. "Can I buy a ticket to Bangkok?" I ask.

"For today?"

"Yes, the 3:30 pm flight. Is it full?"

She types into her computer. The clicks of the keys pound in my head. Can she hurry up? I haven't got all day. "That would be $2650.00."

"Ok, I'll take one. One way. For today. 3:30 pm."

"Great," she says, typing into the computer. "Can I have your passport?"

"Passport?" *Shit.*

I'm running quickly out the door before she even looks up. I need to invent one of those teleportation machines that I saw on *Back to the Future*. I wave down the first cab and jump in. For now, I'll I can do is run.

In the cab, my fingers and toes tap along to Brian Adams' voice on the radio. *Played it 'til my fingers bled. It was the summer of '69.* I'm so jittery, so much energy. It's hard to sit still. Can this guy drive any faster? Sure, it's a Sunday, but we're on the 401. Speed of traffic is at least 120-130 km/hour. FUCK! I NEED TO GET OUT AND RUN. SPRINT!!! I'll race this cabbie home.

I have too much energy. Too much passion. Too much COURAGE to sit around, trapped in this city. I gotta move. Go to the mountains. The ocean. The WILD WILD WEST!!! It's a race now. I must act. The world needs me. Alexander Graham Bell only patented the telephone hours before Elisha Gray. Once an idea comes, you gotta rush to transform it into something real. There's something for me on the West coast. I can feel it.

"Turn around!" I shout to the cabbie, in a panic, like I am calling from outside myself. Am I above me? Below me? Beside me? Under me? Where am I now? I'm in a lost and found. Lost and found at the same time. Everywhere and nowhere. But I need to keep moving. Sprinting!!!

"I have to go back to the airport. I forgot something. Please. Get off at the next exit. Weston Road. We have to turn around. Please. Hurry. It's urgent." We drive past a green road sign, *Algonquin Park 250 km*, then a strip mall with a Canadian Tire, The Brick, and a Tim Horton's and I begin to get really antsy being stuck in the collector lanes on the busiest section of highway in North America and all I want to do is break free.

The idea to go West just fell into my lap from the sky. *Go west, young man.* That's how the best ideas happen. Just out of nowhere. When you're not even thinking. Like they've been created for you and you just have to reach out and grab them before someone else does. This is history in the making. A few years from now, they'll be interviewing me on CBC. *"Mr. Davison, what propelled your success?" "I grabbed an idea by the horns and rode it fearlessly, like a bullfighter."*

Vancouver will be a rebirth. A place where people go for a work-life balance. You step out of the SkyTrain station after a long day at the office, one minute feeling the pressure of a busy city life and the next minute looking up at the mountains and into the ocean. You go from feeling like a caged animal at the zoo to total freedom. That's what mountains do, they taunt you, lure you to the freedom of the wilderness, and it is fucking exhilarating. A constant seduction. None of this *go to work and come home on the goddamn Dufferin bus* with all the creepos and whiners. Vancouver's a bit rainy, yes, but I see myself staring at the striking city skyline along the harbourfront, the sun setting just beyond the mountains, a peaceful pink glow of dusk falling on the electric buzz of the city's nightlife. It has a magnetic pull.

"Sir, are you okay?" The taxi driver looks at me nervously, like I'm some criminal. He thinks I've just robbed a bank and is planning my escape. But then why would I go back to the airport where there is so much security? Other people can be so dumb sometimes.

He won't understand the truth. My right leg shakes as my heel tries to get ahead of the beat. I start singing in my head or out loud; I'm not really sure. *And now the times are changin'/ Look at everything that's come and gone/ Sometimes when I play that old six-string/ I think about you, wonder what went wrong.* I'm just trying to pass the time until I get on the flight. It's agony—knowing what you have to do then waiting for it to happen. Just happen already! I want to scream! *It was the summer of '69, oh, yeah/ Me and my baby in '69, oh.*

Eventually, the driver turns around and we drive further and further away from the CN Tower. The suburban industrial landscape off the highway irritates me more than ever. So bland. Boring. Monotonous. Not the right environment for a big thinker like me. I need inspiration!

"Can you change the station?" I ask the driver. "Something more current. Upbeat." I'm not going to get anywhere by singing about the past.

Emma: May 11, 2014, 5:45 pm EDT

Where the fuck are you, Adam? Geez, just find a phone and call me! How hard can that be? You arrange some elaborate party last night and now you can't even let me know where you are? You know how much I hate not knowing what's going on.

My phone vibrates in my pocket. *Finally, Adam. Thank you!* I look at the screen. *Fuck. Adam, where are you?*

"Hey Katie," I say into the phone.

"Hey, Em, great party last night. Did you have fun?"

"Yeah, it was the most fun I've had in a while. Thank you for coming. I can't believe you guys pulled off the surprise."

"I know. It was fun listening to you try to figure out where Adam was taking you for dinner. You were so… I don't know… *vulnerable*. Usually, you're the one making all of the plans."

Great, now even my friends are teasing me for being a control freak. There're only so many hours in the day. How am I supposed to work crazy hours in the ER, make time for yoga, running, keep our apartment clean, and socialize with friends without keeping to a tight schedule? I'm not Superwoman!

"Yeah, I guess I do tend to initiate things, which is why I'm a bit stressed now. Adam and I are supposed to go to my grandparents' for dinner, yet I haven't seen him all day."

"Seriously? He's probably at the gym."

"That's what I thought too. He left a note saying he'd gone to pick up stuff to make pancakes."

"And he just never came home?"

"No. His phone's here, too, so I can't even call him. It's pretty pathetic. I've called him at least a hundred times, even though I can hear it ring. I don't know what else to do. I called Jeff to see if he was over there. Nothing."

"I bet he went ahead to your grandparents'. Maybe he has something else up his sleeve."

I detect a knowing tone in her voice. Does she know about the proposal? If Adam wanted help picking the ring, he definitely would have gone to Katie.

"That's what I was thinking. He's probably over there already. I'll call them. He's planning another surprise, but even then, why would he drive to frickin' MISSISSAUGA without me? I'm so pissed at him. It will take at least an hour to get there if I have to take the Go Train. It's weird that he didn't come home after his run, though. Should I be worried?"

"It's definitely a bit much that he would leave you worrying for this long. My guess is that he changed at the gym, then went to your grandparents' from there. Maybe since he left his phone, he figured they'd call you. He probably doesn't even realize that you're worrying right now," she tries her best to calm me.

"You're probably right." Still, why did his note say that he was going to get stuff to make pancakes, which suggests breakfast, which means he was supposed to be back in the morning? What if something bad happened to Adam? I bury the possibility. He seemed so happy last night. Life can't just fall apart in an instant, can it?

Adam, May 11, 2014, 3:10pm PDT

I'm strapped in this seat and going fucking crazy. We're high in the air, I'm high as Superman and all I want to do is fly alongside the plane. Everyone will look out the little windows and point in awe. *Look a bird, or Superman!* Glancing out the window, all I see below are miles of green forests surrounding lakes and rivers. There're no houses, no cars, and no people, but there's a great vastness of land and water and it makes me feel small. I'll strap on a parachute and disappear in the wilderness. The west coast is a mecca for wild hearts, wild minds, wild spirits and I'm a WMD—I've got so much energy I'm about to explode. The airplane booze doesn't help. The perky flight attendant's like, "More wine, sir?" and I'm on my third glass. *Yes please! Fill 'er up!* I announce to the whole airplane and I'm immediately shushed by the man beside me. What does he care? He's wearing headphones. I've been dancing to his pulsing beats all trip. I gotta get that playlist for the gym.

Once I get to Vancouver, I'll head north. There's something enticing about the north: a wildness that I feel within myself but don't know how to unleash. All the burpees and box jumps and push-ups I do at the gym aren't enough to tame me. I'm a wild dog. Or a caged bear. A man on the brink of BECOMING. That burning awareness that your work will put a dent on the universe. I'm not sure what my purpose is yet, but the pull WEST is overwhelming.

I finish my wine in one acidic gulp, like after rugby games when I was named the "Man of the Match" for my team and had to challenge my opposite to a beer chugging contest to claim my title. I always won. *"Down in one, down in one, down in one!"*

After tapping the man beside me (an "excuse me, sir" couldn't compete with his beats), I squeeze past him to the aisle and walk to the back of the plane to use the bathroom. Both are occupied. So I wait, shifting back and forth on the balls of my feet like I'm jogging on the spot, waiting for a traffic light to turn green. The bubbly blonde flight attendant flashes me a million dollar smile and I'm so aroused that I'm overcome by the need to pull her in the stall so that we can join the Mile High Club. My fantasy is swiftly interrupted by a man stepping out of the bathroom.

"Sorry 'bout that," he says, avoiding eye contact as he rushes past me.

I shield my face, gagging slightly by the rancid stench. My fantasy deflates as quickly as it came. Oh well, there're lots of hotties in Vancouver. All of those yogis and hikers and runners with their spandex tights and ponytails and positive vibes. But I can't let any of them get in the way of achieving my destiny, whatever that is. When a woman digs her claws into you, that's the end of the journey.

In a flash, I'm back in my seat, breathing easily again. My flight attendant fantasy comes to collect our garbage and she suddenly looks too made up, like she tried too hard to paint herself a cheerful face. Avoiding her gaze, I look out the window. There's so much movement below me. A miniature city: I can't really see the pieces, but I know they're all there and soon I'll be part of it.

"Attention passengers. We are now beginning our descent into rainy Vancouver with a ground temperature of 22 degrees Celsius..."

Emma, May 11, 2014, 7:15 pm EDT

The rest of my family sits stretched out in Granny and Grandpa's living room, watching the Jays' game in peace, but I don't even know the score. It's like I'm perusing *Gone Girl*, about to turn the page before I realize that I'm not even aware of what I just read. All I can think about is Adam. Strangely, no one else seemed concerned when I showed up without him about an hour ago. They all offered logical excuses as to why Adam hadn't arrived yet:

>My brother, Tom: *"He's at the gym, working off last night's hangover."*
>
>Grandpa: *"He's out getting me cigars."*
>
>Granny: *"Last night I asked him to pick up the cake on his way over."*
>
>Mom: *"Has he started going to church again?"*
>
>Dad: *"He's on his way. He's a good man, he wouldn't let you down."*

Acting is not a skill that runs in my family. Besides, in the past couple days, I've watched eight episodes of *OITNB*, so my bullshit radar is way up. They're not telling me something.

"Nice hit, Bautista! We've got this one now, boys. Woohoo!" Tom cheers enthusiastically, clapping his hands.

"I knew he'd get it back," Dad says. "I'd been praying for him. After last game, when he went 0-4, ending his 37 game hitting streak, I was worried something serious had happened to affect his performance. It just goes to show, you can never lose hope!"

"He's not lying," Mom confirms. "Your father kneeled in front of our bed and said a prayer for Bautista each night before going to sleep. God listened to you, Bill. He always does."

"Mom." I say bitterly. "The Jays didn't win because Dad prayed for them. They just won."

"Maybe you don't feel like God listens to us, but he does, sweetie. Besides, what can we believe in if we don't have faith in the Lord?"

I hate to admit it, but these days it seems like Mom has a point. I want to believe in science and medicine, but despite my best efforts, patients still die. I used to believe in love, but now that Adam may have left me for another woman, I'm not so sure anymore.

Besides, no one seems to care that the love of my life has been missing for almost ten hours! They'll call upon God to give strength to the Jays, but they seem unphased by my missing boyfriend/almost fiancé, which is further proof that they know exactly where Adam is and why he's late. Mom and Dad haven't even prayed to God or Saint Anthony (the Patron Saint of missing things). When our cat, Mona, went missing a few years ago, my Mom e-mailed Tom and I, begging us to pray to St. Anthony in the morning when we woke up and at night when we went to bed. I didn't pray. I was too busy and figured that Mona had decided to return to the wild, a place where she felt happier, yet Mona returned two weeks later. Mom invited the whole family for a celebratory brunch the following Sunday to celebrate "God's miracle."

"Kids, the lasagna's ready. May as well eat it while it's hot," Grandma announces, then hesitates, looking at me, "or should we wait for Adam?" She speaks as though she's certain that Adam's coming, playing her role in whatever surprise Adam has planned.

"I haven't eaten all day," I say, realizing only now that I spent the day waiting for pancakes that never came home.

We cram ourselves around the tiny dining room table. All of us focus on the empty place setting: the white China plate, the unused silver, the empty wine glass. Then we pass the dishes around as we do for every birthday dinner: "more Caesar salad?", "pass the salt," "can you fill up my wine?" However, the routine feels forced and uncomfortable today. No one wants to be the one to be the one to draw more attention to the empty seat.

Finally, Dad breaks the silence. "So you're sure that Adam never mentioned what time he'd arrive? We definitely discussed it last night at your party. Adam's always on time for things, so I'm surprised that he wouldn't have said something to me if he knew he was going to be late."

What are you trying to tell me Dad? I'd rather the 'surprise' be ruined than have to continue to worry on my birthday!

"If you're asking if I was too drunk to remember what he told me last night... maybe. Maybe Adam said something to me. I can't remember. I was overwhelmed by the number of people who showed up for the party, so maybe I didn't pay attention when he told me."

"I thought for sure that he was coming. He has to come," Dad replies anxiously. "He would never have asked..." he trails off, like he's revealed too much. He definitely knows something.

"Well, Bill, Tom, it might just be the three of us smoking the cigars tonight," Grandpa comments. He sounds disappointed. He and Adam have really bonded over the years. He told me once that he sees some of his younger self in Adam, a real soldier, a quality that's rare to find in kids these days. ("Don't tell your brother!" he joked.) When I told him that Adam's nickname is "The General," Grandpa beamed. "Yes, just like me. Major General Watters of the Canadian Army."

"Why don't you say Grace, Emma?" Granny suggests. "It's your birthday."

I pause for a moment, as I plan what I'm going to say. *It's been a great year. I feel so lucky to have such a wonderful family, an amazing job, a new apartment...but I stop before adding "the perfect boyfriend."* A broken record of "Where's Adam? Where's Adam? Where's Adam" spins in my mind.

"I can't. I'm sorry, Gran," I cry. "I don't want to start without Adam. I can't. I want him to be here. Do you guys know where he is? If there's some big surprise coming up that I don't know about, it stopped being funny hours ago."

My family looks at each other. I detect the same expressions on their faces. Pity. Again, Dad's the one to speak.

"We don't know any more than you do, Em. He did mention to me last night that he had planned something for you here, so I was sure he'd be here."

"We were so excited for it," Mom adds. Dad glares at her. Something is going on.

"What's 'IT'?" I ask. "Mom, tell me what you were excited for."

"Oh, nothing, nothing," Mom says, picking at her lasagna. "I was excited to celebrate your thirtieth with both of you, that's all."

I look around and see everyone awkwardly picking at their lasagna with their forks. Shit, maybe they weren't part of his 'plan' after all? Did Adam really not show up for my fucking birthday dinner?

Adam, May 11, 2014, 7:00 pm PDT

    I'm close to shitfaced when I'm enticed by a beautiful woman in a purple dress sitting a few seats away from me at the bar. A model. Or a secret agent. She'll seduce me, then knock me out with a tranquilizer, kidnap me, and send me on a private jet to Russia. That stunning blond bob's part of her disguise. If I rip it off, she'll Judo-chop me. Our eyes meet. She has the only violet eyes I've ever seen. I must be dreaming. The desire to rip her dress off and fuck her right here in the middle of the bar is so powerful that I turn my eyes away from her momentarily to catch my breath.

    On the TV just above her, a rainbow of race cars speeds around a track. The Indie 500 or Formula 1 or some big race. I'm not a fan of auto racing. It doesn't seem like a real sport compared to rugby, football, boxing, basketball, or sports where you need to be in top shape to compete. The TV's on mute, but the music in the bar—*I want to Rock n' Roll all night, and party every day! I want to rock and roll all night and party everyday!*--yields to the powerful revving of eight-cylinder engines being pushed to the max as I feel myself pulled into the adrenaline high of the race with my super sexy spy-girl/model cheering me on.

    My mind feels like a race car on the track, getting faster and faster every time I pause to think or blink or try to focus on anything. Nothing can keep up to it, not the other cars, not my body, not anyone else in the bar. It's a rush, pure exhilaration, and I'm having the time of my life. But instead of driving, I'm in the passenger seat, along for the ride, watching myself race around the track from my barstool.

    I notice the empty seat. She thinks she's immune to my charm, but I'll prove her wrong. I order another drink, my fourth or fifth, I can't keep track, but all it does is add fuel to the engine. *Shaken, not stirred.* The revving gets louder and louder. I lead the race, lap after lap after lap. I'm sprinting in a never-ending marathon but have so much energy I can't slow down. Muscles eventually fatigue as they reach the lactic-acid threshold. Crash. But I'll keep speeding until I run out of gas.

I look around the bar. All of the men wear suits and the women look like they've just come from the office. This is the kind of place where the bankers or lawyers or CEOs come to talk business outside the office. It's the kind of place where ideas are put into action, not like the sports bars like Tallboys where I go to drink beers and watch the Jays' game.

I catch a glimpse of the model/spy coming out of the bathroom at the back of the bar. *I've caught you, Pussy Galore.* An animal instinct draws me to her—so deeply rooted, so visceral, so *violent* that every cell of my body shakes. It's like I've already fucked her. Now I just have to get her back.

I approach. I feel so wild and mad that I must be in love. It's a miracle. A fucking miracle. I start speaking to her, but I can't even hear myself. Instead, I'm in the front row at the movies, watching two actors on the big screen.

Next thing I know, it's as though someone hit fast-forward. Like we've gone from the beginning of an eighty-minute rugby match to the final play in a blink of an eye. We're in a cab. En route to her hotel room. Some swanky hotel in Yaletown. I bet she'll have a penthouse with an ocean view. I inhale the salty ocean breeze, taste the freedom, and let it fill my lungs.

"Let's climb a mountain!" I suggest out of nowhere, but it's a great idea. I have too much energy to be in captivity.

She'll say she's not dressed for it, but I'll carry her on my back. Then we'll stay awake, counting stars, talking about our dreams and our plans for the future until sunrise. My heart's racing. I'm in love!!

"Which mountain?" she asks, laughing at me as though I've told some sort of joke. The driver's laughing as well. I look out the window and the mountains are laughing and everything's laughing, but I know that there's nothing to laugh about because I'm fucking serious.

Emma, May 11, 2014, 10:30 pm EDT

"Thanks for the ride, Tom," I say to my brother as I step out of his car.

The house is dark. Vacant. Maybe Adam already came and went to bed, but then he would have seen all the missed calls and texts on his phone, right? Would he have even called me back? He's not the best phone person. Sometimes, when he work consumes him, he makes me wait hours before returning a text. It drives me crazy. I know his phone is almost always in his back pocket. How hard is it to send a quick "Ok" to let me know he got the message? *"I'm not going to start texting other people when I'm face to face with a member!"* he'd argued.

"We live in the digital age, Adam," I responded. *"You won't survive if you can't multi-task!"*

Even I can make time to text him back when I'm at work and dealing with life or death situations when every second counts. While the members at MaxFit may think Adam's workouts are killing them, they're not actually suffering. They don't really need his full attention. Patients who come in with arterial bleeding, gushing head wounds, heart attacks, and anaphylactic shock are suffering.

"Do you want me to come in? Wait with you until Adam comes back?" Tom asks me gently.

He's not worried about Adam. He's worried about me. Tom thinks I'm going to go inside, pour myself a glass of red wine (some shitty Cab-Shiraz blend that was left over from the party), and cry myself to sleep, blaming myself for the fact that my boyfriend fucked up. That's what he thinks girls do: Blame themselves and cry for the shit the men they love put them through. How many times did Carrie cry over Big? Not me. If I could, I'd change the locks and lock him out of his own house. If he fucks up, he'll learn the hard way. No, what I'm going to do is go inside, get cozy in my PJs, and finish Season 1 of *OITNB*. Who am I kidding? I'll likely start Season 2. It *is* my birthday after all.

Tom continues, "One of his friends probably gave him a ticket to the Jays' game last night at the party when he was drunk and he forgot about dinner. He fucked up. We all do. My guess is that he's going to come home when he's tanked and try to sneak in bed in hopes you'll forget about it in the morning."

"I'm pissed, but I'll be fine. I turned thirty today, remember? I'm officially an adult. I'll lock the bedroom door before I go to sleep so he's forced to stay on the couch. He'll know he's in deep shit the second he comes home."

Am I becoming like Red, the Master Chef who is feared and respected by most of the prisoners at Litchfield? Do I really want to show 'tough love' in order to keep The General in line? Punish him when he screws up?

"Ok, if you say so Em, but just so you know. Regardless of how much I love Adam, if he breaks your heart, I'm going to fucking pound him."

"Thanks, Tom," I reply, but if I were going to put money on it, I'd honestly pick Adam over Tom in a fight any day. Actually, I'd even pick *me* over my brother in a fight. He's short and scrawny and a bit of a wimp. When we were kids, I had to come to his rescue to remove spiders, mice or other whatever creepy crawlies lurked in his room.

"I'll admit, I'm shocked that Adam hasn't gotten in touch with you. I thought he was better than that. But then again, judging from some of the shitty things I've heard guys at work brag about, some jerks think they can get away with anything. Did I tell you about the 'ladder' at work?"

"No."

"Yeah, a couple of guys are having a competition over who can sleep with the most women in our building. Apparently, they have some private Facebook group where they update their 'numbers' after each conquest. The guy who's banged the most women's at the top, while the most celibate is at the bottom. They're not even trying to keep it a secret anymore."

"I hope they get fired." I cringe at stories like this one. I remember Adam telling me that the guys on his rugby team had a similar ranking system, except certain categories of women (sorority girls, MILFs, nurses) carried bonus points. While Adam claimed that he'd never be in on the action, he felt it wasn't our place to judge his teammates if "all parties were willing participants." And this was before Tinder. Maybe they found it "empowering." I don't get it.

"Me too," Tom agrees, "but they won't. They're the ones who make all the sales. They're rewarded with trips to Hawaii or the Dominican Republic."

"For their work, but not their sex lives! But, *sheesh*, can we stop talking about people? I'm still hopeful that Adam's upstairs in bed and has a good excuse as to why he wasn't at dinner tonight. I don't want to consider the alternatives." I would never forgive him if he slept with someone else. I couldn't.

Tom nods. "Sorry, Em. But don't you think that if Adam was sleeping around, we would have found out? Like I said before, he's probably at the game. Or at the pub with his buddies."

"Maybe. You're probably right. He never goes out on Sunday nights, though. He gets up early Monday mornings to teach his class."

"Well, you never know. Keep me posted, okay? I'll say a prayer for you."

He watches me unlock the front door of my house and then drives away. I hear that cab driver's voice: *Family is the most important thing in this world.* Whatever happens with Adam, even if it's the worst—that he cheated on me with some bimbo cheerleader—I'll be fine. My family's got my back. I can even picture Granny going after him with her cane.

Right now, I know my parents and grandparents are praying for us. They love Adam like a son and grandson. They know how happy we are together. A family. *"St. Anthony, who received from God the special power of restoring lost things, grant that Adam Davison returns home safely."*

I hope their prayers are answered. If not… if Adam's still out, do I assume he's an asshole like those guys at Tom's work? Or should I be worried? I've already called Jeff. I checked the gym. I creeped his Facebook page for signs of activity. It'd make me seem too desperate if I start calling all of his other friends right now. *Don't go there, Emma. Be strong. Don't suddenly transform into a psycho because your man fucked off. Wait until he comes home.* He'll have to demand forgiveness, then suffer the consequences if I can't forgive him. *Please be in bed, Adam.*

My heart stops when I see the empty bed. *ADAM? WHERE ARE YOU???* After picking my laptop off my desk, I sit on my bed and open up my e-mails. Nothing. I've been glued to my phone, waiting for that text or e-mail, anything to tell me he is okay and on his way home. *Relax, he's probably home already*, I kept telling myself. But now it seems that I wasn't going crazy. I had reason to panic. Next I check Facebook. Same thing. Nothing.

I creep his Facebook page anyways like a desperate teenager. Tyler posted a few pictures from the party. A group shot of the MaxFit team doing a group 'cheers' with their tall cans. One of Adam and I each flexing our biceps (after I drunkenly challenged him to an arm wrestling competition, which he naturally won in seconds after letting me think I could win for a minute or so). A picture of Adam dancing with Granny. Tears roll down my face. *We were all so happy.* However, there are no signs of activity from Adam. He didn't "Like" any of the pictures, add any new friends, or comment on anyone else's posts. It's like he hasn't logged on since before the party.

I decide to send him a message. Should I seem pissed? Hurt? Annoyed? Freaked out? *I* don't even know how *I* feel. I'll be short and to the point. Emphasize that I want a response. I don't want to say anything to push him away more.

Hey Adam. Not sure what's going on, but please msg me back to let me know you are okay. I love you.
-Emma

I read it over ten times to make sure the tone doesn't sound too pushy, then I press send and then I copy the message and paste it into an e-mail and a Skype message. I keep Facebook open, waiting for a sign, an explanation, a notification that he's read it—anything that might suggest what's going on. Should I be doing more? Like call the police? It's too soon, right?

I have no idea what I'm supposed to be doing in this situation. I always avoid crime shows because I watched *Unsolved Mysteries* once with Granny when I was a kid and couldn't sleep because I'd been so freaked out about someone climbing through the window and abducting me from my bed like they did to the girl on the show. Waiting by myself in this empty bed, I know there's no chance in hell that I'll get any sleep tonight.

Adam: May 12, 2014, 3:00 am PDT

    The animal instinct rises inside me. I can't just lie here, looking up at the ceiling with its crown moulding, which seems to be closing in on me. The room is getting smaller and smaller, and I start to feel a pressing weight on my chest. I'm trapped. I need to look up at the stars. The mountains. The ocean. Be in the wild.

    I get up, throw on my track pants and golf shirt and go take a look at what's left in the mini fridge. We finished off the rum and the vodka when we got back, so I open a mini bottle of whisky. Canadian Club. It burns down my throat, both calming and fuelling the urge. I can taste hints of roasted almond, grainy cereal—like Harvest Crunch or Cornflakes—and a macho hint of vanilla. The breakfast of champions. I can feel my blood warming my core, my limbs, my fingertips and toes. It feels fucking great to drink again.

    I take another sip of whisky. My senses feel sharper, more alert than they ever have and everything around me feels, looks, smells, tastes, and sounds better, clearer, and purer. I'm better, clearer, purer. Stronger. I'm overcome with an incredible desire to workout. Hit the gym. Test my strength. I feel superhuman. The Hulk.

    I pick up the phone and call the concierge.

    "What time is the gym open? I'm having trouble sleeping and feel the need to run, run, run it off. Does the gym have a treadmill? What about free weights?"

    "It's 24 hours, sir. Yes, it is a fully stocked gym. Not your typical hotel gym. Treadmills, stationary bikes, free weights."

Oh, fully stocked. Like the bar Pussy Galore and I just ploughed through. Gonna tear this gym up like she's Jan for hangover breakfast.

"Okay, perfect. I never understood why so many gyms are open 24 hours now. But now I get it. It's for people like me who have some extra fuel to burn in the middle of the night. I thought it was just for people who did shift work like nurses or security guards or even bartenders. If I worked at a nightclub, I'd go after work too. I'd have so much energy from listening to loud music all night. I wouldn't even need to wear headphones. Headphones! Do you have headphones I could borrow to plug into the TV. Do you have TVs?"

A late night workout in a swanky hotel: a gym for a king. Suddenly, an idea hits me: I came to Vancouver to open a gym in a fancy hotel. Run my MaxFit workouts for international tourists to promote my brand worldwide. This is going to be big. It makes so much sense. Two and two add up to even more here.

"Would you be requiring gym clothes? We have fitness packages for guests that have socks, a t-shirts, and shorts that you can use. We will send it to your room shortly. What size?"

"Yes. Yes. Yes." It's all coming together as it's meant to. I hadn't thought about workout gear. But I've come to Vancouver with nothing but the clothes on my back, like how all great success stories are made.

I hang up the phone, pick up the TV remote, and turn on the TV. A blond woman with teeth so white she should be a toothpaste model is smiling at me and encouraging me to buy a Power Pressure Cooker for $99. *It whips up quick, tasty meals the whole family will love! It saves you time so you can focus on what really matters: spending time with your family before, during, and after meals!*

The image quickly flashes to a happy family eating delicious, steamy hot beef stew, juicy pulled pork, and even a chocolate cake. My mouth waters. I can taste the sweet and buttery icing, the dark cocoa flavour. *Mmmmmm*....I take another sip of whisky. When did I eat today? Did I eat today? *Three Easy Payments of $33. Call now! Order yours now!* Numbers flash on the screen.1-888-20-it's TOO FAST. I scramble around for a pen. Frantically, I pull the dresser drawers open. Where's a fucking pen?

"Are you crazy? Have you lost your mind? What's going on?" The annoying British accent. I can't take it right now.

"Shshshsh, I'm going to miss it. Goddamnit!" I finally find a pen and I chuck it as hard as I can at the TV, which has cut to an image of a man on a Zamboni drinking his morning coffee. A Tim Horton's commercial.

"FUCK!" I pick up a pillow off the bed and launch it towards her. "You made me miss the Power Pressure Cooker. I was going to order three!" I'm pacing back and forth. Pulling out my hair. My heart is racing, my hands are sweating, my body's shaking. What do I do now? How do I find the number?

"Do you have Wi-Fi? Can I borrow your laptop? I need to order three of those Power Pressure Cookers! It will make cooking quick, convenient, and easy!

She starts laughing. "You're a fucking lunatic! Three pressure cookers?! What are you going to do with THREE pressure cookers?" She sits up, inspecting the messy room that resulted from the chaos that unfolded in my search for a pen and paper. Then she sees the remnants of her minibar. The empty rum, vodka, and whisky bottles. "That explains everything. You are completely hammered and need to sleep."

The thought of sleeping repulses me. I'm still pacing. My mind's racing. Nothing's slowing down. How can I possibly sleep? At once, there's a knock on the door.

"Who the fuck?" She turns the light off and pulls the cover over her head. The knocking continues, so I open the door. I'm greeted by a man who looks to be about my age wearing a three-piece grey suit and a butler's hat holding a small duffle bag.

"Room service."

Right, the 24 hour gym. My workout.

He hands me the bag. *Phewf.* I'll be running in no time.

Emma: May 12, 2014, 5:30am, EDT

    I wake up to an empty bed, which isn't abnormal. Adam's usually up getting my coffee ready before he heads to the gym. But he still hasn't come home yet. I barely slept last night. I kept getting up to check and see if he was downstairs. I kept checking my phone, his phone, and creeping his Facebook page. He still hasn't seen the message. A few of his friends sent him texts telling him how fun the party was, but there was nothing unusual. Nothing to suggest that he'd been planning something else. Nothing to suggest that he wouldn't be making me coffee right now as he always does.

    Dragging myself out of bed, I head downstairs and turn on the kettle. I measure the coffee beans to put in the grinder. Two scoops? Adam perfected the coffee grinds to water ratio. Two scoops will have to do for today. Tomorrow, Adam will be back and he'll insist on making it up to me.

    I pick up the phone and call Jeff. After five rings, it goes to the answering machine. I try again.

    "Hello?" Jeff picks up on the fourth ring this time, breathless. I can hear his daughter screaming in the background. He has enough on his mind right now and definitely does not need to worry about his partner not showing up for work.

    "Hey Jeff, sorry to bug you so early in the morning, but wanted to call you to let you know that… Adam still hasn't come home."

    "Seriously?" Jeff's shocked. "Where could he be?"

    "I don't even want to know."

I'm worried that my brother might be right: Adam was out partying with the guys and forgot about the family dinner. I thought he was done with the drinking. He was pretty shitfaced at my party, but I only turn 30 once!

Adam used to party hard on Saturday nights with his team after rugby games. It's basically a tradition in the sport. Play hard, party hard. The players would pour their hearts and souls into the games, with the General leading the charge. Then they would shake hands with their opponents and buy them beers after the game. Sundays were always Adam's 'recovery days,' but he was really just too hungover to do anything else. Ever since he's been working early mornings at the gym, and isn't playing rugby anymore, he's basically quit the drinking. What if last night set something off?

Or what if he's cheating on me? I can't even think about that as a possibility. After everything we've been through together, another woman would be the ultimate betrayal. I could never forgive him for that. I need to know.

"Jeff, is there someone else?" I ask.

"What? Are you crazy? Of course not! Did you not see how much effort Adam put into making your birthday special for you?" The screams in the background get louder and I'm almost embarrassed for asking such a ridiculous question.

I sigh with a mix of relief and exasperation. If he's not in someone else's bed, why isn't he in his own? "Yeah, I didn't think he could ever cheat, but I had to ask."

"It doesn't make sense to me. Hold on..." He puts the phone down for a minute. I can hear him: *It's okay. It's okay. You'll be fine.* Whom is he talking to: his daughter or me?

"Ok, I'm back. Sorry, I don't know why this little munchkin won't stop crying!"

"Well, I hate to say this because you sound pretty swamped, but I called to say Adam probably won't make his 6:00 am class this morning. Unless he comes from wherever he is."

"You're right. Okay. Shoot. Thanks for calling, Em."

"Sorry. I wish I didn't have to. Fingers crossed he shows up."

"Yeah, hang in there. I'll let you know if he's at work."

I hang up the phone, slide along the wall onto the floor, and start crying. What am I supposed to do now? Just sit around and wait for him to come home? Do I call his friends? Post on Facebook: *If anyone's seen Adam Davison, please tell him I'm PO!* Should I call his mom? What about the police? Ten years of university didn't prepare me for this shit! I have to make quick decisions at the hospital, but overall, my responses are fairly procedural. In the case of missing persons, I'd inform the police and the social worker. If it's a death, call the coroner. I pass it on to someone else. Detach myself from the situation. But Adam's my family and that makes everything so complicated and confusing. My phone vibrates in my hand. Adam?

Katie: *On my way!*

Oh yeah, Monday Run Day. All I want to do is crawl into bed and return to the moment when I woke up hoping Adam might be home. Adam's been gone for almost 24 hours now and I can't handle worrying about him for much longer. As much as I want to sulk on the kitchen floor, I know that running is the best medicine for me right now. Hopefully by the time I come back, I'll have a message from Jeff saying that Adam showed up for work and I can stop freaking out. *Get up, Emma!*

I pull myself off the kitchen floor and pour myself a cup of coffee. I take a sip. *Too weak.* Adam's brew tastes way better than mine does. Bringing my inadequate coffee upstairs, I change into my running gear: black Lululemon capris and my t-shirt from when Adam and I ran the Sporting Life 10k race last year. After all the running Katie and I have been doing, I thought I'd have a chance at beating Adam in the next Sporting Life marathon. With all of his MaxFit training, he hardly ever makes time to run. However, he's freakishly fit and never shies away from a challenge. Like everything else in his life, when he competes, it's with an all or nothing mentality. He's in it to win it. While I managed to get a personal best time of 47:34, Adam smoked me, finishing with 42:03.

"See, running's a sissy sport," he'd teased.

"It's not," I argued. "It takes discipline to stick to a training regime. And running's more of a mental challenge than a physical challenge. Most people give up before their bodies give out."

"Yeah, but all sports take discipline. These charity races seem too predictable. You train to hit a certain time, not to win. The guys out at the front, competing to cross the finish line first, are the real athletes. The rest of us settle for a time we know we can achieve. We're happy to just cross the finish line and get a participation medal. It's kind of...boring."

For a second, I wonder if Adam took off because our relationship had become too routine and comfortable. Instead of a Saturday morning run, he's looking for a more high intensity, interval-based workout, something that would push life to the extremes. Maybe he doesn't see me as the finish line or as a PB, after all.

Well, I'm definitely a runner. I love the comforting monotony of doing the same routes over and over, waving to the same people walking their dogs, passing them at the same spot on the street corners, and seeing the same cars drive by on their daily commute to work. It's therapeutic. My body craves the familiar stride, the endorphin high, and the cleansing feeling of my muscles detoxifying. The steady pace and predictability of my morning runs prepare me for the chaos I experience at work.

As I start looking around for my FitBit so that I can keep track of our kilometers, I hear the doorbell ring. *Katie can wait*. I look through my dresser, under my bed, and scavenge through the dirty laundry. Maybe it fell out of the pocket of the running shorts I wore on Friday. *Oh, yeah, Adam took it to the gym on Saturday so he could track his heart rate*. As usual, his gym bag is sitting on the floor beside his bed. Unzipping the main pocket, I feel around for the FitBit. Shoes, socks, towel, water bottle. I unzip a smaller inside pocket and pull out a sleek wallet-sized leather case. It's a bit thin to hold a FitBit, but I open it anyway out of curiosity. When I fold open the case, a sparkling diamond ring pops up like a beautiful flower blooming. It's exquisite: princess cut, classic setting, white gold band. It's simple yet elegant. Perfect. I'm stunned. This surprise is not what I was expecting.

For what feels like several minutes, I stare at the ring. *If Adam was planning to propose, then where is he? Did he freak out and realize he doesn't really love me?* This discovery explains why my family seemed so convinced that he was going to show up last night. Maybe he was planning on proposing at dinner and had told them in advance. But he didn't propose. He didn't even show up. Did he just decide that it's over between us and take off?

I instantly regret having looked through his gym bag. Now I'm stuck with a secret I'm not supposed to know, like the time I carefully unwrapped and then re-wrapped the present Granny had sent me for Christmas when no one was home. I had to pretend I wasn't excited to be getting a Polly Pocket. I was excited, though. I just couldn't tell anyone. But now it's the opposite. I'm devastated. Adam's left me and I have to pretend I don't know why. He's had second thoughts about our relationship and he's going to come back in a day or two to tell me it's over.

The doorbell rings again. *Katie.* I go to the bathroom and splash water on my face to wipe off my tears. You hear of people having cold feet over getting married but I never thought it would happen to me. I mean, I wouldn't stay in a relationship where I wasn't absolutely sure that the other person loved me as much as I loved him. I had imagined our future together. Our family. I envisioned us spending a few more years in Toronto and then buying a cute little place in Parry Sound where we'd raise our kids. Grow old together. All I want to do right now is lie on my bed, pull the covers over my head, and disappear.

I hear my phone ring. Adam? Jeff? I'm disappointed when I see the caller ID. Katie. She thinks I've overslept.

"Hey Emma! I'm here! Get your butt out of bed!" she says enthusiastically.

"Hey, I'm trying to find my FitBit. Be down in a second," I tell her then hang up before she can tell that I've been crying.

Again, I splash some water on my face. *You're creating crazy stories in your head because you're upset and worried, but you have no idea what's going on. The mind can really mess with you. Turn you into something you're not.* I take a deep breath. Maybe he'll change his mind. He's freaking out right now, but he will come to his senses soon. He'll be back by the time I get home from work. He'll get down on one knee and propose as he always planned.

I go downstairs and open the door.

"Hey, sorry about that. I couldn't find my FitBit. I think Ad…" I almost choke. Feeling tears start to form in my eyes, I bend down to tie my shoelaces. "Adam must have left it at work."

"No worries," Katie says. "We can use the GPS on my phone."

"Great." I reply, as I step outside and lock the door to the house. "Do you mind if we run the stairs by Casa Loma? I feel like I need to burn some steam this morning. Start the day fresh."

"Sure," Katie agrees as we start running north on Dufferin. "I'm guessing things weren't good when Adam came home?"

"He didn't come home," I tell her. "I have no idea where he is. I even called Jeff this morning because I figure Adam's not going to show up for work. I don't think he's ever missed a shift before." I wonder if she knows about the ring. If Adam would have asked anyone to help him pick out a ring, it would have been Katie or Nancy.

"This doesn't make any sense. He just left Sunday morning and hasn't been in touch with you since?"

"No."

A dark haired man with curly black hair and a Toronto Blue Jays t-shirt bikes by us. I stop and turn around, desperate for clues that it might be him. But I already know it's not Adam. He has a road bike. That man was riding a mountain bike. Katie, understanding my thought process, puts her arm around my waist and pulls me in to give me a quick hug.

"Sorry, every time I see someone I think it might be him. Last night, I looked out the window and saw someone walking down our street in the distance. I ran outside to greet 'him' but it turned out to be an old woman. Katie, I'm going nuts. I don't know what else to do. His cell's at home and I've tried e-mailing him, Facebooking him, texting his friends. I feel like a crazy girlfriend." *Ex-girlfriend?*

"Do you think you should call the police?" Katie asks as we turn at Sunny's Convenience Store and head east on Dupont. The rising sun warms the vacant parking spots reserved for customers of the Modern Furniture Knock-Off Store and Zip Car users. We jog past the Casa Do Alentjo Community Centre, Harry Motors Auto Collision and General Tech Automotive, landmarks that I pass by every day but barely notice. I'm suddenly aware of how easy it could be to hide in a big city when people don't even pay attention to what's around them.

"What? Do you think I should? He's been missing for almost 24 hours, but I'm sure he'll come back today. All of his stuff's at our place." He'll come home. End it. Move out. Or he'll come home, beg my forgiveness, spend a few nights on the couch, and then we'll be back to normal.

"I wasn't going to tell you because I didn't want you to freak out. You seemed so happy on Saturday. I didn't want to burst your bubble."

I slow to a walk so I can process what she is going to reveal, but I already know what she's going to say. *He was planning on proposing. I helped him pick out the ring.*

"What? Katie, you have to tell me. Omigod, did you see Adam with someone else?" That's why he panicked. He was going to propose, but then he met someone else at the party. This can't be happening.

"No, it's not that. Emma, come on. We both know Adam would never cheat on you. I don't know if he was involved, but at the party, James was offered some sort of drug by some guy he thought was one of the doctors you work with."

"What?" I bet it was Neil. It has to be. He told me that when he was in undergrad, he used to take amphetamines so that he could pull all-nighters to cram for exams. Did he convince Adam to do drugs? Would that explain his disappearance?

"Yeah. James said he didn't see anyone actually do them. So maybe it's nothing."

"Still, I can't believe it." I was surprised by how much Adam was drinking at the party, but drugs? He treats his body like a temple, carefully measuring out the appropriate quantities of flax seed, protein powder, berries and milk to put in his breakfast smoothies. We don't keep junk food like candy, chips, or chocolate in the house. Adam wouldn't do drugs. Would he?

"Uh, one more thing." I have to ask her about the ring. It will eat away at me if I don't. "Katie, when I was searching through Adam's gym bag for my FitBit I found something."

"Drugs? You found the drugs?" She asks in disbelief.

"No. An engagement ring. It is so beautiful. Did you help Adam pick it out?"

She hesitates, looking at the ground, "I did give him some suggestions about a month ago but I didn't realize he was planning on proposing so soon. Wow. How do you feel?"

"Confused. I'm worried that he didn't come home because he panicked about the engagement. But now that I've learned about the drugs, I don't know what to think anymore."

"I'm sorry you have to go through this, Em. I'm sure he'll be back today. You'll get the answers you need," she squeezes my hand.

Somehow I find the energy to continue the run. Part of the high that comes after finishing a long run is overcoming the wall, that point when your body crashes but your mind keeps moving you forward. I just want to turn the clock back to

Saturday night when Adam and I were dancing in the middle of Christie Pits park and it felt like there was no one else in the city but us. Who am I kidding? I can adjust the time on my iPhone, but it still won't change the fact that today is Monday and Adam's still not home. I bet iPhones automatically sync with some virtual world clock anyways and won't let me lie to myself as much as I want to. Saturday night can only ever be a memory now. Life, like time, is linear; you can never go back, only forwards.

Finally, we reach the concrete Baldwin steps that connect the two sides of Spadina Road while functioning as a public Stairmaster. A man who looks about our age descends the stairs towards us, breathless from a set of sprints. I nod in encouragement as he passes us.

"Five sets?" asks Katie.

"Yep."

"Ready. Set. Go!"

I pump my arms as I sprint up the stairs with all of my might, driving the balls of my feet into the concrete and propelling myself uphill by lifting my knees. *Push! C'mon, you got this.* Katie pulls ahead slightly and I recruit more power from my quads, glutes, and hamstrings. *Faster. Faster. Let's go, legs!* But I can't catch her. We give each other a high-five at the top of the cliff at the edge of Casa Loma.

As we walk slowly down the steps to catch our breath, I stare at the CN Tower rising up and piercing the sky before Lake Ontario. The city looks vacant. Deserted. In a few hours, the downtown core will be a rat race of bankers, lawyers, and business people rushing to meetings amidst the chaos of bumper to bumper traffic and never-ending construction. But now, the centre of trade and commerce lies dormant except for the odd dog-walker or early commuter. Adam could be anywhere, but the emptiness of the city makes me wonder if he's even here at all.

Adam, May 12, 2014, 9:10 am, PDT

I pick up the phone and dial the operator. "Hi, I'd like to order breakfast to room 612. Eggs Benedict. Pancakes with maple syrup. Sausages. Breakfast Smoothie. Waffles. Orange juice. *Whoa, $9 a glass.* Make that three glasses of orange juice. I'll also get the Steak and Eggs. Toast on the side. Brown toast."

"Would that be everything, sir?"

"Yes. Actually, no. I'd also like a ham and cheese omelette. Can you make it with egg whites?"

"Of course we can, sir."

"Wonderful. I need all the protein that I can get for my big day. Today is the first step on my path towards greatness. I'll hit the gym again and then hike a mountain or go camping. Spend some time alone in the wilderness. You know, really let my mind wander. Be creative. Dream. Successful people always talk about how nature inspires the ideas that change the world. Bill Gates escapes to his wilderness lodge for a week every six months to develop his strategy for Microsoft. He's the richest man in the world because he makes time to think. Are you a baseball fan? Did you catch the score of the Jays' game last night?"

"Sir, you sound quite excited. That's a busy day, and I would be happy to help you coordinate your camping excursion. Unfortunately, I'm a soccer fan, not a baseball fan, but I'll have a copy of *The Globe and Mail* sent to your room so that you can check out the scores. Anything else I can help you with?"

"Cirque du Soleil tickets. I saw a poster on the SkyTrain. Is it in town? I heard the acrobats fly through the air and contort their bodies into pretzels. I'm always amazed whenever I see the human body pushed to the limits. Nowadays, the only body parts people workout regularly are their thumbs, playing Angry Birds or Tinder swiping. When I played rugby, I used to work my body to the extreme. I'd lift hard in the gym and work my butt off on the field so that I'd have the stamina to pick myself off the ground in the pouring rain and hammer my opponent before he made the gain line. Against the toughest teams, like Alberta and BC, I'd get driven into the mud over and over but I always got back up, even when I fractured my arm."

There's a slight pause on the other end of the line.

"Uh, you sound like quite the athlete, sir. Yes, Cirque du Soleil is performing Friday night. How many tickets should I try to get?"

"Two. We'll go to dinner somewhere first. Is there a sushi restaurant you would recommend? Someone told me that Vancouver sushi rocks. Shoot, I'll need hiking gear. Boots. A tent. Backpack. The works. Where's the best place to go for gear?"

Again, there's a long pause, like the concierge is looking up information on the computer. *Hurry up, it's your job to know everything about the city. I don't have much time.* I hear him take a deep breath and then clear his throat.

"Okay. I'll send up the information about the Cirque du Soleil tickets for Friday's show and a map to the nearest outdoor stores along with your breakfast. Should I charge your order to the room?"

"Yes. Yes, of course." I'm sure that Pussy told me to order whatever I want. We're king and queen, indulging in life's pleasures because we deserve it. When I hang up, I'm overcome by the urge to call Emma and tell her about this suite, with its pillow top king-sized bed, brown suede couches, cream carpet, and art that must be on loan from a gallery. The floor-to-ceiling windows and oceanfront view would take her breath away. Yuck, my workout gear reeks like leftover curry mixed with spicy fajitas, and I could wring out the sweat.

Once again, I pick up the phone. "Hello. I called a minute ago. Room 612."

"Right, the breakfast and Cirque du Soleil tickets."

"Yes, can you add fitness gear to that order? After breakfast, I'm going to hit the gym. Last night it was chest and legs. Today, it will be back and shoulders. I'll probably add some intervals on the treadmill. Must be the ocean air because I have so much energy to burn."

I'm a machine, like a gladiator or an autobot. Where's Optimus Prime? I'd pulverize him. Without any protection. Rugby-style. The General versus The Machine. *Crouch. Touch. Engage.* Dump-tackle him the way I do a hefty prop. I'm a steel crusher. Mark Wahlberg ain't got nuthin' on me. I should do a *Transformers* movie marathon. Watch 1-3 before the new one comes out. "You seen the *Transformers* movies, bro? When's the next one out?" I ask the receiver.

I start doing bodyweight squats while I wait for his response, keeping my chest lifted and my back straight, driving my weight through my heels for maximal glute activation. He takes so goddamn long to reply that I can probably finish a set, or even hit the floor and do ten pushups before he opens his mouth to speak. *8. 9. 10.*

"No, I haven't seen any of the—"

I hang up the receiver as I transition into pushups, putting my hands outside my shoulders and engaging my core. *One. Two. Three.* I execute the move like I'm on fast-forward, bringing my nose as close as I can to the floor during the concentric phase. My blood's pumping. Beads of sweat run off my forehead and onto the floor. I'm cleansing the shit from my system and I feel amazing. *Two more. Nine. Ten. Nice work, champ. Time to up your game.*

I bound to my feet and jump as high as I can towards the ceiling, land, and then put my hands on the floor and kick my feet back to complete the burpee. *One.* I spring back up, reaching for the sky. I land softly and then I drop into a pushup position. *Two. Back up, come on. Don't quit now, man.* I push myself up, jumping higher than I ever have, like the floor's a trampoline and I'm an acrobat. *Is Cirque hiring?* I shave a second off this rep, shooting my legs back before my hands hit the floor. *Three.* Then without hesitation, I push the floor away, catapulting myself through the ceiling. I'm in robot mode. *Four. Don't stop. Don't rest. Just move.* My pecs scream and my heart pounds, but I won't quit. *C'mon, five more.* I continue the reps of shooting myself towards the moon, then falling to the center of the earth. I couldn't cut the engine if I tried.

Emma, May 12, 2014, 1:00 pm, EDT

"It hurts! It hurts!" As soon as I touch his thigh, Alex wails in agony. Didn't he say the pain is in his abdomen? Something's not right here. There's a strong odour of alcohol on his breath. It's like Dr. Gregory House is peering over my shoulder, shaking his head, tapping the floor with his cane. *"Tsk. Tsk. Dr. Watters. Don't be fooled. Everybody lies."*

"Sir, we are trying to help you." I bend and then straighten his right leg. "Where does it hurt?"

"It hurts!"

"Sir, we are trying to help you," I repeat in frustration, looking at Melayna and Eliza for support. "You have to tell us where the pain is."

The 24-year old patient, Alex Roberts, checked himself into the ER about an hour ago. He told the attending nurses that he'd been assaulted outside the Eaton Centre and that he was experiencing severe pain in the abdomen. Now he's complaining of pain everywhere. While he shows some signs of injury, bruising on his forearms like he'd been grabbed and a recent scrape on his knee, he shows no evidence of abdominal injury.

"Mr. Roberts, this is a very unreliable exam," Melayna speaks up more assertively. "You need to let me know if you have pain when I push on your spine." She winks at me.

Eliza follows along, and starts setting up the monitors. "Sir, if the doctors can't see any physical evidence of bruising then it's probably something pretty serious. You will be in here a long time while they run the tests."

Immediately, Alex winces. "Aww it hurts. Aww it hurts. Right there. I want some morphine."

Melayna stares at me. *I knew it.* Eliza is fuming. She just came from the triage desk and reported that there's over thirty people in the waiting room and they keep coming in the door. *"Must be the full moon," she'd joked, "Everyone's getting injured doing risky things they know they shouldn't be doing."*

Maybe she's onto something. But if Adam comes home tonight claiming that the full-moon made him turn into a werewolf and disappear into the night, I'll remind him that I was never a fan of *Buffy* or *True Blood* or those other vampire shows, and that he can find some other human to prey upon. I know it seems like a ridiculous explanation for his disappearance, but for some reason, I have an easier time believing that The General transformed into a supernatural creature than believing he used drugs at the party.

"Mr. Roberts, I'm not touching anything," Melayna admits. Eliza covers her face with his chart to hide a giggle.

Alex groans. "It hurts everywhere!"

"At the party, James was offered some sort of drug." What Katie told me finally sinks in. What if Adam's hooked on drugs? If it's something hard, like speed or heroin? Who knows what effect it would have on his body? Omigod, what if Adam's shooting up under a bridge somewhere or in some dealer's apartment? One day you're smoking a joint at a party and then next, you're stealing money from your friends to pay for heroin and you end up in prison like Nicky in *OITNB*. In a way, we're all addicts by nature. (I'd ever miss my morning run!) Some

addictions just destroy your life while others make you stronger and less aware of the side effects.

I watch Melayna palpate the patient's spine, gently pressing her fingers on each vertebra to feel for bumps and swelling. Even though we both know it's an act, we have a professional obligation to rule out the possibility that his pain might be real.

I remember that when I started watching *House* during undergrad, I thought that Dr. House's credo, *"Everybody lies,"* was too cynical. Shouldn't we believe everyone is telling the truth until they prove us wrong? (Have "faith" in people, as my mom says?) I think Dr. House just doesn't want to admit that even top-notch doctors like him make mistakes. The symptoms doctors see in patients never lie. Instead, our possible misinterpretation of the symptoms leads to misdiagnoses. If we see the symptoms as they are, then we see the problems as they are.

Alex complains of pain. I see very little bruising or evidence of injury. He claims he was assaulted. After I run a few tests and check for internal bleeding, I may determine that he shows no symptoms of it at all. Then I'll send him home and know I've covered my bases before signing off his chart. The worst case scenario would be to assume that he is lying and send him home before I've done a thorough examination. What did Prof Williams tell us in med school? Assumptions lead to lawsuits.

"Fuck you, it hurts. Did you hear that? I'm going to sue you for malpractice."

Glancing out a small crack in the blinds covering the window of the patient room, I notice Neil hurry down the hall carrying his clip board. *There's someone I'd like to sue for malpractice.* It looks like an average day for him, saving lives and breaking hearts.

While he rubs me the wrong way, he seems to value his job too much to risk getting caught stealing meds. Real doctors don't use prescription drugs recreationally. But then again, Dr. House sometimes puts his career on the line for Vicodin, despite Dr. Wilson encouraging him to go to rehab.

"Alex, please tell me again about the assault so I can make sure I have all the details for the police report. The cops will need to speak to you as well."

"I already told you. Now give me the morphine. It hurts everywhere."

I flash to an image of Adam begging a dealer for drugs in a run-down Toronto Community Housing Unit, one that's infested with cockroaches. It's hard to picture Adam asking anyone for anything. If The General wants something done, he does it himself. But then again, no one's immune to addiction, not even a brainiac like Dr. House. Who knows what effect the drugs would have on The General's freakishly healthy system.

I prepare the ultrasound while Melayna continues the physical examination. "Listen to me," she tells Alex, "I'm going to give you some pain medication. You let it work its magic."

She's giving in too quickly by giving him the drugs he wants. He's going to learn that all he needs to do is whine a bit and some gullible doctor to feed his drug addiction. Usually I have more patience, but after being up all night worrying about Adam, I can't deal with any bullshit. Not today.

"Actually, Dr. Santos, I'm just going to do an ultrasound on his abdomen. Alex seems to be suffering a lot. It's important that we get to the root of the problem to get Alex the help he needs." I turn my head and catch Neil walking back down the hall. "Actually, Eliza, do you mind running this test? I need to step out for a minute."

"Sure," Eliza replies.

I open the door as Neil approaches. I know it's inappropriate to confront him now, in the middle of the hospital, on what seems to be one of our busiest days of the month, but I need answers. *Where is Adam? What did you give him?* He greets me with a smile, like he has nothing to hide.

"Hey, it's the BDG. Fun party. Everyone was pretty fucked up. I haven't partied like that in a long time, like since before I started working here. But we all need to let loose every now and then. Glad I was able to make it."

"It was really fun." I feel a pit in my stomach. *"This is the happiest I've ever been,"* I'd said to Adam. I thought he was happy too, but what if it was because of the drugs? Maybe the party sobered him to the reality that life's dull and boring without drugs. The thought stings. *So am I dull and boring to him without drugs? We seemed drunk on love in the park! Is that why he didn't propose? He realized how BORING I am?*

"Your boyfriend's a cool dude by the way."

What is this, high school? "Cool dude?" *I tested out your boyfriend's cool or not scale by offering him amphetamines. Verdict? Cool.*

"Ya, about that. I don't appreciate that you were handing out drugs at the party like they were candy or something."

His face goes blank. He doesn't try to look away, avoid me or fiddle with anything. Instead, he appears surprisingly stunned. *And the Emmy for Outstanding Lead Actor in a Medical Drama goes to...*

He looks me directly in the eye. "Emma, I haven't done drugs in years, not since my stint with the uppers in med school. I care about my career…" his face softens, and he pleads with his eyes, the kind of desperate, wide-eyed look that's landed Nicolas Cage multiple Razzie nominations. "…and the people I work with too much to do anything stupid."

I'm onto you, Neil. Everybody lies.

Adam, May 12, 2014, 11:30am 2014 PDT

    I throw five bottles of OFF! Insect Repellent into my cart before heading to the checkout. This shopping spree at Mountain Equipment Co-op fuels my urge for adventure more and more. I need absolutely everything in the store. There are no excuses now. Everything: kayaks, canoes, backpacks, camping stoves, wetsuits, and mountain bikes all entice me to DREAM BIG. They inspire me to embrace the chaos of the wild, wild west. It's entropy at work.

    "The universe tends towards disorder," my eccentric grade 11 chemistry teacher, Mr. MacDonald, told me when he saw how messy my locker was in high school. I'd crammed all of my rugby gear into it and had to slam my whole body weight against it. *"See, reversing the ever-increasing tendency towards disorder requires energy. A clean locker goes against the Second Law of Thermodynamics: that all closed systems tend to maximize entropy."* That's probably the only thing I remember from high school chemistry, other than when you burn magnesium, it yields the most intense light you'll ever see. Mr. MacDonald made us wear glasses and told us to avoid looking directly at the light, they way you avoid looking directly at the sun. However, I couldn't take my eyes off it. It was the most brilliant white light.

    "Big trip coming up?" asks the cashier, a scrawny eighteen-year-old with long hippie hair and a t-shirt that says *"Life is Good."*

    I nod, making an inventory of my gear as he scans the items. Did I forget anything? *We can't control what happens when we step onto the field, all we can control is how prepared we are for battle.*

    I've got a tent. Sleeping bag. Tarp. Sleeping pad. A couple sets of t-shirts and shorts. Rain gear. A hat. Sunglasses.

Water bottles. Dehydrated food. A bear resistant food canister. A stove and three fuel bottles. An expedition pack and a smaller day pack. Two pullover sweaters. A fleece jacket. Four hammocks. Five t-shirts (one in each colour they had). Five pairs shorts (one in each colour they had). Hiking pants. Long underwear. Six pairs wool socks. A toque (it can get cold in the mountains). Bowls and cutlery. A cooking pot and pan. A Thermos. But none of those bullshit camping stainless steel wine "glasses". The call of the wild calls for real camping.

"Do you think I forgot anything? I just came from Ontario, but I feel the pull to go camping now. Like, right now. I can't wait any longer. I need movement, risk, challenge; a chance to test myself. Alone."

The kid quickly surveys my purchases. "In my opinion, it looks like you actually might have too much stuff. I always try to pack light. You probably only need one hammock." *Fucking minimalist.* "Are all of those t-shirts and shorts for this trip?" *I bet you're living in your parents' minivan in some hippie commune.*

"Yeah. I don't know why I got every colour. I'm just excited. I guess you can take those back. Leave the white t-shirt and khaki shorts. Get rid of the hammocks. I'll be spending too much time climbing mountains to be swinging between the trees, anyways."

The kid removes the excess purchases from my bill. "That will be $2637 even. How would you like to pay for that?"

Without hesitation, I hand him my credit card. Small price to pay for the experience that's going to change my life.

"Where are you going?"

"I'm not sure yet. No plan. I'm thinking I'll head north up the coast. Find a mountain to climb. I'll drop my gear at the bottom and sprint to the top." I shove the clothing and kitchen gear into my pack, and my arm shoots through a dark, dark tunnel. I stuff the t-shirts, shorts, and socks right to the bottom, filling every space. I'm sweating now; it takes energy to stuff the void as densely as possible. "Everything needs to fit in here. I'm going to hit the grocery store and then be on my way. The adventure awaits."

"At this time of year, I'd suggest you take the ferry to the island. It's milder there. Lots of rain, though, but you got your rain gear. The western coast of the island's very rugged and mountainous in spots. You can catch a bus from Nanaimo north to Campbell River or Ucluelet and eventually set up camp somewhere in Strathcona Park. Seems to fit what you're looking for."

I hadn't even thought about going to Vancouver Island, further WEST. But I'm about to embark on a new chapter in my life and it makes perfect sense to start it in a place I've never been to before but always wanted to visit.

"The trees are amazing. Some of the biggest you've ever seen. Douglas fir, Sitka spruce, western hemlock. The central interior north part of the island's just itching for adventure. Every time I go there, I find somewhere new to explore. How much time do you have?"

"Not sure," I admit. "A week maybe. Right now, my past is holding me back and I gotta break free."

"I know what you mean. I can't wait for school to be done so I can get out of that prison. If you want a real adventure and have more time, I'd suggest going further north to Prince Rupert, then meander to the Great Bear Rainforest up the coast towards the Alaska border. I went on a trip there with my dad last summer and it was life-changing."

He comes to the end of the checkout to help me stuff my purchases in the sack. After inspecting the mess I made, he takes everything out to start the process over.

"You have to put the bigger, heavier items, like the bear canister, your tent, and your sleeping bag in the bottom. Then stuff the smaller things into the empty spaces that remain. Try to make it as symmetrical as possible." *Does he know who I am? I don't need a fucking lecture on how to pack from some hippie teenager.*

Clearly, he's got a system. *Fuck. Just stuff it all in and make it work, man. Life's not supposed to be neat and tidy. I guess you haven't gotten to the thermodynamics unit in chemistry yet.* I pull the sack away from him so I can stuff my shit in my way. He doesn't seem to notice. He just keeps talking.

"It's paradise. I'm trying to get a job working as a trail guide up there this summer. We went hiking in one of the most pristine rainforests in the world and even saw the spirit bear or ghost bear, the kermode, the white black bear population up there."

Spirit Bear. That should be my new nickname. The General never got me anywhere anyways. I'm starting life fresh so I should take a new name. *Spirit bear. Kermode. Kermie.* The best players in Raptors' history all have nicknames. Mighty Mouse. Psycho T. Air Canada (or Half Man, Half Amazing). Popeye. The Red Rocket. The General was for my past life. Kermie sounds too wimpy though, like Kermit the Frog. I need something tougher. A name of champions. A brand.

Something wild and threatening. Like a wild dog or a lone wolf. *Lone Wolf.*

The Lone Wolf's on his own now, but he's become fiercer, more aggressive, more dangerous than the pack wolf he once was. He doesn't follow the rules. Before he was the alpha, he kept the chain of command in place, but he's better on his own. He does what he wants. When he wants. He fights. He survives. He fucking lives.

"Seeing the spirit bear was the most unbelievable experience. It's not an albino bear or a polar bear. It's a black bear with a recessive gene. My Dad said that nature's diversity is what makes life interesting."

Pretty soon, the locals will be telling legends about me. The Lone Wolf. One man among many who came to the island to dream. But unlike all of the dreamers who think about changing the world but do nothing, my legend will be that of the Lone Wolf who transformed his BIG IDEA into action.

I stuff the final pair of socks into my pack and haul it up over my shoulder like a firefighter putting on his oxygen tank before walking into a burning building. I thank the kid for his advice and step onto West Broadway and the sky's grey and dark. I've entered a rain cloud. The fog's so thick I could reach out and grab a piece of the sky. As I begin walking west, always west, towards Broadway City-Centre station, I pass an African art shop, a few more outdoor stores, a tailor, a pizza place, and I'm stung by a light sprinkle of rain. A bus drives past and I'm nauseated by a whiff of exhaust. Then rotting fish. The rancid stench of sewage. *Is it garbage day?* I'm trapped in the pungent fog, in the dreary suburban-style shops, the rat race of city life. The city, even on the west coast, has the power to beat us down, to suck us of passion, to crush our dreams. It's no place for a Lone Wolf. I'm too restrained. Caged in. I need to be free, and roam the land, test myself against the harshness of the wilderness, and let my imagination wander.

Seeing a payphone, I get the overwhelming urge to call Emma and tell her about the big adventure. I dig through my wallet and find fifty cents to place the call. Lifting the receiver, I key in her cell number.

"This is a long distance call. Please insert additional funds and try your call again."

Looking through my wallet, I see all I've got is a couple of dimes and a few pennies that we can't even use anymore. So I hang up the receiver and walk into the corner store next door. Then I withdraw 500 bucks from the ATM and continue towards the Sky Train to start my adventure.

Emma, May 12, 2014, 7:30 pm EDT

Please be home. Please be home, Adam. I hold my breath as I open the door. The lights are off. There's no dinner on the stove. No barbequed chicken and steamed vegetables. No pasta with sausages and roasted red peppers. No baked salmon and asparagus. No evidence that he's been here.

"Adam! Adam!" I call out. No response. There's always hope until there's not.

"Adam?" I run up to our room, just to make sure he's not having a nap. No one's in our room or in the bathroom.

Maybe he's still at work, doing an extra training session for the upcoming regionals. He's been so committed to making sure his team is at their peak going into the competition. I rummage through my purse and pull out my phone. There's no way he'd let the team down this close to the competition. But I didn't think he'd ever bail on me like this, either. I dial Jeff's number, surprised that I hadn't heard from him already today. *No news is good news.*

He picks up after the first ring. "Emma? I was surprised that I didn't hear from you earlier. How's Adam?" he asks desperately. "He came home, right?"

"No. He's not here. Did he show up for work?" I feel hopeful. Jeff expects Adam to be at home, so Adam must have stopped in at the gym.

"No." My heart sinks into my gut. "He didn't call into the office and he didn't show up for practice tonight. He didn't text or call anyone on his team, either. I don't get it. In the ten years I've known him, he's never been late for work. He's never called in sick or missed a shift or anything."

"I know. I'm trying to understand what happened, but I'm so confused. One day, we're on our dream date, and the next, I'm living a nightmare. All I can think of is…" My voice cracks. I've been trying to remain calm for the last two days and I can't control my emotions any longer. The tears pour out like Niagara Falls. *This is the happiest I've ever been.* The memory plunges to the basin below.

"All I can think of is," I repeat, "that Adam got scared about how serious our relationship was and he freaked out. Saturday night DID feel a bit like an engagement party. Maybe my grandparents or parents said something to trigger him. Maybe they put pressure on him to propose or something."

"Em, I don't know if this will make it better or worse," Jeff takes a deep breath, collecting his thoughts, "but Adam wasn't getting pressured to propose. He *wanted* to. In fact, I thought he was going to do it yesterday. I'm as shocked as you are." *So he knows about the ring.*

"Are you saying that you think he's had second thoughts about us? Did he say anything to you?"

"Emma, listen to me. We both know that Adam would never abandon something he's trained for. You guys have put a lot of work into building your life together. I know how much he wanted to propose. He wanted to start a family with you."

Everybody lies. Not Jeff. He tells the truth. Or is he just giving me these lines to protect his business partner?

I take a deep breath. In through the nose, out through the mouth. "You didn't hear anything about him doing drugs at the party? I heard a rumour that some guys were doing something."

"WHAT? Are you kidding? I didn't see anyone doing drugs or hear about anyone doing them. But the Adam I know would never put that crap in his system. I was surprised to see him drinking. It's been so long since he partied. He measures out his food and everything. He's too committed to his routine to do that stuff."

There's silence on the other end, like Jeff needs time to mull it over. "The only drugs he'd maybe consider would be performance enhancers, like steroids or something. But he's too honest to cheat, too driven to be the example for his clients, and he's not even competing in Regionals, so why would he need to try them out now?"

"I know. That's what I thought too. I'm just so confused. But what do I DO now? Jeff, what should I do?"

"I don't know. I was wondering that too. As far as I know, no one's heard from him in a day or so. But it seems too soon to panic. Have you contacted his family? Maybe he went to visit his mom?"

"Ya, that's what I thought too. But his mom already thinks I'm controlling. I'll give it another day or two before I call her. If he wants space, he should have it. We all need some breathing room every now and then."

I hang up the phone, go upstairs, and find Adam's phone, which I'd placed on our dresser. There are six new texts.

Jeff:	*Hey buddy, u around?*
Nicky:	*U forgot to call me yesterday!*
Jeff:	*Bud, u comin to work?*
Jeff:	*Practice?*
Tyler:	*Coach!!! Where r u?*
Rosa:	*COACH?! R u coming?*

Nicky's text worries me. Maybe he's not in Parry Sound, after all. Or maybe he was on his way when she sent the text. Should I call her? What would I even say? *"Hey, Nicky, you wouldn't know where the fuck your son is, would you?"* I don't even know what she could do at this point. It's only been a day. He'll be back soon. Tomorrow at the latest.

There's a voicemail. "Hello, this is the Royal Bank of Canada security calling to report that we've detected unusual transactions on your RBC credit card and have placed a freeze on future transactions on your card. If you could please call our 24 hour toll- immediately at 1-800-769-2512 to discuss this further. Thank you."

What? Unusual spending? If Adam's not at Nicky's, maybe he's staying in hotels, using the Four Seasons to network with his druggie friends. In *OITNB*, Alex lived in luxury when she worked in the international drug trade. Adam never spends money on himself: he'd be more likely to camp in the woods somewhere than spend a night in a swanky hotel. But what else would he spend money on? Unless he's the victim of fraud or someone's stolen his identity.

In a complete panic, I scavenge our bedroom for a credit card bill or something that might have Adam's banking information on it. I search through our desk and dresser and look in the closet. Nothing. I'm pretty sure Adam does all of his banking online like I do. Actually, it's rare that either of us gets any mail these days. Although I can't find Adam's banking info, I call RBC, desperate for clues as to what's going on.

Breathe. Breathe. Breathe. I close my eyes and try to calm myself down, practising the meditation techniques I learned in yoga, as I'm put on hold. Right now, Adam could be in danger, being manipulated into smuggling drugs like Piper was, and they are making me WAIT. GEEZ!

I listen to a list of at least ten options. Press "1" for account information. Press "2" for Credit Card information. Press "3" for branch information. *Blah blah blah. No wonder there are so many victims of credit fraud. This is taking freaking forever!* I press "0" to speak to an agent.

"Hello, Miss?" The voice on the other line sounds distant. Probably at some call centre overseas. How the heck are they going to be able to help track Adam down from across the ocean?

She runs me through a list of security questions. *Just hurry up and tell me where he is and what the fuck's going on.* What is his date of birth? What is my relationship to him? What was his last transaction? This is one of those instances where being married and having one of those joint bank accounts would definitely be helpful. I have to keep nagging and nagging and nagging.

"I don't want to access his account," I say. "I haven't seen him in days and want to know what is going on!"

There's a long pause.

"Hello, Miss? Hold on, I'll transfer you to my manager."

Another long pause. I know security is important and all, but can someone please just tell me what's going on? Where's Adam? What happened to his account?

"Ms. Watters?" A man's voice this time. French accent this time.

"Yes?"

"Hi…I checked the status of the account for Mr. Adam Davison. A freeze has been put on spending on this account, so please have him contact us to reactivate his card."

"I told you. He DISAPPEARED. I have NO IDEA where he is or how to contact him. I would like to know what the charges were so I can try to track him down or figure out what's going on." I'm snapping in frustration, the way my grandma does whenever a telemarketer has the nerve to call during our family dinners.

"Miss, unfortunately, due to security reasons, I can't provide you with any additional information about this account. However, if you are concerned about his safety, I highly suggest that you contact the police. Or I can connect you with our dedicated team of fraud experts if you think he might be the victim of identity fraud."

"Can't you just tell me what the charges were? WE'RE BASICALLY MARRIED!!"

"Sorry, miss. It's not a joint account so I have to protect his privacy. We take identity theft very seriously so I have to protect our clients. Again, I would suggest you contact the police if you have concerns about his safety."

I hang up the phone in complete frustration. Then I lie on my bed, scream into my pillow, punch my bed like I'm a toddler having a meltdown, and cry my face off because I don't know how to get what I want. When's the last time I felt this helpless, this desperate? I can't even remember. No amount of yoga or meditative breathing could control the rage. I keep screaming and crying and punching my pillow and kicking my feet on the bed like a total whiny baby. "AHHHHHHH!!!!" Finally, when I can't scream anymore, I turn on my laptop in hopes that the cyberworld might be able to give me more answers than the woman I just spoke to.

I Google, "When should you contact the police when someone you love goes missing?" Still sobbing, I click on one of the first sites that pops up, "Ontario's Missing Adults," and try to skim the information through my tears. The crying slows to a trickle as I concentrate on reading the text.

"When someone you love goes missing, please contact your local police to file a missing person report as soon as possible. Law enforcement is the single best resource in helping to locate missing persons. Even where the person has disappeared years or decades before, you can still file a missing person report."

YEARS OR DECADES?! I wonder how many people were in my position ten years ago and are still waiting by the phone for a sign. Adam's coming back tonight, or tomorrow at the latest. He has to. If he doesn't, should I call the police? What does "as soon as possible" mean? 24 hrs? 48 hrs? It's already been over 24 hrs. Does the canceled credit card mean that this really is a criminal case after all, and that Adam didn't just freak out about our relationship?

Desperate for more answers, I try another website, The Canadian Centre for Information of Missing Adults. I speed-read through the information, pulling out the key points. *"No reasonable explanation for disappearance. Contact the police. The sooner the better."* My eyes stop when they find what they are looking for. *"There is **no** waiting period for filing a missing person report in Canada. Having to wait 24 hours, 48 hours, or any other set time period is a myth."*

Does this news mean that I should contact the police? It seems a little ridiculous to file a missing person's report for Adam. If The General disappeared, it's because he wanted to vanish.

My heart sinks as I read on. I already feel sick with fear, worry, and regret and Adam's only been gone for a day. Another day of this torture seems unbearable. I hadn't considered the possibility that Adam might not come home. But there's a whole database of unresolved missing persons cases in Ontario! What if Adam becomes another statistic?

"It is not a crime for an adult to sever all contacts and voluntarily walk away from her/his life to start over elsewhere. As a result, police have the difficult job of balancing the missing adult's right to privacy with finding out the reasons for the disappearance.

In some cases, the person no longer wishes to remain in contact with her/his loved ones. When this happens, police have to respect the missing person's decision. In most cases, the searching family is notified that the missing person has been located but no further details are shared without the missing person's consent."

How can someone be legally allowed to just disappear from their family's lives? People must feel really imprisoned by their families if they break contact. Maybe if they don't escape their families, they'll end up in jail themselves. In *OITNB*, family ties can be a prison that holds people back. I wonder if Daya would have ended up in jail if she'd have broken free from her Mom when she was younger?

We all need family to survive, so if the one we are born into isn't working out, there's always the option to cut loose and create a new family, like Nicky does with Red. What if Adam felt imprisoned by our relationship and needed to escape like Nicky did with her mom? What if Adam wants to cut ties with me so that he can be with someone else who understands him more than I do?

Could anyone understand him more than I do?

Adam, May 12, 2014, 6:00 pm PDT

The pulse of the wild wild west beats and draws me into the spirit of adventure, the instinct to roam free that lives within all beasts. Placing my front paws up on the ferry railing, I close my eyes and inhale the salty ocean breeze. It's the adrenaline rush of a winning rugby game but better. Then I throw back my head, let the wind sweep my mane, and release the feral cry of willing prisoners trapped in the city. *Ahooo! Ahhahhahhooooo!*

Let's go, boys. Fight for that inch. Look your opponent in the eye, then drive your shoulder into his thighs the instant he gets the ball. I'm the Lone Wolf, the Alpha of the West. I've abandoned the fear of men. I can either hunt or be hunted. Men are more cowardly than the beasts of the wild. *Ahooo! Ahhahhahhooooo!*

I open my eyes and see a pod of porpoises swimming and jumping in the ferry's wake. The wild has answered my call.

A crowd of tourists rushes to the deck, taking pictures of the porpoises as they dive in and out of the wake. Snap. Snap. Snap. Snap. Snap. Click. Click. Click. Click. Click. The tourists push each other out of the way, competing for the best photo to post for all their friends to like like like, as the porpoises flip around carefree, riding the wake, having the time of their lives.

Emma, May 13, 2014, 6:30 pm EDT

As I walk towards the house, I notice that the tulips Adam planted are wilted. Was I supposed to water them? I approach the garden and bend down low to get a better look. Only yesterday, their bright green stems seemed strong and firm. Their pink petals closed together tightly around the stoma, much like I used to close my palms around a butterfly when I was younger. Today, their petals droop open like the leaves of a weeping willow tree.

I glance at the neighbours' garden next door. Their yellow tulips look robust, much like mine did yesterday. Are they a more resilient strain? Mr. and Mrs. Rizzuto wave to me from the porch, where they sit on Adirondack-style chairs reading various sections of the newspaper.

"Just noticing your flowers. How do yours thrive while mine look like they're basically dead?"

Mr. Rizzuto stands up and walks down off the porch to check out my tulips. He shakes his head. Then he bends down, picks up some soil and rubs it between his fingers.

"Soil okay," he says. "Maybe frost?"

"Wouldn't yours be dead too if there was frost?" It doesn't make sense why similar flowers in neighbouring gardens would respond so differently to the same weather conditions.

Mr. Rizzuto shrugs. "My wife does garden. She have green thumb." Upon hearing her name, Mrs. Rizzuto comes to join us.

"Can you revive wilted tulips?" I ask her. Tears start to form in my eyes. I want to stay hopeful, but I've always been too busy to garden and don't really know when to let go.

She's already on her knees, inspecting Adam's planting job, testing the soil quality, feeling the stem and the petals for damage.

"You can try watering them, but it looks like it might be best to let them go. Even when you've taken the best care to make them healthy, sometimes they just die for what seems like no reason." She looks up and sees my tears. Then she stands up and gives me a hug. Mr. Rizzuto doesn't really know what to do so he goes back to the porch and continues reading the paper.

"Don't be so hard on yourself. You did the best that you could with the experience that you had," she consoles me. "Each year, you'll get better. No one's perfect."

"It's not that. It's just..." I pull away from her and look towards the house, hopeful that Adam's come home. I called Jeff in the morning and at lunch, and Adam still hadn't shown up for work. Is that a light on in our bedroom? Did I leave one on before I left for work?

"Have you seen Adam? Do you know if he came home today?"

I can't look at her directly. I want her to see me like one of the tulips in her garden, strong and robust. Instead I'm wilted, unsure of whether or not to give up hope that Adam will come back. It's been two and a half days now, so if he's not here, I feel like it's time to take stronger action to figure out where he is. But what do I do? What if he doesn't want to be found?

"No, I haven't seen Adam since the weekend. He helped me bring in groceries from my car Saturday morning."

She catches me staring at the wilted tulips.

"Hey, Al, have you seen Adam lately?" she shouts.

Her husband looks up from the newspaper and shakes his head, "*Niente.*"

Mrs. Rizzuto squeezes my hand gently and looks at me in the eye. I can't hide my tears from her any longer. "Is everything okay, Emma?"

"I don't know. He left Sunday morning to get some groceries for breakfast and hasn't been back since. I don't know what to do."

I haven't told anyone else except for Jeff, Katie, and my family that Adam's been missing. Hearing myself say it makes it sound real. And terrifying.

She gives me another hug. "Is there anything we can do? Would you like to come for dinner?" she asks me.

I smile. "No thank you, I'm okay. I have some phone calls to make." I really hope that Adam's upstairs cooking dinner for me. Tuesday night is usually fish.

She lowers her voice to a whisper. "I know how you feel. Al left me for about two weeks once, when I was pregnant with Matteo. That was the worst two weeks of my life, wondering whether or not I would have to take care of the baby myself and find some way to pay the bills. But he came back. He said he panicked. He didn't know if he would be a good enough father. Everyone makes mistakes." She squeezes my hand again. "Adam will come home. He's a good man."

We stand looking at the wilted tulips, unsure whether to stay hopeful that they will come back to life.

"I hope so too. Thanks for the advice about the tulips," I respond, as I head towards my house to go inside. When I open the door, I don't smell supper being cooked, I don't hear *Call of Duty* being played upstairs—nothing to keep me hopeful. I know Adam's not home.

Adam, May 13, 2014, 3:30 pm PDT

One minute I'm walking with ancient giants, 800-year-old cedars with tree trunks so big that a whole family could encircle it holding hands and they wouldn't even connect. The forest is blanketed by the greenest ferns and moss and bonsai-like trees, a wild majesty that beckons hobbits and pixies and elves and dreamers. I make it past the gain line and then BOOM! I'm face-to-face with a tempest that sculpts the coast of pristine beaches, a paradise for surfers and artists and drifters.

The cries of eagles are replaced by the howling roar of nature as furious tides and swells sweep the shores. A rainbow of invertebrates clings to the rocky bluffs and jagged cliffs. It's a personal encounter with the raw, unrelenting power of nature and the violent extremes of the open Pacific. As I bear witness to the madness of the ever-changing moods of the wild, I'm overcome by a sense of peace. I like like LIKE it.

Emma, May 13, 2014, 7:05pm EDT

Like I've done obsessively the last two days, I check my e-mail and Facebook accounts. Nothing from Adam. As I scroll through my Facebook newsfeed, I'm struck by a post by this girl, Abby, with whom I went to Queen's, but haven't seen in years:

Sometimes love comes in big gestures, like buying a house, moving to a new city, or even an "I do". Other times, love appears in small actions like bringing you flowers for no reason, making you coffee, early morning drives to work, or even making pancakes. I am so lucky to receive both from you Erik Lawrance *- xoxoxo!!!*

It's so nice that Abby is so happy, but I can't help but want to comment, *"Everybody lies."* I do it in my head and keep scrolling. When I see posts like this one, I wonder if the couples who feel the need to broadcast their love on social media are actually happy. Why do they need thirty "likes" to validate their relationship? Adam and I never posted anything like this to each other's Facebook pages. I didn't feel like it was something to share with the world. I re-read the post. *Making pancakes.* A "small action" Adam was going to do the morning he disappeared.

Skimming through my newsfeed, I notice that Erin and Kevin posted pics of their trip to Mexico from their joint account. The sunny shots lift my spirits. *Aww, they're so cute. What a beautiful beach. Ooooooh I like Erin's bikini! I'll have to ask her where she got it!* Erin and Kevin are one of those really cute couples that seem so happy that it's disgusting. I bet they've never had a fight in their life. They publicize everything from where they go for brunch to books they read in bed together. But then again, if everything's so wonderful, why do they need to rub their love in our faces? To make the rest of us feel bad about having such flawed relationships? Or are they putting on a show to hide what's really going on at home, like Charlotte on *Sex and the City* did when Trey couldn't get it up?

Then I see a picture of a young teacher from Tennessee holding a sign: *I'm talking to my 5th grade students about Internet safety and how quickly a photo can be seen by lots of people. If you are reading this, please click 'LIKE'. Thanks!* I click the "Like" icon. *WTF? Over 300 000 Likes? News travels fast!* Maybe that's how I should find Adam. Take a picture of him and post it to social media: *Have you seen Adam Davison? Please Like and Share!* He's been missing for almost three days now.

After going through the routine of checking his phone and creeping his Facebook page, and finding no sign of Adam, I decide it's finally time to call his mom and go to the police.

She picks up after the first ring. Has she been waiting by the phone like I have? "Hey, Nicky? It's Emma."

"Hello, Emma. I was just going to call you. I've been trying to reach Adam since the weekend. Is something wrong with his phone? He hasn't been returning my calls. He usually calls me back right away." *She must be freaking out, as she's called him at least ten times in the last three days.*

I take a deep breath. *Be honest with her, Emma. Family is the most important thing in this world.* "Uh, actually, I was hoping you would be able to know something about Adam. He left Sunday morning to go get groceries to make my birthday breakfast and never came home. I've been in touch with his friends and no one has heard from him. He hasn't been at work all week."

Nicky explodes in disbelief. "SUNDAY? My son has been missing since SUNDAY and you only call to tell me NOW? Geez, Emma, it's Tuesday night! What if something bad happened to him? Have you contacted the police?"

"No," I admit sheepishly. "I assumed that he'd freaked out about our relationship and took off. Maybe I should have contacted the police earlier. His bank called and said they froze his card due to unusual spending. I really thought he would come home." *I guess I didn't want to admit to myself that he wasn't coming home.*

"Emma, you should have called me. You know how Adam loves you." She's lecturing me the way she would to one of her students.

"I thought he would be home by now. I don't know what to do."

"I don't really know what to do either, but I think we have to contact the police at this point. Did you have any reason to suspect that something was wrong? Was he acting differently in the last little while? Was he having problems at work?"

"No." I reply honestly. "He seemed really happy. I'm so confused. This doesn't make sense."

"Well, I'm certainly as confused as you are. But you work pretty long hours so maybe you weren't home enough to recognize what's been going on." *Is she blaming me for Adam's disappearance? Accusing me of working too much to realize that her son, my partner, was suffering? What if he ran off like his dad did? Is it in his genes?*

"Nicky, I'm sorry. I told you all I know. To me, he seemed really happy. He even threw a surprise party for me on the weekend."

There's a long pause. "Well, people often hide their problems from the ones they love the most. Maybe Adam didn't want you to know if he was in trouble."

"I've been replaying the last few weeks over and over in my head and I can't think of anything that would have suggested something was wrong." I won't tell her about the drugs yet. I don't even know for sure that he did them.

"Maybe he's okay, but if you haven't seen him since Sunday, it means he's been missing for about four days now. Emma, you have to call the police right away. I'll call my principal and see if I can take a personal day tomorrow to come into the city. I'm guessing the police will probably want to talk to me as well."

While I often have to file incident reports for cases that come into the ER, I've never contacted the police for something personal, other than getting cleared for a few criminal record checks. I haven't needed to contact them.

"Ok. I'll call the police and let you know what they say. But shouldn't you stay at your place in case Adam goes to Parry Sound? That's the only place I think he'd go to outside of Toronto."

"You've got a point, Em. But if he was planning on coming home, don't you think he'd be here?" Home. Where is home for Adam now?

Adam, May 14, 2014, 3:30 pm PDT

Scrambling over a cluster of loose rocks, I get a whiff of familiar scents: struggle, discipline, and perseverance. The Lone Wolf moves ahead of the pack when all the forces of nature have been pushing him back. Last night, before he set out on the trek, he looked up at the mountain and it seemed like an impossible feat to get to the top. He endured the gruelling trek with nothing but animal instinct. It's been harder, steeper than anticipated, especially with the heavy load on his back, but these four strong legs shoulder the burden.

***

Next stop: Everest. Without any oxygen, as the real heroes do. I'll climb the Seven Summits, travel the world, push myself, abandon comfort and mediocrity, and really LIVE. Fight for the extra inch. Great men, like George Mallory, risk their lives for the mountains. They dare to live. What man has gone down in the history books for dying doing a boring office job or walking down a sidewalk in suburbia? To really live, you must be prepared to die.

At this altitude, I inhale the purest, freshest, coolest air that my lungs have ever known. At the top of the mountain, the spirit of the wild is THUNDERING. It's terrifying. Exhilarating. Clawing further and further towards the top, I stare out at the islands scattered across the wild ocean and watch the waves rage into the rocky shoreline. I'm pulled by the mountains jutting out on the horizon, the distant peaks still to be climbed, and see a power beyond the grasp of normal men. A hunger for imagination. The wild freedom of the mountain lives within all of us. It just needs courage to be unleashed.

I adjust the straps of the heavy pack on my back and then grab hold of a piece of jagged rock cutting out through the steep cliff face. Digging my claws into a shelf, I prowl stealthily up the mountain. I hesitate and linger for just a second: I look down, even though I know I shouldn't, and the long drop overwhelms and inspires me. It's an abyss; an omen of darkness and another challenge to come. I hold myself for a minute, teetering on the brink between life and death. I thrust one paw upward, and then the other, defying reason and gravity with each ascent. When I finally get to the top, I throw my head back, let the spirit of the wild blow through me, and I listen as the wind whispers history: this is how it feels to triumph.

My eyes stop on an orange tent at the south end of the summit. I'm not alone. Only dreamers like me would choose to camp atop the mountain. The descent, the return to the valley, is the worst part of the climb. After putting my heavy pack on the ground, I wander over to the tent. Two sets of hiking boots rest in front of the door.

"Ahoooooo! Ahahahoooo!" I howl with the wind. "Is anyone in there?" I'm shouting through a megaphone, the call of the wild coming through me with each breath.

The zippered door to the entrance of their tent opens slowly, then a man, who looks to be about forty or so, pokes his head out. I can see the shape of another body cocooned inside a sleeping bag. His eyes are droopy with the fatigue of hitting the summit.

"Huh?" He looks up at me in confusion, not expecting company.

"Hey," I say, so excited that more disciples have answered my call. "You guys spending the night up here too?

Where are you from? Did you take the trail? I veered off course within the first hour of the hike and followed a stream up to the top, but then had to bushwhack my way through the wild cedars until I reached the cliff face. It was pretty intense. But I kept pushing. One foot after the other. Left-right. Left-right. All the way to the top. There were some tricky scrambles up near the end. You hit those ones too?"

"Whoa, slow down man," he says, crawling out of the tent. "You've got a lot of energy for someone who's just hiked a mountain."

"Well, just look around at this view. It's incredible! There's so much light up here. It's like you can see life in its most purest form. The harsh blows of the sea. The ancient rainforests. The sun shining on jagged peaks. There's no watches. No schedules. No cell phones. No stress. No judgement. No control. Just life as it's meant to be lived. We're just out here, IN IT!"

The man shakes his head in disbelief, like I've told some awful joke. "It *is* a pretty fucking awesome view. I guess if you're going to be camping out here too, you may as well join us for dinner. That's my girl, Mary, in there. Having a little cat nap after the big hike. I'm Rain." *The Lone Wolf shakes hands with the Rain. He's face to face with his destiny.*

A striking golden-haired lioness lifts up head. She licks her lips like a predator stalking its prey and I'm instantly aroused. Her eyes remind me of the Pacific: Raging. Fearless. Restless. I can feel her hunger for the wild of the jungle, the desire for freedom one senses in the caged lions at the zoo. She's on the top of a mountain, amidst one of the wildest places on earth, and still she wants more. We either can hunt or be hunted.

"You guys come up here often?" I ask.

"We climb mountains whenever we need to find our strength. We're going to be putting our bodies on the line tomorrow," Rain replies.

"Yeah, the descent's always painful. It puts so much pressure on the joints."

"No, that's not what I meant. We're going to the mainland to protest drilling and survey related to the proposed pipeline expansion."

His eyes blaze with fiery passion, energy that I rarely see in other men but it's now burning within myself. There's a reason I met this man. I can feel it.

Emma: May 14 2014, 7:00 pm EDT

I stare at my computer screen in disbelief. Police investigations involve other people, not anyone I know, yet the man in the picture is certainly Adam, the love of my life, in his Team Ontario rugby jersey. The police report passes under my eyes for what must be the hundredth time today.

Toronto Police Service News Release
Missing man, Adam Davison, 30

Broadcast time: 09:14
Thursday, May 20, 2014

14 Division
(416) 808-1400

The Toronto Police Service is requesting the public's assistance locating a missing man.

Adam Davison, 30, was last seen on Sunday, May 11, 2014, at 10:00 a.m., in the Bloor Street West and Dufferin Street area.

He is described as a Caucasian male. 6'2", 195 lbs., athletic build with brown short hair and dark brown eyes. He was wearing a black Rugby Canada t-shirt, red Nike basketball shorts, and yellow Reebok running shoes.

Police are concerned for his safety.

Anyone with information is asked to contact police at 416-808-1400, Crime Stoppers anonymously at 416-222-TIPS (8477), online at www.222tips.com, text TOR and your message to CRIMES (274637). Download the free Crime Stoppers Mobile App on iTunes, Google Play or Blackberry App World.

Then I share the link to my Facebook page. *Please help me find Adam!*

Within minutes, the post has been shared six times. Friends post comments of reassurance.

Joyce Webber: *What?! What happened??*

Alex Tomlin: *Thoughts and prayers.*

Tom Watters: *Thinking of you and Adam.*

All I can do is stare at the screen, waiting for someone somewhere to give me a tip or clue as to Adam's whereabouts. The police weren't much help when I reported that Adam was missing last night. Since it's not illegal for an adult to go missing, all they could do is have me come into the station, fill out a pile of paperwork, and answer one ridiculous question after another.

"Did you have any reason to suspect he might be having an affair? Does he speak about any women? Does he go away for long periods of time? Has he been coming home at irregular times? Does he have a history of alcohol or drug abuse?"

At first, I answered "No. No. No. No. No. No" with confidence. However, as more time passed, I began to wonder. What if Adam's been duping me like Walter White does to Skylar in *Breaking Bad*, telling me he's going off to a respectable career when he's really cooking crystal meth? Or what if he's on Tinder? From what my friends tell me, it seems like there's a ton of married men online looking for casual flings.

I tore our room apart, searching between the mattress and box-spring, smelling the sheets and pillowcases for a scent other than mine, looking for evidence—a hair, an earring, underwear, traces of make-up, or anything to tell me that he was sleeping with someone else. I was shocked when I found the ring. Was it for me or someone else?

"Have you tried calling the local hospitals or the coroner? I don't want to worry you more, but there are over 200 unidentified-remains cases at the Ontario Coroner's Office. Sometimes when people go missing, it means that something has happened to them."

The statistics haunt me. I won't let Adam become another statistic. But I've already called the police, shared the police report on social media, called his friends, what else can I do?

When my cat, Mona, went missing, my family walked around the neighbourhood, calling for her in alleyways and backyards. We knocked on neighbours' doors and put up signs with her picture. After a couple of hours of searching, one of the neighbours found her inside his backyard shed. We found Mona the old-fashioned way, so I run downstairs and put my shoes on and grab a light cardigan and set off to find Adam myself.

Walking north on Dufferin towards Dupont, I desperately scan the storefronts that serve the Portuguese, Italian, and Ethiopian communities now becoming gentrified by young urban professionals looking to pay cheaper rent in the city center. As I hurry past the Santo Antonio Coin Laundromat at Hallam Street, I make eye contact with a young woman about my age folding her laundry. I feel sadness at the sight of her. Despite being one of 8.1 million people in the Greater Toronto Area, she seems desperately lonely.

I glance inside the Home Hardware, where Adam got a drain snake to clean our clogged kitchen sink a couple of weeks ago, then the Unisex Hair Salon and the Fried Chicken Shop, where we always joked about going to for a mid-week date but never tried. For a brief moment, I contemplate spending twenty bucks on a psychic reading, but decide that I should probably wait to call upon the spirits since I just called upon the police. I feel haunted by the strangers speeding past in cars or on bikes. Have any of them have passed Adam along the way?

I look in the alleyways, between the two or three story Victorian houses, full of neighbours I've never met but acknowledge every now and then as I walk by them. An older Portuguese man stares at me as he smokes a cigarette on his front porch and I wonder how long he has lived in that house, how many evenings he spends smoking cigarettes on his front porch smiling at pedestrians as they pass by without ever asking their names. Each one of us participates in similar daily routines, passes the same shops, and takes adjacent commutes to work, but we navigate our lives independently, never allowing our paths to cross. In Toronto, the city of neighbourhoods, community is something you create yourself but are not automatically a member. Making connections means crossing the boundaries of independence and interrupting busy schedules.

I pass the Olympia Supermarket, where bouquets and hanging flower baskets cram the storefront. Is this where Adam bought my birthday roses? A young employee winks at me as he sweeps some dust from inside the store out front. Maybe he can help.

"Have you seen this man?" I ask, showing him a picture of Adam on my phone.

He inspects the picture for several seconds then looks up at me. "No. He's your husband?"

"My boyfriend. Adam. He went missing a couple of days ago. If you see him…" *I should go to the library and print off some copies of the police report to hand out.* "Call the police," I tell him. It's hopeless, trying to recruit a stranger to help me find someone who's a stranger to him. But then again, we are all strangers to ourselves, caught up in the monotony of daily life, stuck in our routines, never really stopping to think about what will happen to us if we fall off track.

As I hurry by the grey angular chiropractic office at the corner of Lappin Avenue, a wave of pure misery stings me as the overcrowded Dufferin bus drives past the corner. As usual, it's jam-packed with moms with baby-strollers, seniors with shopping carts, chatty teens, men with their hockey bags, and professionals frustrated with the routine disappointment of their commute home. Despite being sardines in a can, everyone's on their phones, connecting with anyone in the cyberworld or typing random keys to look busy and avoid catching the interest of that lone passenger on the bus who inevitably wants to make a friend. Only crazy people talk to you on the bus, like that old man who asked me to marry him or that teenager who claimed that she was overpowered by the sense that I was her spirit friend. Better to keep the headphones in and avoid conversations altogether.

Moving to the left side of the sidewalk to make space for a young couple to pass by me while walking their dog, I realize that avoiding people is not going to help me find Adam. *If they're out walking their dog, they're probably from the neighbourhood. Just ask them.* I take a deep breath and then step towards the middle of the sidewalk, slowing them to a stop.

"Excuse me, I'm just wondering if you've seen this man?" I ask, showing them the same picture I showed the employee at the supermarket.

The couple looks at each other, seemingly annoyed that I've interrupted their evening walk. The woman, who appears to be slightly older than me, shakes her head.

"Does he run?" her husband asks. "I feel like I may have seen him or someone who looks like him running through High Park. But it's hard to say. I'm kind of in my own world when I'm running."

My heart starts racing, fueled by the hope that Adam's nearby. But what do I do? Set up camp and watch runners go by in hopes that Adam is one of them? "When did you see him?"

The man thinks for a moment. "It would have been at least two or three weeks ago. I pulled my groin so I haven't been running lately." Their dog starts pulling on the leash, suggesting that their break has gone on for too long.

My heart drops. Any hope that had started to build has disappeared as quickly as it came. It's like I revved an engine then cut it out before switching into first gear.

"Ok, well, his name's Adam. He works at Dufferin Grove MaxFit. He disappeared on Sunday. If you see him, can you call the police?"

The couple looks at me like I'm a desperate housewife, avoiding the reality that my husband is cheating on me by convincing myself that he's in trouble. It was foolish to think that I could do anything to find Adam. He could be anywhere.

The tears are now rolling down my face, so I turn into Wallace Emerson Park. I sit on a bench and watch a group of guys playing basketball on the outdoor court, something Adam does every now and then when he's not too busy with work. I keep wiping the tears from my eyes, trying to hide the paralyzing grief, the real possibility that Adam might not be coming back and that there is nothing I can do about it. The world continues without him. It's like I'm the only person in this city who even cares or notices that he's missing. Toronto will be the same city with or without Adam in it, but my world has transformed into something dead, empty, hopeless.

Everywhere I look, I see people I don't know and feel the haunting weight of Adam's absence. Everything reminds me of the times we shared together in the city: Sunday morning croissants from the Portuguese bakery, bike rides to High Park, even the mundane shopping trips to Fresh Co. or Dollarama at the Galleria Mall. It's like he's always around, in my memories, but he's not actually here to share them.

Adam, May 15, 2014, 1:00 pm PDT

"NO TANKERS! NO PIPELINES! NO TANKERS! NO PIPELINES!" We hold up signs and walk in front of Burnaby Mountain, shouting with everything we have. It's exhilarating being part of something. Making history. Changing the world. A line of cops stands like soldiers in front of the mountain and defends the ideals we're fighting. We've been told that we'll be arrested if we cross the line, and I know Rain and Mary are willing to go there if necessary.

"NO TANKERS! NO PIPELINES! NO TANKERS! NO PIPELINES!"

An Elder takes the stage. The crowd hushes out of respect as she raises her hand the way a kindergarten teacher does to her rambunctious but obedient class. She respects the land and knows it's part of her roots, her heritage, her legacy. She stands tall like the trees that awed me on the journey here: wise and beautiful and fierce.

"I've been coming to Burnaby Mountain every night for the last month to keep the sacred fire alive. It's our sovereign right to defend this mountain. It's unceded traditional territory for the Tseil-Waututh, Musqueam, Sto:lo and Squamish Nations, but it is not only sacred for First Nations people. It is sacred for all people. We have one Mother Earth. It's our duty to protect her."

"Ahoooahahaahoooo!" I shout, banging on my chest as members of the Squamish Nation bang on traditional drums and lead the crowd in a song. "We will all save Burnaby Mountain. We will all save Burnaby Mountain. WE WILL ALL SAVE BURNABY MOUNTAIN." I'm screaming at the top of my lungs, gearing up for battle. The louder the roar, the stronger the fight, yet I know I need to do more. I look around. Anyone bring a chain? I'll lock myself to the mountain and make 'em drill through me.

The crowd goes silent as the Elder lifts her hand again to speak.

"The proposed pipeline is symbolic of a way of life that causes more harm than good, one that is dependent on fossil fuels to service our notion of wealth. The corporations that seek profit from this pipeline could care less if we have healthy relationships with each other, with our communities, with the land. Their goal is to make as much money as possible for foreign investors. That is crazy logic. Why are we putting the market over the land we depend on to survive?"

"FUCK FOSSIL FUELS!" Mary yells beside me. Rain holds her hand and they punch the air, two fists raging against a way of life that they feel is destroying them. They're getting me fired up, like a pep talk before a big game. I lift my fist with them. Courage is contagious. "FUCK FOSSIL FUELS!" I repeat.

The crowd goes wild. People bang on drums and dance around and start chanting. "Heyhey! Hoho! Fossil fuels have got to go! Heyhey! Hoho! Fossil fuels have got to go!"

The Lone Wolf's hungry for his prey. He's out for blood. Every cell in his body is on fire now and the urgency to fight is about to erupt. "FUCK FOSSIL FUELS!!!" I yell again. "Ahoohoooo!" The yelling releases some pressure, but it's not enough. There's more I can do. I'm so hungry for purpose I can almost taste it, but it's an angry, bitter taste. For months, concerned citizens have been putting their bodies on the line and I didn't even know about it. I'm here now, though. Time to make a difference. The future of all of humanity is at stake and I've gotta fucking *do something* about it.

"The regulatory process for protecting the earth from harm have been gutted by unjust laws. If we allow our LEADERS—"

"BOO!" "SHAME!" The crowd explodes in disgust. It's like we're a bunch of hockey fans doing what we can from our seats, believing that if we cheer enough, believe enough, shout enough, wave our signs, then maybe we'll get the outcome we want. We're all part of something. A team. (*Go Leafs Go!*)

Standing beside me, Mary is fueled by rage, pumping her fists and shaking her head, with so much passion that I want to throw her onto the ground and fuck her right there. Her long blond hair is absolutely glowing, like a golden mane, and she's so fucking beautiful that I can't take my eyes off her. Beads of sweat drip off her brow and there's fire in her eyes. Her energy inspires me. This isn't just part of her. It is her. No matter how many times she gets knocked down, she'll get right back up and keep fighting for more. "FUCK FOSSIL FUELS!" Mary will chain herself to one of the giant cedars, cross the police line, and risk her life before she gives up the fight.

Once the crowd calms down, the Elder resumes, "If we allow our LEADERS to continue to look at the land and the world around us just in terms of dollars and cents then we are going to destroy the things that keep us alive and healthy."

If we allow our leaders. The phrase fires me up like Mary's feline spirit. I can do more to fight for the future of humanity than scream my head off in front of a bunch of cops. I've never been good on the sidelines. I'm meant to be wearing a uniform, not cheering for the uniform. I'll be a leader. Become the next Prime Minister. The world needs me.

*

"Hey buddy, sorry to bug you, but I thought you should know you still have the tags on your jacket."

A young surfer dude carrying a Hollister bag approaches alongside me as we exit the Pacific Centre mall. He points at a tag hanging over the back of my neck. "Oh, thanks," I say, tucking it inside my new jacket. "I just bought it. I'll cut it off when I get to my hotel."

"No worries," he replies, smiling all happy-go-lucky, "Great suit by the way. It looks sharp." *Idiot. 'Sharp' is a word you use to describe your two year old nephew's Christmas outfit, not the next Prime Minister. But I do look amazing: dressed for success.*

I'm a hot air balloon, drifting between the tall buildings and fancy hotels along Howe Street as yellow cabs, Smart Cars, mini-vans, cyclists, and pedestrians flood the concrete below. The traffic below me gets smaller and faster as I'm lifted higher in the sky and eventually it looks like I'm watching a car commercial on fast forward. Today is the beginning of something big, even bigger than myself. A day for the history books.

Emma, May 17, 2014, 5:45 am EDT

I hold my breath as one of the paramedics delivers the report to my team while his partners continue to perform chest compressions. I desperately scan the limited sections of the patient's face not covered by the oxygen mask. Whenever a patient Adam's age comes in, I expect it to be him. *Where is he? What happened to him? Why hasn't he contacted me?*

"This is an unidentified Caucasian male, appears to be about 30-35 years old. Bystanders saw him walking across the intersection at the corner of Queen and Lansdowne and he just collapsed on the street corner. Vital signs absent, we've been doing compressions for about fifteen minutes now."

"As soon as possible, let's get the patient on the bed and on the monitors, please," I assert, directing the paramedics into the emergency room.

As they transfer the man off the stretcher and onto the hospital bed, my heart stops for a second. I notice a wedding band on his left ring finger. I think about the ring Adam never gave me. *He's someone else's husband—not yours.* Then I take a deep breath to calm myself down as my eyes begin to water.

"Let's get some bloods drawn, including a full tox screen, and two peripheral in stat," I direct the nurses to assess his vital signs as one of the other doctors takes over chest compressions. "Eliza, can I get you to check the tube placement? And Marc, can we get an arterial blood gas from him right away?"

The man in front of me is someone's husband. He's someone's son. Maybe he's someone's father. What if another doctor is with Adam right now, wondering the same things, not quite understanding what led to his crisis but treating him to the best of her ability?

As time is critical when vital signs are weak, I respond quickly.

"So, on the count of five, we are going to stop CPR so we can do a check on the monitor for a rhythm. So, one, two, three, four, five. Stop CPR."

I examine the monitor and hold my own breath as I check for pulses. Nothing.

"Okay, guys, so, urgh...we've got pulseless electrical activity. No pulses palpable anywhere. Let's continue CPR."

I look at the ring on his finger. Was he with his wife last night? Why was he wandering the street so early in the morning? Is his wife she waking up for work right now, wondering where her husband is? Do they have children? What will she tell them when their dad isn't there for breakfast? How long will she wait before calling her friends, her parents, or the police?

Maybe she's playing it cool. *He's probably planning another surprise for me.*

"So, at this time, our downtime has been how long?" I ask.

"It's been one hour and five minutes," Meg responds, reading the chart of the unidentified man in front of her.

"From his initial arrest? Ok." I take a deep breath and look back at the monitor, willing it to reveal some sliver of hope. I turn to my team, "Let's do another rhythm check." I stare long and hard at the monitor for several seconds. A flat line stares back at me. There's no pulse.

In a painfully monotonous voice, well-rehearsed from years of training and mock-situations, I tell the team my decision. "At this point, there's been significant downtime since the initial arrest and the monitor is showing no cardiac motions, so unless anyone has any other suggestions, I'm going to call it."

"Ok."
"Ok."
"Ok."
"Ok."

"Alright, time of death is 5:51 am. Can we make sure we check his clothing carefully for ID? I'll notify the social worker and the coroner," I tell them, hurrying out of the room. Tears are running down my face. I don't want anyone to see me. It's always hard to deal with a patient's death, but I'm not crying for the patient, I'm crying for Adam. I'm crying for the loss of a life I imagined for myself. I'm crying at the fear of having to start my life over again. Alone. Where am I going to go? What am I going to do?

Finally, I make it to the washroom. I run into the stall and quickly close the door behind me. Collapsing on the toilet seat, I put my elbows on my knees and my face in my hands and start sobbing uncontrollably, the helpless cries of longing and loss. Grief pours out of me. I feel numb. How long can I go on like this, trapped within my own despair, clinging to the memories of a time when I was the happiest I've ever been? I may never see Adam again. Maybe he's not even alive. How long can I stay trapped in this prison of pain, guilt, regret, sadness, and hope? How can I move forward with my life when I'm stuck in the memories of the past? Everywhere I go in the city, I'm watching another re-run of moments when I felt happy and alive and excited to share my life with Adam. I just want to hit the replay button and watch them over and over, like a ghost stuck in a dead past. I can't go on like this, stuck in the re-runs. I need a new reality, a new life.

    What I need to do is to leave.

Adam, May 17, 10:00pm PDT

Seeing a cab approaching, I wave it down excitedly. The driver pulls up alongside me. Clearly, he sees how important I am, as he immediately gets out of the cab and comes around to my side to open the back passenger door for me. In no time, I'll be taking limos or being chauffeured around by my own personal driver.

"Hotel Georgia," I slur. How many drinks did I have?

"Sir, you're already there."

"Just drive around the block then. I wanna go where the action is." The words have blended together like a protein shake. Too many tequila shots burned through my wad of twenties. I'll be the fucking best Prime Minister this country's ever seen.

"Turn left at the lights!" I shout urgently, seeing a man in a Leafs jersey. Phaneuf. That's my jersey! What the fuck is that man doing with it in Vancouver? Madness overtakes me like a rabid dog. Time slows. I can see every hair on his head. Every wrinkle on his face. He is laughing so fucking loud it's giving me a headache like I'm wearing headphones and my iPod's stuck on full blast because I can't even hear the music in the cab.

The traffic light turns red as the driver pulls into the left lane. Once he stops, I open the door and release myself into the night, a mad dog breaking off his leash. My eyes zero in on the royal blue maple leaf logo and the white lettering *Toronto Maple Leafs*. As I do before every tackle, I visualize the attack. *This one's yours, man.* The Lone Wolf's salivating. He's hungry for the win.

Crouch. Touch. Pause. I shift my weight onto my hind legs. *Engage!* I attack driving my shoulder into his quads. Then I wrap my arms around him and pull him to the concrete. It feels so good to be in the game again.

Part 4: Two months later

"Some birds are not meant to be caged, that's all. Their feathers are too bright, their songs too sweet and wild. So you let them go, or when you open the cage to feed them they somehow fly out past you. And the part of you that knows it was wrong to imprison them in the first place rejoices, but still, the place where you live is that much more drab and empty for their departure."

-Stephen King,
Rita Hayworth and the Shawshank Redemption

Emma: August 5, 2014, 4:00 pm EDT

Jay, the mental health nurse I've been working with over the past few weeks, scrunches his face pensively to focus his camera lens on a tiny purple flower blooming out of the grassy tundra. For him, photography is a serious hobby, as he uses his camera to zoom in on the elements in life that people rarely notice.

"I think Arctic wildflowers are the most beautiful in the world. Knowing how hard it is for them to survive makes them even more special in my eyes," he comments.

With his shaggy golden hair, free-spirited personality, and caring demeanor, he reminds me of Adam Galloway, the rugged humanitarian/photographer from *House of Cards*. I wonder if, like Adam, Jay's honesty has made him the victim of power. There must be a Claire buried somewhere in his past.

Everyone who comes north must be escaping some sort of toxic love affair or career, hoping that the Arctic, with its myths of adventure and possibility, will capture their romantic imaginations. However, the land is as unforgiving as it is healing. On the tundra, you're exposed. There's nothing to hide behind, no distractions.

"I didn't even know there were flowers in the Arctic," I reply honestly. "I'm amazed that something so beautiful and fragile could survive in this extreme climate."

I've been told that southerners come to the north for three reasons: missionary, mercenary, and misfit. I'm not yet sure into which category I fall, but I hope that being here will be a fresh start. A new purpose. I mean, I never would have come here if things hadn't fallen apart with Adam. But I had to stay strong and see the breakup as an opportunity to do something that I never would have done if we were together.

"Even the tiniest of flowers can have the toughest roots," Jay laughs.

I suppress a tingle in the pit of my stomach. I had such a crush on Adam Galloway while watching *House of Cards*. Like Claire, I was drawn to someone who allowed himself to live so freely, so passionately and in the moment, a contrast to my dependency on calendars and to do lists for survival.

He continues, speaking like a sexy British artist seducing the First Lady.

"I've met southerners who see these flowers as victims of extreme conditions. But I hope that my photos will help people see them as they are: survivors."

"The only photos I'd ever seen of the Arctic were of polar bears or glaciers or Inuit in traditional clothing. Nothing that shows how life actually is up here." I admit.

Before I came here, I thought the Arctic was an archaic wasteland, frozen in the ways of the past. However, many Inuit Elders I've met were born in igloos and now use iPods. Survival's not about preservation, but about the constant adaptation to the changing world.

Instead of being stuck in the past, the Arctic is a site of contention over competing ideas of the future. While some northerners resist the changes being imposed on them by resource extractive industries, others embrace them. Many Inuit fight to incorporate traditional knowledge and culture into development projects ensure that their communities contribute to shaping the future, and ultimately are not lost within it.

"Yeah, most southerners have this idea that the Arctic is just a big sheet of ice and snow. I thought the same thing when I arrived here six years ago. It's hard to really know something until you experience it with your own eyes."

After taking a few pictures, Jay stands up and points at the stretch of the Arctic Ocean in front of Bylot Island.

"Just look at that iceberg. It's massive, yet about 90% of it is below the surface. Something can appear a certain way but if you make the effort to dig a little deeper, you discover that things are rarely what you expect them to be."

"That's the first iceberg I've ever seen. Aside from watching *Titanic*!" I joke.

"When you live in the extremes, like we do up here, life is full of surprises. Just wait until you experience the dark season. The darkness messes with your mind. You need to take every opportunity to get outside and be with other people. Even when it's minus 40."

"Oh, I've already made a plan for living in 24 hours of darkness: a natural sunlight lamp, lots of Vitamin D, a treadmill in my living room, and a goal to re-watch all 10 seasons of *Friend*s. There's no way I'm going to let myself get depressed!"

Jay shakes his head. With his greying hair sticking out from under his toque and the wrinkles around his eyes, he must be at least ten years older than me.

"I thought I'd be able to handle the darkness better than I did my first year. I tricked myself into believing that I was much more alone than I actually was. You have to stay connected. I'll help you out."

"Thanks, Jay," I say honestly.

Turning his camera away from the pristine landscape, Jay takes a photo of the town, capturing clusters of run-down government housing units and failing infrastructure. The poorly maintained facilities like the potholed outdoor basketball court and abandoned youth centre, reveal a poor foundation laid by settlers looking to find richness in the land. As Jay pans his camera, the desolation extends to the crumbling infrastructure: dirt roads, inadequate housing, and the neglected waste facility site with its frozen piles of garbage, broken snowmobiles, and stacks of junk. It is easy to see the beauty in the surrounding mountain ranges, picturesque icebergs, and stunning fjords, but once the camera points inward, it forces the photographer to confront realities one would rather avoid, such as the high rates of poverty, unemployment, addiction, and domestic violence that an overwhelming number of people in this community endure daily.

"You're sure you're okay about what happened yesterday?" Jay asks softly.

I know he asked me to go for a hike in order to look out for me. It's not the first suicide I've responded to, but in Toronto, I found it easier to separate myself from the patients. It's always difficult to tell their loved ones about what happened and see the intense feelings of sadness, shock, and anger as they react to the news. But at the end of my shift, I go home and go to yoga or watch Netflix to detach. But with the few fitness classes that are available here, and the limited bandwidth we get through our Internet providers, I can't keep up my usual 'coping routine' here, so I'm finding it difficult to escape the community's grief.

"It's hard to understand why someone so young could take her life," I say, "but I didn't really know her, so I'm sure I'm doing better than everyone else. Besides, I have to be able to stay strong so I can support community members through their grief."

Stay strong. I tell Jay the same message I've been telling myself. *You need to be able to hold it together when everyone else is falling apart.* That's what strong women do. The Claire Underwoods of the world don't allow themselves to have emotional breakdowns. Not in public anyways. Instead, they suffer privately. Disappear. Have affairs with hunks like Adam Galloway and come back stronger than when they left.

But the truth is, last night, I was a mess. As soon as I came home from work, after consoling grieving family member after grieving family member, I start sobbing. Conscious that someone from the community might come over to check on me (Elisapee, the high school principal did), I had to take a hot shower to help hide my tears.

Ever since Adam and I broke up, I'm no longer immune to the suffering of others. I've put thousands of miles between us, but the distance does not erase the pain of losing my best friend. Witnessing community members' intense reactions of shock, anger and sadness to Lynda's death yesterday released the pain I'd been suppressing over the loss of my relationship with Adam. It's truly hard to grieve the loss of someone close to you when they're still alive, so my pain must come out in little droplets, through the suffering of others.

"That's the thirty-eighth suicide in this community since I came here six years ago, and it's always a difficult time, no matter how well I know the person." He crouches low to the ground to take another picture of the purple flower; a reminder that life persists even in the most unforgiving places.

"Wow, it's so tragic that such a small community would have to endure so much suffering. Were you close with Lynda?"

He nods, looking through the pictures on the screen on the back of his camera. Some relationships can only exist as memories. But unlike ephemeral digital images that can be sorted and deleted, we can't erase the past. We have to learn to live with all the images that are stored in love's archive, memories tagged good and bad. No Photoshopping. Accept the negative before moving forward.

As much as I blame Adam for fucking things up by taking off, I've begun to wonder what I did to drive him away. If only I didn't work so much... if only I'd recognized that he was in trouble... if only I hadn't put so much pressure on him to be perfect... IF, IF, IF. *Come on, Emma, stop. You have to let it go. You could only do so much with the information you had. Look at Claire. She clearly regrets that she and Frank didn't have a baby, but she hasn't let that destroy her. (Yet, anyways.)*

"She came to Hip Hop regularly. She had a lot of trouble concentrating at school and, every now and then, would do things that were delusional. I suspected that she had a mental illness, maybe schizophrenia or something, and I had actually referred her for a psychiatric evaluation in Iqaluit about a year ago, but the system's so backed up that she never got a diagnosis.

"Last year, during Hip Hop, she ran outside at night with no shoes or jacket and it was minus 40. She claimed to have a superpower to protect her from the cold. I actually had to go outside, pick her up, and carry her in. Maybe I should have pushed harder for her to get assessed after that. But she was never in serious trouble at school or with the RCMP, at least not to my knowledge, so she flew under the radar. I kind of rationalized her delusions as being symptoms of a moody teenager."

I don't know how to respond, so I stare out at the town from where we are standing on the tundra. It's really hard to detect mental illness in someone if you're not an expert. The sun shines off the green metal roofs of the Greenlandic-style houses and I wonder what the families are doing to support each other during this tough time. These moments of tragedy and despair make us realize how much we need our families for support. When we suffer, we need the unconditional love of our families to give ourselves the permission to let out our emotions without feeling judged. When we're alone, we preserve our pain, like a dead caribou carcass on the frozen tundra, delaying the process of decay until the climate is warm enough to break it down.

"I try to do as much as I can to help and make life better for the kids here," Jay says softly, "But I've learned that the only way we can really help someone in pain is by listening. The change has to come from within them. During my first few months here, I was obsessed with implementing interventions, like after-school programs and support groups. I became frustrated when things weren't going well. It took me awhile to realize that I never asked the community what it wanted from me. I never took the time to listen."

At once I begin to shiver, so I take off my backpack and pull out a down pullover jacket, something I would never dream of wearing at this time of year in Ontario. However, it seems these extra layers are crucial for survival up here, as the wind coming across Lancaster Sound is a cruel kind of cold, piercing through my clothes and skin, and right into my soul. After I pull the hoodie over my head I feel chilled, haunted. It's like no matter how many layers I have to protect myself, I can't hide my loneliness. I thought Adam and I were going to be a family. Now I'm on my own and I'll have to find other ways to gain strength during the tough times.

The Arctic breeze disappears as I turn my attention to Jay. The vast landscape of the Arctic, where you could wander for hundreds of miles without coming into contact with another person, inspires the terror of solitude. Even though Jay has been through this before, he probably needs the warmth of human connection as much as I do, a friendly reminder that he's not alone in this immense wilderness.

"It's impossible to know what's going on in someone else's head. Sometimes the symptoms of illness aren't obvious from the outside. It's like you said, you can only ever see the tip of an iceberg, but the bulk of it exists below the surface."

After pausing to take a wool sweater out of his backpack and put it on, Jay responds cautiously. It's like he suddenly has realized the burden of his isolation and the threat of revealing too much to someone he doesn't know very well. When you allow yourself to get close to someone when you're away from home, there's always the risk that they will leave and you will be alone again, but this time, you're aware of how much better life was when they were there.

"I know," Jay continues, "but when you're part of a community, you feel a certain responsibility to protect each other. I can't help but wonder if there is something more I could have done to prevent this. But, sadly, suicide is not only a problem in this community. It's a huge public health issue across Nunavut. The rates across the territory are ten times the national average. It's hard to find someone in the territory who hasn't lost a friend or family member to suicide."

"That's so sad. Why are there so many suicides?"

Jay looks past the town at the dramatic presence of Sirmilik glacier on Bylot Island, as though the hundreds of thousands of years of history contained within its densely packed layers of ice and snow could inspire a simple solution to a complex issue. These glaciers are incredibly powerful, as their history proves they sculpted the surrounding mountains and carved out their valleys. However, while looking to them for hope, we aren't prepared to discover that the compressed ice sheets also contain thousands of years of suffering and despair. When we begin to search a little deeper into the heart of the glacier, into the wisdom preserved in the remains of the last Ice Age, we can see that all life contains elements of light and darkness, and that to live truthfully, we need to be able to accept the joy as well as the pain.

Earlier on our hike, Jay pointed out an area where remains of bowhead whale ribs were overgrown with layers of moss and grass, which he said were likely remnants of houses occupied by the Thule, the prehistoric ancestors of today's Inuit, who lived on Baffin Island sometime between 900 AD and 1100 AD. With thousands of years of history frozen in time, it's no wonder that many southerners like me romanticize the north as a place where we can freeze our former selves, thaw, and then bloom anew. Here it's just you, the land, and your thoughts, and you can't leave until you've wrestled with yourself and emerged a survivor. But then again, the light is much more intense up here and everything looks different because of it. The sun hasn't set in a couple of months, and you can see things much more clearly when it is light all of the time.

"It's hard to know why one person would take her life and another with a similar background doesn't. But in the majority of suicide cases I've experienced, the victims were diagnosed with severe depression before their deaths. And there's a lack of services available in the communities to support people suffering from mental illness. I mean, you're not a psychiatrist, but it's rare for us to have a medical doctor in the community for longer than a week."

"I'm not even here permanently." I remind him of the new trial Northern Health Outreach program that I'm participating in. "I'll be between here and Iqaluit."

"Hey, Jay! Jay!"

Jay turns and waves as we're interrupted by the shouting of a few kids sitting on the back of an ATV. It approaches us and then slows to a stop.

"Jay! *Qanuippit?*" A boy, who looks about twelve, wearing an Ottawa Senators jacket and jeans, jumps off the ATV, runs towards Jay, and gives him a hug. His younger sister follows. She has a lollipop in her mouth and a Dora the Explorer backpack hanging off her left shoulder.

"Hey Robert. Hey Julie-Anne." Jay greets them with a smile. "You guys coming to Hip Hop tomorrow at the C-Hall?" They nod in such excitement that Julie-Anne's lollipop falls out of her mouth and onto the tundra. Like many of the kids I used to work with as a camp counsellor when I was a teenager during the summer in Parry Sound, she brushes off the dirt and puts it back in her mouth.

"Who are you?" Robert points at me in confusion. While there are daily flights bringing tourists, nurses, teachers, researchers, government workers, and community members in and out of the town daily, an unfamiliar face attracts a lot of questions from locals. No one is anonymous in such a small community. Despite the vastness of the tundra surrounding the town, it's difficult to disappear or hide.

I remember that Jay told me that nearly every winter, someone from the community goes missing on the land while hunting or camping. As soon as friends or family members realize the person has not returned home as planned, they notify the local search and rescue team, and community members rally together, coordinating searches on the land and sea-ice on snowmobiles, and staying in contact through radio and Facebook. I guess it's tough to get lost when a whole community is looking for you.

"I'm Emma. The new doctor." He opens his eyes wide.

"*Ittuq! Ittuq!*" He calls towards the older man who is carefully watching our encounter from the ATV, and then points towards me. "*Luutaaq!*"

Looking slightly weathered and a little wrinkled around the eyes, he reminds me a little bit of my grandpa, a soldier who, despite being burdened by years of struggle to defend his territory, has found peace in the time spent with his grandchildren and the hope they offer for the future.

"He has the cancer," Robert tells me, "you can fix him so he don't go Ottawa."

"I'm liking your positivity, Robert," Jay says walking towards the old man, "but your grandpa will still need to go to Ottawa for his treatment. He needs special equipment that they only have at the hospital."

"*Unnuksakkut* Elijah." As Jay shakes his hand, I notice the old man wince, suggesting that his afternoon on the land with his grandchildren was not enough to mask his pain. Julie-Anne runs up to the ATV and hops up onto her grandpa's lap. Then holding his hand, she points to me the same way her brother did. "*Luutaaq!*"

"They're telling him that you are a doctor," Jay tells me. "Elijah's one of the community Elders. He doesn't speak much English."

I try to recall one of few phrases of Inuktitut that I've learned since I've been here. I gesture towards myself. "*Kinauvit* Emma," I enunciate the words slowly and carefully, as though I was teaching a kindergarten class the alphabet.

Elijah chuckles then shakes his head and waves his right index finger from side-to-side. Then he points to himself. "*Uvanga* Elijah."

Ooops. I blush then try again, copying his introduction. "*Uvanga* Emma."

He smiles then shakes my hand. "Welcome... doctor," he says in forced English. He turns to Jay and winks. Then he says something to his grandchildren in Inuktitut.

Robert translates. "He go seal hunting tomorrow if there no funeral. He wants you to come."

I smile. "I have to work. But please tell him that I would love to go another day."

After climbing up onto the ATV, Robert whispers the message to his grandpa. Elijah looks at me disapprovingly then mumbles something in Inuktitut.

Robert nods, translating. "He says you *Qallunaats* work too much. No time for family."

Adam, August 5, 2014, 7:30am EDT

Her long blond hair falls across her face. She brushes some away before taking a sip of her coffee so that it doesn't dip into the cup. She looks up at me, a bit embarrassed.

She's cute, but looked much hotter in the pictures. I should've known better. All women have to do is cake on some makeup, purse their lips, play with the filters on their phones, and suddenly they transform into someone better. Guys just end up looking shittier and shittier by comparison.

Third match and they're all going downhill. First an eight, then a seven, and now a six.

"So, Alex," she looks at me shyly. I don't correct her. What does my name even matter? Adam's who I used to be.

I don't say anything, but just keep staring at her, trying to figure out how long ago she took those pictures. I didn't remember her cheeks being so round, like one of those stupid Cabbage Patch dolls.

"Do you want to get a dog someday?" she asks. She puts down the coffee and bites into her turkey bacon club wrap. A bit of bacon falls from her lips and onto her plate. She just picks it up and puts it in her mouth.

My chest feels heavy. Compressed. It's like I'm being wrapped in plastic. My body is being squeezed tighter and tighter the longer I sit here.

"I don't know," I spit out.

We were supposed to have a beer and talk about the Jays or Raptors or *Game of Thrones* or working out. None of this deep, personal do-you-want-a-dog shit over the exact same fucking lunch that Emma always ordered. I take a bite of my toasted tuna sandwich. It tastes bland, generic, uninspiring. Empty. I couldn't go for the usually Philly Steak Melt. Why did I take her here anyways? The past is over. *You gotta accept it, man.*

She just keeps talking. *Blah blah blah blah blah.* The pressure gets heavier. A fucking herd of elephants steps onto my chest as she tells me about how nice the dog parks are in Parry Sound. How wonderful it is when she brings her lab retriever to the park and lets it run free in the off-leash area with the other dogs so it can make some fucking dog friends. "Run free." *Bullshit.*

"Hardy loves to play fetch in the park," she continues. "We have this ratty old tennis ball that he's been chasing for years. The other day, I, like, whipped it way too far and it went in the bushes. He just kept sniffin' and sniffin' and sniffin', looking in all the bushes until another dog snatched it and ran off. Hardy was so pissed. He took off after the other mutt to get it back—"

"Oh." I say, because I can't say anything else. Sweat drips down my face and my instinct, for some reason, is to cool myself down with steaming hot coffee. When I take a sip, I burn my tongue. My throat's constricted and my body's clammy and I'm having an allergic reaction to the image of freedom as an off-leash dog park.

Within every dog is the primal urge to roam wildly in the Rockies. Dance across the Great Plains. Prey upon the coastal shorelines of the Pacific. But something always pulls us back. An unwritten yet sacred attachment. Commitment. Loyalty.

Of course her dumb Lab's going to do whatever it takes to retrieve the ball. What he craves more than freedom is companionship.

"In the end Hardy brought that ratty tennis ball back. He had to fight extra hard for it this time, but that dog, would like, never let me down. Thank God because the few minutes when he disappeared were torture. For a moment I thought he was gone forever. Like seriously. I couldn't imagine a worse feeling."

The elephants stomp on my chest now and I can't handle the heat anymore, so I just get up and leave before I can hear anything else about dogs and leashes and how wonderful it is to let a dog roam free.

Emma, August 11, 2014, 5:20pm, EDT

As soon as I get home from work, I turn on my computer. *Geez, the Internet up here is almost as slow as dialup.* Good thing Katie lent me her *Homeland* DVDs. (All four seasons!) With a limit of 10 GB per month, I wouldn't be able to watch more than an episode or two per week on Netflix (I usually watch one to two episodes per night), and I doubt the Internet speed is fast enough to stream shows online.

I skim through a few e-mails after deleting all of the updates from stores I've shopped, non-profits I've donated to, and blog subscriptions. There's a short 'Hi, how are things?' from my mom, another update from Melayna about how creepy Neil's been at work ("He keeps asking when you're coming back, though!") and a message from Jess that she caught my subletters smoking weed in the apartment again. ("All the secondhand smoke really put me to sleep!")

I should really return Jeff's e-mail from last week. What do I say? While it's great that he wants to keep me in the loop about what's going on with Adam—he was my best friend after all—Adam's not my responsibility anymore. I thought that putting thousands of miles between us would help me to move on, but, unfortunately, the past chases us wherever we go thanks to technology, which makes me wonder if it's possible to escape anything anymore. You don't need to be a criminal these days to be haunted by your past.

Feeling a bit guilty, I read the e-mail again.

Howdy Emma!

I hope you haven't been eaten by a polar bear yet. LOL

Just wanted to give you a quick update about our man, Adam. Remember how I told you he seemed back to his normal self at work before you left? Well, things kind of fell apart in the last few weeks. He took it pretty hard when you moved away (not that I'm blaming you or anything. You did what you had to do).

He started coming in really late again, was rude to our members and then even missed a couple of shifts. I know something must be seriously wrong with him, so I tried to be understanding. But his behaviour really started to hurt business.

He was still staying on the couch with Nancy and it got a bit uncomfortable. He wasn't helping out with any of the meals and started spending all of his time lying around playing video games. I think he must be depressed or something. I told him to go see a doctor to get the help he needs. There's no shame in asking for help! But you know how he is. You'd have to drag the man to the hospital with a broken leg. He has too much pride to admit that he's suffering.

Anyways, I suggested he take some time off. Go live with his mom in Parry Sound until the trial. Hopefully, she'll have better luck convincing him to get help.

Again, I'm not telling you this to make you feel guilty or anything. I just thought you would want to know.

Stay warm,

-Jeff.

I'm sad to learn that Adam's having such a hard time, but I don't have much sympathy for him. People endure greater hardship than he has, and they find a way to get through it. Look at the people in this community. They're forced to deal with the consequences of a century of colonialism: broken families, alcoholism, drug addiction, unemployment, and suicide. What problems has Adam ever had, other than getting cut from some rugby team? Maybe he's going through an early mid-life crisis or something, but he DID bring his problems upon himself. He's the one who chose to disappear for over a week, go on a bender and get into some stupid bar fight.

What was he thinking? Our life in Toronto was so perfect and he threw it all away. How can a man get lost within himself?

Like Jeff, I also thought Adam was suffering from some sort of depression, brought on by the shame of getting arrested, destroying our relationship and disappointing the members he was coaching by not showing up for the MaxFit games. While I know that depression is an illness people can't control, I guess I saw Adam as immune to it. He doesn't allow anything to break him or get in his way. He's one of the strongest, toughest men I know. He's an athlete. A fighter. The General. During rugby games, he always got back up when he got tackled. Even when he got injured, he'd never just lie on the field. Instead, he would try to keep playing despite the pain. We were happy together, too, right until he left.

I decide not to reply just yet. I can't. It's too soon. Every time I think about him, the feelings of hurt and anger re-emerge. While I'm not going to let it destroy me... I've chosen to move forward, I've also had to accept that certain dreams might not happen for me. Sometimes our heroes let us down.

I log into Facebook and creep Adam's page. I look through all the posts and his pictures. There's nothing to suggest he's in a new relationship. I know I shouldn't care, but the thought that he might meet someone else makes me feel sick. What if this is just a phase, and someone else gets to be with the amazing man I fell in love with? *Emma, stop torturing yourself. He treated you like shit. You can't tolerate that. You'll meet someone better than him and if you don't, you'll still have an amazing and fulfilling life!*

My heart stops when I check my News Feed and see the topic that's trending: *"Robin Williams dead in apparent suicide."* I'm shocked. How could someone so amazing and talented be dead? I click on a link to a *Toronto Star* article that Katie posted:

"Actor-comedian Robin Williams, 63, is dead and an investigation is underway into his apparent suicide, the Marin County Sheriff's Office said in a statement on Monday.

Williams, who won an Oscar for his performance in 1997's Good Will Hunting, *was found unconscious and not breathing in his Tiburon, Calif. home around 11:55 a.m., the Marin County Sheriff's Office confirmed in a news release."*

We were worried about copycat suicides following Lynda's death and we worked with Elders to encourage community members to talk about their grief and suffering, so I've been preparing myself to deal with another suicide. Still, I'm completely shocked and saddened by this news. From his roles in *Patch Adams*, *Mrs. Doubtfire*, and *Jumanji* at least, it seemed like Robin Williams was one of the happiest men alive, always cracking jokes and having the biggest smile on his face. Tom and I must have watched Mrs. Doubtfire at least fifteen times when we were kids. My favourite part was when Daniel (Robin Williams) kept calling his wife (Sally Field), acting as potential nanny candidates (all seemingly crazy) for his kids. Tim and I would try to impersonate the wild characters. *"Figaro!" "I do a great impression of a hotdog." "I am job... I am job."*

I skim through the article, desperate for answers as to why this tragedy happened. One sentence stands out: *"Williams had been battling severe depression recently."*

Depression? Robin Williams suffered from depression? How did I not know this? How can a man with so much sadness inspire so much laughter? The Robin Williams I know and love had a contagious spirit and energy that brightened my childhood. Yet, I *had* noticed that he played some darker roles in later years, like in *Insomnia* and *One Hour Photo*. Isn't that what great acting is, though, being able to play the polar opposite of oneself?

The article says that Twitter has also been flooded with reactions of shock and sadness alike from celebrities. Clearly, the world is mourning the loss of someone who warmed their hearts and brightened their days. Fellow comedians publicly grieve their loss:

@SteveMartinToGo: "I could not be more stunned by the loss of Robin Williams, mensch, great talent, acting partner, genuine soul."

@TheEllenShow: "I can't believe the news about Robin Williams. He gave so much to so many people. I'm heartbroken."

@jimmykimmel: "Robin was as sweet a man as he was funny. If you're sad, please tell someone."

Jimmy Kimmel's comment hits me. Would Adam have told me if he was sad? What if the whole time I thought he was an asshole and a fuck up--getting in trouble with the police, lying around on the couch, ignoring me at home--were his ways of masking his pain? For Adam, being a man means showing no weakness, being invincible, and never asking for help. As a matter of fact, he would probably do whatever he could to make sure I couldn't see he was suffering.

Reading on, I'm taken aback by a Tweet from @TheAcademy, "Genie, you're free," which has been re-tweeted nearly three hundred and thirty thousand times. Are they suggesting that suicide is liberating? Maybe people are living in complete hell when they are trapped in their own minds, like a genie in a bottle that needs release. But what escape is death?

Omigod. Adam. What if he was really suffering and I didn't notice it because I aspired for an easier, happier kind of love, like the kind I see in photos my friends post of their trips to Hawaii or New Zealand or Mexico? I guess all the time I spend on social media has made me believe that love exists above the surface, that it's supposed to be light all of the time. Life's too stressful to endure struggle at home. To me, it seemed like Adam had decided to throw his life away, and I wasn't going to allow myself to get pulled down with him. But what if I abandoned him when he needed me the most? The trouble is that Adam kept pushing me away, causing himself to plunge deeper and deeper into the darkness like an anchor.

At once I pick up the phone and dial Adam's number. I'm greeted by a woman's voice. *"The person you are trying reach is unavailable. Please try your call again later."* Did he block my number? I try again. Same message. Then I log into my Skype account and try calling from it. *"The person you are trying reach is unavailable. Please try your call again later."* Okay, so he didn't block my number...what's going on with his phone? Does he not have enough money to pay the bills?

Almost as soon as I hang up, the phone rings. The sliver of hope that I have, that it might be Adam, that somehow he was able to see the missed calls, quickly dissipates when I hear the voice on the other end.

"Hey Em, Jay here. Whatcha up to?"

"Hey Jay. Did you hear the news about Robin Williams? I'm just reading it now!"

"Yeah, it's really sad. I could watch his stand up over and over."

What makes it even harder to diagnose is that people who suffer from mental illness have a hard time seeing the symptoms within themselves, just like how Robin Williams' sunny demeanour made us think he was okay. When the chemistry in your brain is imbalanced, you see the world through a warped lens. Also, there's so much stigma around mental illness that people would often prefer to ignore symptoms if they suspect them. In particular, Dr. Marcuse, my supervisor during med-school psyc rotations, told me that some mood disorders like bipolar disorder are often misdiagnosed, especially when people self-medicate using drugs or alcohol which can mask their symptoms.

I quickly Google "diagnosing bipolar disorder" and am flooded with memories of Adam when I read the symptoms. "Excessive happiness, hopefulness, and excitement, or irritability," "restlessness, increased energy, with a tendency to become over-involved with many (often unrealistic) plans and activities," "less need for sleep," "rapid speech," "racing thoughts," "impulsive behaviour," "inflated self-esteem or feelings of grandiosity," "reckless behaviours," "impulsive sexual indiscretions," "lavish shopping sprees." I think of his intense workout regimes. His unstoppable energy on the rugby field. Impulsively going to Vancouver. Beating up a stranger. Buying a suit he can't afford. Any of these could be understood as a 30 year-old man determined to prove his masculinity. Or they could be symptoms of mania.

Then I read the symptoms of depression, like "feeling sad or blue," "loss of energy," "feelings of guilt, hopelessness, or worthlessness," "thoughts of suicide or attempting suicide", increased need for sleep or inability to sleep," "loss of interest or enjoyment from things that were once pleasurable," and run through the memory bank. Adam getting bummed out after getting injured. His anger at being cut from Team Canada. Lying around on the couch playing video games after he returned from Vancouver. Acting irrationally angry towards me. Pushing away the person he loves. Any of these could be natural reactions to frustrations, but with Adam, the anger became irrational and the disappointment almost debilitating. He always picked himself back up, though, so I never really considered that he might have an illness.

"Most people with bipolar disorder are often misdiagnosed several times," Dr. Marcuse explained. "Currently, there's no test, no brain scan or anything that doctors can use to make a proper diagnosis. Unless patients come to see them in a severely manic state or during a psychotic episode, doctors have to rely on the patient's self-reported history of their experiences with mania and depression. Often people mistake their highs for normal behavior or for parts of their personality. Many people have symptoms that have gone undetected or untreated simply because they were unable to identify their problem, or were not asked the right questions about their symptoms."

Jay's voice interrupts my thoughts. "But anyways, Micah and I are going on a little hike up towards the cliff by the dump. Someone just went on the radio saying that there's a whole pod of narwhal sighted by there. Wanna check them out?"

"Okay."

If I don't leave now, I'll probably spend all night glued to my computer, trying to understand what happened to Robin Williams. At work, we always joke about how sites like WebMD drive our patients crazy, as people will get a little cough or rash and then spend hours trying to self-diagnose their symptoms as part of some serious illness. (Before I came up north, a man came in with a little poison ivy rash on his thigh, yet was convinced that he had flesh-eating disease. He had been preparing himself to lose a leg.) It's like people have started taking physical illness too seriously and mental illness not seriously enough.

"Great," Jay says. "It would be good for you to get to know Micah before you dog-sit him when I go to Iqaluit next week."

Adam, August 11, 2014, 6:00pm EDT

The knock on my door's soft.
"Wake up, wake up.
Time to go to school."
Babying me like she did in high school.

Michael Keaton's eyes mock me
From the poster above my desk
Fuck you, Batman.
You're not even real.
Nothing I believed in was real.
Not rugby. Not my business. Not love. Not myself.
Nothing.

I pull my duvet over my head.
To shield my eyes from all the awards.
Certificates. Medals. Trophies.
All lies to make me believe I could become SOMEBODY.
But I'm not somebody. I'm nobody.
Nothing.

It was all a waste of time.
The trying. The believing. The dreaming. The training. The fighting.
I'm a fuck up and a criminal and I've ruined my life.
I'm a fuck up and a criminal and I've ruined my life.
I'm a fuck up and a criminal and I've ruined my life.

Knock. Knock. KNOCK. KNOCK. KNOCK.
BANG! BANG! BANG!
Stop convincing me I'm someone I'm not, Mom.
She needs to accept it.
I'm nothing but a fucking disappointment.

"Adam, are you up? Don't you have an appointment with Dr. Mitzel?"
She knocks again. *Fuck you, Mom. I can take care of myself.*
Then she knocks again. Louder. Louder. LOUDER.
Smashing my head with a sledgehammer.
Just stop. Go away. Leave me alone.

She opens the door and comes in.
Who does she think she is?
Does she have no fucking RESPECT for me?
This is an invasion of privacy!
One step closer and I'll call the cops, Mom.

"You're still in bed? Adam, get up!
 Your appointment is in less than an hour!"
Fuck. Mom, it's not your business.

I want to tell her to go away.
GO THE FUCK AWAY, MOM.
But I do nothing and say nothing.
I just lie in my childhood bed.
Pull the covers tighter over my face.
Hide from the world.

My heart rate rises. I'm pressing over 200 lbs.
Striving for an extra rep.
But my muscles can't handle the tension.
The pressure builds and builds and builds.

"Your life isn't over just because Jeff suggested you take a leave of absence before your trial. He really cares about you. We all do. He wants you to get the help you need so you can get back to work when you're ready. I'd be really surprised if you actually go to jail. The lawyer thinks you'll probably have to do community service. People have it a lot worse off than you.

You can't give up on life because you made a couple of mistakes."

ENOUGH. JUST STOP. FUCK!

I'm an elastic band stretched past its limits. Her naggy teacher voice is fucking annoying.
You're not at school, Mom, lecturing one of your kindergarteners.
You're in a MAN'S BEDROOM. A PRIVATE SPACE.
Want to come to the fucking bathroom with me too?

Instead of going away.
The woman keeps talking.
Same annoying Charlie Brown teacher voice.
Whaa whaa whaa whaa....

"I know you've had a hard go of things since moving from Toronto. But that was months ago. At some point you need to move on with your life. You can't lie in bed like this forever."

Whaa whaa whaa whaa....

A wildness comes over me.
Something terrifying and powerful and monstrous.
Me but not ME.
I throw off the covers and sit up.

"MOM. STOP. YOU'RE BUGGING ME.
I TOLD YOU. I DON'T WANT TO GO SEE SOME IDIOT DOCTOR.
I DON'T NEED HELP.
I'M NOT SUFFERING. I'M NOT GOING THROUGH ANYTHING.
THIS IS WHO I AM."

Instead of leaving, she comes closer.
Crouches low beside my bed.

GET OUT. GET THE FUCK OUT.
GET OUT, MOM. GET OUT.
GET OUT!
GET OUT!
GET OUT!

"Adam, I'm not leaving. The courts put ME in charge of YOU. I need to make sure you get to your appointment with Dr. Mitzel. It's not too late to turn your life around."

Whaa whaa whaa whaa....

She grabs my paw. Tries to pull me out of bed.
I recoil quickly, growling.
Don't touch me. Stay away. Go away.

Instead of respecting me, she comes closer.
She's on my bed now. My FUCKING SPACE.
Again, she grabs me, more forcefully this time.

The rage forces my claws into a fist.
Without warning, I attack.
One hard blow across the face.
Then quivering.

Emma, August 12, 2014, 2:10pm EDT

After driving the small aluminum fishing boat west out of the bay into Eclipse Sound, Elijah slows the motor to an idle.

"So we just wait now?" I ask.

Elijah opens his eyes wide. "*Ii.* We wait." He stares at the waves calmly flowing in front of the hoodoos, eroded rock pillars jutting out from the glacial basin across the channel. In a couple of months, the ocean will be a frozen highway of sea-ice, and instead of his fishing boat, he will be traveling by snowmobile, likely pulling his family members behind in a wooden qamutik as they go to the floe edge to hunt for seal, narwhal, walrus, and even polar bear.

"This will be good for you, Em," Jay jokes. "Seal hunting teaches patience. You're still trying to live that fast-paced lifestyle of the city. You know, wanting everything now but not having time for anything."

"Hey! I *am* patient!" I reply as he rubs my back teasingly, the warmth of his hand seeping through the three layers of clothing covering my upper body. I'll admit, though, he does have a point: I *did* peek at the online spoilers for *OITNB*. (I couldn't wait a *whole year* to find out if Piper and Alex end up together.)

Michael, Elijah's twenty-something-year-old grandson aims the scope of his .22 rifle, which is held together with layers of electrical tape, at the water. Zipping up the neck of my Gortex coat to shield my face from the frigid Arctic air, I realize how terrified I am of the ocean. I panic at the thought of a 50 ft bowhead whale surfacing beside our helpless fishing boat. The ocean is so deep and so vast that it's hard to see what's below the surface even when we want to. I mean, efforts are still underway to locate the wreckage from the mysterious Franklin expedition that went missing more than 150 years ago!

BANG! A split second after a ring-seal pokes his head out, Michael fires his rifle quickly. *BANG! BANG! BANG!* The gunshots echo off the ancient layers of glacial ice, a sound that, in the last century, has replaced the quiet splash of a harpoon piercing the seal's pelt.

"Shit. Missed." He scoffs dejectedly. We wait longer. Elijah lights up a cigarette and eyes his grandson intently, the way a coach would critique an athlete on the field. Michael shoots again. And again.

"Ay!" Elijah cheers, keeping his eyes focused on the bloody seal head, bobbing at the surface as he accelerates the motor towards it. Michael carefully places his rifle down and grabs what looks like the wooden shaft of a hockey stick with a metal hook, a *niksik*. When we pull up to about a few feet away from the seal, Michael reaches the niksik into the water, hooks the seal, and pulls it towards the boat.

"Nice one, Mike," Jay congratulates him. Then he turns to me. "Their family will use the whole seal. The skins will be probably be used by Ragilee, Elijah's wife, to make *kamiks* or sealskin mitts or crafts to sell at the market. And they'll share the meat with others in the community."

BANG! We look at the water and see another dead seal surrounded by a ribbon of red blood. Elijah slings his rifle back across his back and drives the boat towards the seal. Again, Michael reaches the *niksik* into the water and hooks the seal.

"Grandpa doesn't always get it on the first shot," Michael mutters.

"Do you guys go out hunting often?" I ask, knowing that many families rely primarily on country food such as narwhal and seal meat for sustenance, in addition to the food flown up from the south.

Elijah opens his eyes wide and continues driving the boat, keeping his gaze focused on the water. Out on the ocean, he looks how I feel when I'm doing yoga, or when I'm out on a run. No matter how difficult the day, it allows me to refresh, recharge, and find my strength again. It's like when I let go of all the stresses, the distractions, the busy schedule, I can just be myself, alone with my thoughts.

"Yes, my grandpa hunts two or three times a week," Michael adds, hauling the seal over the edge of the boat. "Sometimes I join when I'm not out working at the mine. This is the way Inuit have always existed, hunting seals. But fuel is getting very expensive. Lots of families, they don't have the money for fuel, or expensive *Qallunaat* food."

I move away slightly from Jay, separating myself from the gentle grip of his hand resting on the back of my neck. I hadn't even noticed that it was still there. Adam often squeezed or rubbed my neck and I've been feeling the warmth of his touch when I've been alone, like a phantom limb, mostly when I'm drinking my morning coffee, or eating dinner, or lying in bed at night. I feel a chill go through my spine, as though I'd betrayed myself in some way, broken a promise to protect my heart from any more pain. I guess part of me was trying to preserve the past, not yet ready to embrace the future.

Jay continues, "One thing I've learned from living with Inuit is that culture is not frozen in time. It's not static. Inuit have embraced modernization but want to have a voice in what the future looks like. Sometimes you have to fight for the past to have a better future."

"*Ii*," Michael agrees. "Our culture is very important to us. It's who we are."

Perhaps he wasn't sure how much of the past to hold onto and how much to let go as he spoke in a way that suggested he longed to be part of something that no longer existed, the way that my brother sometimes retells Grandpa's stories from the war. In some ways, I guess we're all envious of a time when people used to fight for what they believe in. Today, it's so easy to replace the old with the new. It was so expensive to fix my old camera before I came up here that I just bought a new one on sale at Best Buy.

"Do you think people were happier before contact, when they lived off the land?" I ask.

Elijah stares silently at the open Arctic Ocean, keeping his focus on the few subtle ripples in order to be ready for when the seal surfaces. Michael translates the question his grandfather has been asked many times before.

As we sit in silence, Jay adjusts his position in the boat so he can look directly at me, taking his hand from my neck and placing it gently on my forearm. *So the warmth was his touch, not Adam's.*

After several minutes of staring at the shadows dancing below the surface of the ocean, Elijah finally responds, in

English this time. His voice is low, soft, distant; his words nearly lost in the crisp Arctic breeze.

"Life is different now."

Then he fires off another shot while Jay interlocks his fingers with mine. This time I don't pull away. Sometimes you have to fight for the past and sometimes you have to let go.

Adam, August 13, 2014, 3:15 pm EDT

I've been standing here for hours.
Staring into the crystal blue water.
Teetering on the spine of the Niagara Peninsula.
At the edge of the white limestone cliffs, at least 50m high.

I can see the bottom clearly.
The graves of sunken ships and old Coke cans.
Resting peacefully in the shallow bedrock of Lake Huron.

I feel absolutely dead inside.
Rock bottom.

Emma, August 13, 2014, 3:30pm EDT

  A strong tug nearly pops my shoulder out of its socket. As I tighten my grip on his leash, Micah flails his ears and tenses his back, exposing the cuts of muscles underneath his grey and white fur. Then he turns around impatiently and the frustration in his piercing, sky blue eyes strikes me with their familiarity. *Sorry Micah, I want to let you run free, but Jay says that if I let you go, you'll sprint across the tundra for hours before you come back. I don't want to be worried about losing you.* As Jay said, huskies put the 'H' in Houdini!

  How long have I been standing here, staring out at the calm, clear, sparkling ocean, an image you'd see in bottled water ads? With the massive white iceberg floating above the surface, and the mountains in the background, it's like I'm staring at a perfect postcard. *"Greetings from the land of the midnight sun!"*

  I bend down to stroke Micah's thick grey coat. He moves closer to me, rubbing his head against my hand to suggest he wanted me to scratch underneath his white chin. *Don't worry, we'll continue our walk soon.* When I first met Micah at Jay's house, he instantly ran up to me, wagging his tail excitedly as though I had a pocket full of bacon. Then he rubbed against my legs, encouraging me to scratch underneath his chin and between his ears. It was an instant connection, like I was being reunited with a long lost friend, but then I figured it was just because he resembles Bran's direwolf in *Game of Thrones*.

  Apparently, Micah can be a bit of a growler around strangers, so Jay was shocked by how comfortable he was with me. *"It's like love at first sight!"* he'd joked. My family is more of a cat family, so I was surprised that I was as taken by Micah as he was with me. I was glad to dogsit while Jay's out of town.

Micah tugs again. His leash nearly slips free of my grasp as I wipe a tear. I've been crying sporadically ever since I found out about Robin Williams' suicide. Did I really try my best to help Adam? Was there something deeper going on with him? What else was I supposed to do when my partner disappears and then phones from prison a week later, screaming at me that he doesn't love me? Piper's discovery of Larry's affair with her best friend was probably the closest guide for me and Adam. *Everybody lies!* I guess love distorts our perception of reality, and it's even harder to recognize the truth when it's buried underneath layers of what we imagine relationships should be like.

But since learning of Robin Williams' suicide, I've started to see Adam's behavior from a different light and I want to make sure he doesn't experience the same tragic fate. I'd tried calling him again earlier today. No luck. So I impulsively called Nicky. If I couldn't do something to help Adam, maybe she could. She sounded upset, like she was hiding something horrible. Or perhaps she is angry that life didn't turn out the way she wanted it to. Like many parents, I think she saw her son as a flawless angel. Adam's arrest shattered her idea of her perfect little boy, and I think she's been agonizing over the fact that her perception of Adam might have masked his problems from her.

"Emma, what are you doing calling him?" she said before I even had a chance to explain. *"You broke up with him. Let Adam move on."* I felt foolish for clinging so tightly to the past, for refusing to accept things as they were and for wanting to change them for the better, so I hung up. I felt ashamed, like my love for Adam had transformed into something horrifyingly desperate.

Just as I'm about to continue walking along the shoreline, the left third of the iceberg breaks off suddenly and crashes violently, like a high-rise apartment building imploding in the heart of the city. Tears roll down my face uncontrollably as I watch the two distinct halves of the iceberg drift further and further apart from each other. It's devastating to watch something that seems so strong and unbreakable crumble in an instant. Even more devastating is the feeling that there's nothing I can do about it.

Detecting my moment of weakness, Micah bounds away aggressively, pulling his leash out of my grasp. He runs along the beach, leaping over icy boulders, piles of seaweed, and seal carcasses. A team of husky sled dogs barks as if they're cheering him on, the way prisoners would encourage an escaped convict. Like a deceived jail-guard, I try to sprint after him, chasing him up over a wall of permafrost and onto the tundra.

"Micah! Come back!" I shout, struggling to keep up over the uneven mounds of grass, moss, lichen and rocks. My heart is racing as I chase the past I had held onto so tightly. I'm helpless as he sprints further and further into the distance, the leash still attached to his collar and dragging behind him.

"Micah! Micah!"

As he disappears down the backside of a hill in the distance, I fall to my knees, crushing the tiny yet resilient purple petals of a cluster of moss campion growing between lichen covered rock. I start sobbing.

"MICAH! MICAH!" I wail. The intensity of my grief hits the mountains across Eclipse Sound, and then echoes throughout Arctic. There's nobody around. I can barely see the town below the hill, nestled within the valley of barren tundra, across from the tiny airport, my only access to the south. I'm alone amidst this desolate landscape and there's nowhere to hide. No trees or buildings or distractions. It's just me in the depths of my suffering and all my faults and mistakes of the past are exposed underneath the spotlight of the midnight sun.

"Adam…" I whisper as I stare at the hill in the distance, a little speck on the vast Arctic horizon, waiting helplessly for him to come back.

All I want to do is disappear, go back to our little apartment on Dufferin Street and sit on the porch holding hands with my best friend, watching our tulips grow in the garden. I feel a visceral tug on my heart, the rip of a bond being severed.

I long to reach out and grab him, stop him, hold him close the way I used to. But I watch in despair as the leash travels further and further away and he escapes into the wild and beautiful and terrifying wilderness.

Acknowledgements

See What Flowers would not have been possible without the support of my incredible friends and family. First, I would like to thank my brother, Pat Mullen, for his ongoing encouragement, editing skills, and critical comments. This novel is as much a product of his labour as it is mine.

Next, I would like to thank readers who read drafts of the novel and provided feedback at various stages. Megan Valois, Jill Holmes, Ashley Peak, Sarah Sibbett, Stephanie Dodds, Ali Duyck, Erin Bailey, Yvonne Kwok, Katie Wrobel, Pat Ahearn, and of course, my Mom: I really would not have continued writing had it not been for your interest in my work.

I would also like to acknowledge Louise Johnson, Rachael Glassman, Keira Loukes, and Brian Mullen for their assistance with the Toronto Book Launch.

Furthermore, thank you to all of the participants in the "Book Cover Design Contest" that I held through 99designs.ca and to my online community of supporters who provided feedback and comments on the covers. I am especially grateful to Estella Vukovic for designing a cover that truly captures the essence of *See What Flowers*.

An enormous thank you also goes to Jim Keohane and Monika Skiba for welcoming me into their home in Toronto on several occasions. This alleviated many financial pressures and gave me the space to make time for something I always wanted to do.

Lastly, I would like to thank my friend, Laura Moore, for encouraging me to make time for writing because it adds joy to my life. I never would have started this novel without that gentle nudge.

Oh, and thanks to my parents for being amazing and for always supporting my wild and crazy adventures.

- *S.M.*

About the Author

Shannon Mullen is a high school teacher and writer currently based in Toronto, Canada. She has previously taught in northern British Columbia, Nunavut, England, and Colombia. While this is her first novel, Shannon's writing has been published in *The Globe & Mail*, *Thought Catalog*, *Rebelle Society*, and *Elephant Journal*. She blogs about her adventures in teaching, writing, and travel at shannonmullen.me.